Equal Opportunities

So, to sum up what I'm hunting down here:
imagine a guy who looks rather like some kind
of 70s heart-throb, with slightly too-big messy
lips and unfashionably curly hair. In fact, if you
can, imagine a boy with that look, a look that
is so far from contemporariness and sexiness
that it's actually the last word in both.

Then put him in a wheelchair.

Because even though the way he looks is
rapture-inducing-perfection that demands that
I flout the standard library anti-stalking rules,
the way he looks is only the start. Only the tip
of the iceberg of reasons why I'm not thinking
or breathing right now.

If I saw this guy walking down the street
I'd probably look – look and lust, even – but
this, this is far, far more than that. Because,
well, how can I put this? I have a thing. A bad
thing. A perverted thing. A heart-stopping,
lust-inducing, bad, secret, kinky thing.

A thing for boys who can't walk.

By the same author:

Peep Show
Mad About the Boy

Equal Opportunities
Mathilde Madden

BLACK LACE

Black Lace books contain sexual fantasies.
In real life, always practise safe sex.

First published in 2006 by
Black Lace
Thames Wharf Studios
Rainville Road
London W6 9HA

Typeset by SetSystems Ltd, Saffron Walden, Essex
Printed and bound by Mackays of Chatham PLC

ISBN 0 352 34070 3
ISBN 9 780352 340702

For more information about *Equal Opportunities*
and Mathilde Madden's other books please visit

www.mathildemadden.co.uk

Part One: **February**

Mary

I don't normally do this sort of thing, let alone in a place like this.

But he's just so pretty. Too pretty to resist. And I've been trailing him too long to turn back now. I've been acting like some sort of lapdog in the dusty silence, all the way from 'large print' to 'historical romance' and back again. I just can't stop staring.

There's a lot to stare at. He's such a symphony of delights, from his slender, but still just-buff-enough, body – biceps and pecs both defined through his white T-shirt – to his hair that is wildly curly and a little bit too long, a little bit out of control, dark glossy cork-screws that almost explode out of the top of his head, looking just as untamable as he does himself. His eyes are dark – brown, I think – but eye colour isn't so important in the bigger picture of this particular – and particularly perfect – face. His eyes are just supporting players here, crowded out by his loose, over-sized, melting-candy mouth. Oh god, that mouth! It's a mouth I could easily kiss all day, just to see if it got any more deliciously pink and pouty.

Maybe this won't make sense to anyone but me, but there's another edge to this whole sexy-boy pack-age that really does it for me. I love the way there's something kind of retro about him. Something a bit man-out-of-time, something sort of 70s-throw-back. It's hard to pinpoint exactly – and maybe it's mostly just down to the hair – but he's got shades of Tucker in *Tucker's Luck*, by way of Adam Ant and David Essex, or one of the teenage sons in *Butterflies*, and even, obliquely, a young Mick Jagger. Basically, he's everyone I ever fancied when I was aged, like, about eight.

He also looks rather uncannily like this guy I work with, who I have a kind of pathetic crush on. Proof, if proof were needed, that he has practically bottled My Type.

So, to sum up what I'm hunting down here: imagine a guy who looks rather like a 70s heart-throb, with slightly too-big messy lips and unfashionably curly hair. In fact, if you can, imagine a boy with that look, a look that is so far from contemporariness and sexiness that it's actually the last word in both.

Then put him in a wheelchair.

Because even though the way he looks is rapture-inducing-perfection that demands that I flout the standard library anti-stalking rules, the way he looks is only the start. Only the tip of the iceberg of reasons why I'm not thinking or breathing right now.

If I saw this guy walking down the street I'd probably look – look and lust, even – but this, this is far, far more than that. Because, well, how can I put this? I have a thing. A bad thing. A perverted thing. A heart-stopping, lust-inducing, bad, secret, kinky thing.

A thing for boys who can't walk.

And, no, I have no idea why. Of course, I've tried to work it out. Of course, I've got nowhere.

Is it just the helplessness? Is it the bravery – the heroic, injured-war-hero thing? Is it a macho, cyborgy, man-and-machine-in-perfect-harmony, hard-body hard-steel sort of thing? Is it just a sadomasochistic thing? I expect it is all of those. But it's also just a pure, hard-wired, born-kinky sort of thing.

But I guess it's always this way with things like this, isn't it? I mean, your body doesn't do 'why?' does it? Your blood doesn't explain why it pumps the way it does. Your heart doesn't tell you why it beats faster. Your tissue, your bones, they're not going to scribble you a quick enlightening Post-It about why certain strange things equal certain strange feelings. Your body doesn't explain the backstory of why some thing turns your head a particular way. Because during those moments your body is far too busy doing something else. Working in a different, more urgent, more real way.

I guess what I really think is that – for me – if you can explain exactly why something turns you on, pinpoint some life- and lust-changing event that skewed your sexuality one way or another (like some foot fetishist who was once made to shine shoes as a child by a domineering stepmother), then it really can't turn you on all that much, not if you can analyse it in a clear-headed way like that. It can't be getting to you in a proper, deep, right-there-in-the-bone-marrow kind of a way.

Well, that's my theory.

So don't expect too much in the way of cold hard reductionism about exactly why I like boys in wheelchairs. I just do. Like some people like firefighters and some (rather more dubious people) like choirboys.

And that's the thing about me, that's my dirty secret. It doesn't mean I spend all my time hunting down disabled men to fulfil my twisted desires. Far from it. I try not to encounter disabled men as far as I possibly can. And when I do stumble upon one, like this, I don't normally pursue them. It's too much. Too confusing. Too questionable. I know very well that disabled people, in general, are not very keen on people like me.

So what's different now? Why am I stalking this guy like a woman possessed? I don't know the answer to that one – hence my current introspection overload. I guess it's just that I've never seen anything quite like him before. Quite as perfect. Quite as button-pressing. And this time I just don't think I am strong enough to resist.

Oh god. I should speak to him or stop following him around. I have to choose between fight and flight. And there's really only one choice. I am going to get up the nerve to approach him. (If only to check he is not some kind of library-dust-induced hallucination.)

And having made that decision I find I'm checking myself out, doing a quick head-to-toe once-over. I really wish I hadn't borrowed (without asking) my flatmate Carrie's unbearably homespun, brown shaggy cardigan today, but it's still so cold and I seem to have made it through the entire winter without owning a proper coat. God, I really am such a student. But noticing my inappropriate clothing isn't enough to put me off now, and I slip the cardie off and kick it under the trolley of books to be shelved. Sorry, Carrie. I can always go back and get it from lost property. It's not like anyone is going to steal it.

Yeti-like cardigan shed, I walk over to my quarry, putting all my acting skills into pretending I haven't been shadowing him for the last fifteen minutes.

As I approach, he reaches up for a book on a high

shelf, and I sweep in to assist him, driven by anything but altruism.

David

First things first: I don't go to the library. I am not a library person. If I want a book – which is a rare enough occurrence in itself – I get it from Amazon, like a proper person.

But my mum asked me to return her library books and get her some new ones while I was in town. And so I'm just having a vague look round at the same time. I'd feel sort of ungrateful if I didn't. They are so falling over themselves to make the place wheelchair accessible, with ramps and automatic doors all over the place, so it would practically be a snub if I didn't take advantage of their Equal-Opps-legislation-following facilities.

But I'm not going to be writing a glowing letter of praise to the local paper just yet, because about half of the shelves are far too high for me to reach. Oops. No matter how many automatic doors they might boast, it's not a lot of use if crips like me can't reach the merchandise. Shame. And they were doing so well, up until that point.

Typically, one of the books my mum specifically asked me to get is almost out of reach, but I reckon I can probably manage it if I stretch. I twist in my chair and extend my arm to its limit, managing to get a fumbling grip on the spine, and pull.

And at that moment this woman, who has just popped up out of nowhere, leans over and whisks the book out from my tentative grip. No doubt in an attempt to help me out. Which annoys me – if I need help I will ask for it.

'I can manage,' I growl at her, all ungrateful teeth.

But she ignores my complaint and smiles, deliberately keeping the book she has retrieved for me just out of my reach.

She turns the fat volume over in her hands in an irritatingly smug manner. 'Ooh, Jackie Collins,' she notes in a stage whisper, and I can't tell if she is talking to me or to herself.

She's standing very close to me – too close, it's a bit overwhelming. But I like the dress she's wearing, tight-fitting white cotton with a print of red cherries and matching red buttons from top to bottom. In fact, with her neat button-down frock, heavy framed specs and clumpy shoes, she has a sort of sexy librarian look about her. I'm pretty sure she isn't really a member of staff, though. The look is just too much to be real. She's like a parody of a librarian. Too prim-looking, too schoolma'am, to be meaning the look seriously.

I realise then that, despite my interest in her clothes, I'm mostly staring up at her lips. It might be a trick of the light, but they seem to be exactly the same shade of red as the cherries on her dress. They make me think of other kinds of lips.

But I can't just stare at her all day; she's still looking at the book she's holding, waiting for me to react to her comment about the type of reading I was so eager to get my hands on. Bitch. 'It's for my mum, OK?' I keep my voice deliberately low, suddenly feeling strangely exposed and guiltily conscious of the desk staff.

Cherry girl seems far less bound by convention. 'Well, of course it is,' she says, levelly. 'A beautiful man like you wouldn't need to read about it.' And then her tongue flicks over her lips turning the matt to gloss. And I have to inhale sharply thorough my nose to keep control of myself.

Then the conversation takes on a slightly surreal, slightly dreamlike quality. She bends down slowly, so her eyeline is level with mine, and I can see straight down the top of her cherry-covered dress. Her voice drops even lower. 'You'd be surprised, though, just how dirty these books can be,' she informs me with flashing eyes. 'I think it's quite amazing that you can find the filthiest things right here in the public library.'

I feel my face start to redden and she suddenly drops the book briskly into my lap and walks away without another word.

I sit there for several moments, my heart beating fast and my mouth dry, but I don't move. For a while I don't even register what has just happened.

Two years ago – before my accident – I wouldn't even have questioned such a blatant come-on. I would have known for sure that she wanted me after an exchange like that. I probably wouldn't have followed it up, though, but for a completely different reason. I would have frowned on her clunky shoes and specs and almost certainly decided that she was not good enough for me to bother pursuing. Didn't I once tell my mate Larry that life was too short to bother chatting up brunettes?

But now, when I stay put as she walks away and I don't even consider following up her offer, it's because things are different these days. I don't go after her because I'm in a wheelchair, and girls like her don't come on to pathetic cripples like me.

So it couldn't have been a come-on, no matter how it seemed. I must have been mistaken. No doubt she just feels sorry for me and thought she'd talk to me for a few moments. Brighten up the day of the poor boy whose legs don't work any more.

So I just get on with it. I push the girl out of my mind, find the rest of the books on my mum's extensive list and check them out. Then I exit through the automatic doors and wheel my way down to pavement level on a shiny ramp, a new addition to this ancient building.

But it's not over yet, because as I zig and zag downwards – the library is set a little way up and back from the street – I see her again. Cherry girl. She's sitting on the low wall at the bottom of the steps, eating an incongruous ice cream. A 99. God knows why, she must be freezing. It's really cold today, and she doesn't even have a coat on, in February. I can practically see the goose pimples on her bare arms from here.

She doesn't seem to have noticed me though and I wasn't planning on speaking to her, but as I roll past her she says, 'Hey.' So, not wanting to be rude, I stop right in front of her.

'Oh, hi,' I say, pretending to be cool. Pretending that her weird behaviour in the library hasn't shaken me one bit. I try not to find her sexy, which shouldn't be too hard. I try to concentrate on her plain brown hair, her heavy spectacles and her strange, slightly studenty, slightly geeky mode of dressing. I insist, quite firmly, to myself that this type of girl, this type of quirky, dowdy, hard-worky type of girl – woman, even – really isn't my type, which is weird, because I don't think of myself as having a type any more.

'Come to the park with me,' she says and winks –

actually winks – and jerks her head towards the iron gates over the road.

'I can't,' I mutter, 'I'm in a hurry.' I gesture at the books in my lap and then wish I hadn't, as they are all embarrassing mum-friendly titles and I cringe inwardly that I have just implied that I can't wait to get home and read them.

She raises her eyebrows at me, then stretches her leg out and sticks the chunky high heel of her so-not-my-type-of-girl brown shoe into the spokes of my wheel. 'Go on,' she says, pulling the ice-cream-smeared chocolate bar slowly out of her 99. 'I'll let you have my Flake.'

I don't reply. I look down at the chunky heel jammed in my spokes, trapping me. What can I do? Well, tell her to fuck off, I suppose, but somehow my mouth is not doing that. My mouth is too busy hanging half open.

I look at her cherry-print dress and her cherry-red lips. I meet her eyes and something in her expression seems to break through my million and one reasons why I shouldn't do this and become the one reason why I should. The not-my-type rationale I had been clinging to seems to be twisting out of my reach, away like the leaves blowing up and down the road.

It really is far too cold for ice cream.

I nod my head.

As she leans forward and slides the chocolate bar into my mouth, I feel as if I'm falling under a spell. Somehow I have no choice but to obey when she whispers hoarsely, 'Don't bite it now.'

Part of me wants to close my eyes, but I don't. I watch her expression as she inches almost the entire

Flake into my mouth, a fraction at a time, and then slowly begins to pull it out again. Then in it goes again, then out, gradually picking up speed. My breathing quickens. It's unbelievable really, I haven't had so much as a chaste kiss from a girl in months and now, suddenly, I'm fellating a chocolate bar for this one, outside the public library.

I can't remember the last time I was this turned on. I didn't know I could still *get* this turned on.

All the time we stare at each other. Stare and stare. And I find I'm trying to will her on with my gaze, begging for more – wanting nothing in the world except to let her fuck my mouth for ever with her makeshift chocolate phallus.

But then the wind seems to change direction. She sighs and shifts. I hear her heel click against my spokes and the sound somehow breaks the spell. I remember in a rush why things like this don't happen to me any more. I remember that I'm sitting outside a library in a wheelchair. I remember what is wrong with this picture. I bite down through the Flake and pull my head away.

I chew the chocolate quickly, feeling awkward, embarrassed. I lick stray flakes of it from my lips and wipe the last bits away with the back of my hand.

Once my mouth is empty enough I say, 'Thank you.' Trying to save face after my wanton display by sneering, keeping my voice cold and sarcastic.

But she seems utterly unconcerned by my attempts at macho detachment, and just smiles seductively at me. 'Well, that's my part of the bargain over with, now it's your turn.'

'What?'

'The deal was, I'd give you my Flake if you came to

the park with me, so, off we go.' And without waiting for an answer she hops down from the wall and starts across the road to the park.

I'm right behind her, crossing the road and following her through the Victorian wrought-iron gates. I don't even consider doing anything else. She keeps walking a little way ahead of me, and my wheels crunch on the annoying gravel as I trail after her. Round and round the garden like a crippled teddy bear.

She doesn't say much as we follow the main path, which loops all the way round the edge of the park. I guess she prefers the ultra-intense unspoken thing. Now and then she stops, looks back and lets her eyes slide over me, as if she can't bear to tear herself away. I feel weirdly self-conscious under her gaze, and bow my head and hunch my shoulders. But deep down inside I like this prickly feeling. There is something between us, something in the air, and it scares me, but I know I can't resist it.

And maybe that's what scares me most of all.

After an interminable age of gravel paths and bird-song, internal confusion and some distinct stirrings from my cock, Ms Cherry stops and plucks a petal from a very dark-red rose.

'Look at this one,' she says, her eyes glowing, 'it's exactly the colour of blood, but it feels so soft.' She rubs the petal briefly on her cheek in a gesture that is kind of seductive, but in a fake sort of way. Weirdly, though, like her nerdy spectacles, she seems to be able to get away with things like this – things that if someone else tried them would be risible.

As if to prove it she leans forward and trails the petal across my flushed cheek. Her face is inches away from mine, and I feel sure she's about to kiss me, but she doesn't. She just says, 'Let's go to the pavilion and get some tea.'

And so we do. In a bizarre change of tone, we end up settling ourselves at a sticky table and making perfunctory conversation about nothing. At one point, she picks up one of my library books from the table and looks idly through it for a couple of seconds, before replacing it on the stack.

'So,' she says, 'are all these books for your mother?'

'Yeah.'

'She has, uh, consistent tastes.'

I shrug. The last thing I want to talk about right now is my mother. Least of all her tastes in semi-seedy literature.

'You need to drop them off today?'

'No, I'll probably do it tomorrow.'

'Right.' She drains her teacup and places it carefully on the saucer. 'Let's go to your place, then.'

'Why?' I use the last part of my resolve to try and resist her, reminding myself that it has to be just pity. If she really is trying to fuck me, it has to be a pity fuck. And I don't need her pity. Really.

Anyway my student-shagging days are long gone. (As I suspected right from the outset, she is, indeed, a student. A mature one, she told me.) And even back when I was a professional student-shagging machine (to the extent that I ought to have been made officially part of the Fresher's Welcome Pack), I so didn't go for girls like her. I mean, mature students! Postgraduate students! As if!

I stuck resolutely to the type of giggly first-years who were slightly in awe of a man with a job and his own flat (and his own legs). Not dissertation-obsessed, given-up-career-for-academia types like her, with serious brown shoes and serious brown spectacles and serious brown hair.

I like her dress, though. It's really tight.

She looks hard at me, her face completely matter-of-fact. 'Why?' she says, repeating my question back to me. 'Why do I want to go to your place?' She seems puzzled that I should even ask. 'Well, partly because my place, lots of stairs – sorry. But mainly because, well, every time I look at you, I want to tie your wrists to your armrests and then get on my knees and run my tongue along your footplate, until you're desperate for me, rock-hard and writhing in that chair like an animal in heat.'

I stare at her, concerns about her appearance suddenly draining away. I can't speak.

She smiles a smile that I just cannot seem to resist, and continues, 'And I'd rather not do that right here.'

And I'm not stupid. I get it now. I know what she is. What's she's about. I've heard all about women like her.

And I don't care. I don't care about that, just like I don't care about the fact that she isn't my type. I really don't care about anything except the fact that I am absolutely, definitely, going to get a shag. In a matter of hours.

What can I say? It's been a long time.

I hurriedly show her around my bungalow, because it feels like it would be rude not to do something, anything, beforehand. She surveys each room with a forced politeness and a distinct lack of interest. Until, finally, we reach the bedroom.

We both stare at my unmade bed. At first, it's like neither of us can say anything.

Time passes.

'You can get into bed without any help, right?' she whispers eventually, as if not wanting to disturb the charged atmosphere in the room.

'Sure.' (How does she think I usually manage?)

'Well, go on then.'

And in less time than it would take to think it, we are both in bed, both naked, and her lips are viciously clamped on mine. She's rough with me, driving her way inside my mouth and sucking brutally on my lower lip.

Her skin against mine feels so good. Did I mention it's been so long? Too long? I feel like I'm going to come just from the sound of her rapid heartbeat and the feel of her hot breath, hot skin, hot hotness.

She moves away from my mouth, nipping her way across my cheek until she reaches my ear and hisses, 'I want to fuck you with my mouth.'

I laugh. 'Don't you mean you want me to fuck your mouth?' (OK, I know it's hardly the time or the place to get all semantic, but she did tell me she was an English student.)

'Nope.'

She rolls me over on to my stomach with a long and impassioned sigh. She doesn't seem to have any qualms about manipulating me into the position she wants, and I know I shouldn't but I kind of like that.

Once I'm positioned the way she wants me, she straddles my legs and bends down to flick her tongue across my exposed buttocks.

I flinch, uneasy, not sure if this is something I want, but somehow I can't find the words to tell her to stop – I can't find any words at all. So I lie there and quiver beneath her, as she lets her hard pointed tongue dart everywhere. Absolutely everywhere.

I gasp when she nudges at my hidden little hole with her tongue, at the same time splaying me with one hand, so open and wanton for her. And then I find myself moaning as she teasingly lets that tongue – soft and flat now – lap over that hot little spot, again and again, until it's so hungry, so wanting, that I am screaming with every languid caress. Screaming and aching. Aching for something. Anything. More.

Responding to my desperation she pushes the very tip of her tongue gently inside me. I'm so needy for her now that I make a noise like an animal in response, half begging and half sobbing. My face is buried in the pillows and my desperate erection is pressing itself against the mattress, so hard it feels like I'm going to drill my way right through it.

Thankfully my frustration doesn't last long. In minutes, one of her hands snakes underneath me, forming a lubricated fist around my aching cock. I thrust into the warm softness gratefully, and seconds later her tongue, which was starting to feel hopelessly small inside me, is replaced by a finger, then two, and the most amazing sensation, as she strokes me to peaks of pleasure I didn't know I was capable of, fucking me decisively with both hands. I've never felt anything like it.

And in moments, with her manipulating me from every direction, and me feeling like I'm her prisoner – captured, pinned, by her expertise – I'm spasming for her, soaking the sheets beneath me, half screaming, half blacking out . . .

* * *

She holds me for a long while after that, brushing my hair away from my face, waiting until I recover. Eventually I find I can speak again: 'If that was a pity fuck,' I breathe, 'then I think I do need your pity.'

She props herself up on her elbow and looks down at me. 'It's only a pity if we don't do that again,' she says brightly, emphasising her point with a brief kiss. Then she asks, 'Could I get a glass of water, or something?'

'Sure,' I say, suddenly a little self-conscious to be back in the real world, naked and sated, with this complete stranger. But coping. After all, I used to do this all the time. The whole one-night-stand thing.

I manoeuvre myself from the bed to the chair and wheel my way into the kitchen. When I return and pass her the glass she is sitting up in bed, grinning. 'Stay in the chair,' she says a little dreamily, watching me as I park up next to the bed.

'Why?'

'You look so beautiful, naked in your chair. Please. I want to see you come while you're sitting there.' She flips back the bedclothes, crawls across the bed and kneels next to me.

I look at her expectant expression. 'Are you going to make me come again?' I ask in sated disbelief.

'More than that.' She licks her lips. 'I will suck your cock every time I see you naked in that chair, and that's a fucking promise.' My sudden erection twitches in excited agreement.

And then, with one final hungry look, she buries her head in my lap, sucking greedily, almost before I have time to engage the brake.

As her tongue swirls around the head of my cock, coaxing and teasing me to my second orgasm, I barely have time to wonder whether I will be able to climax again so soon, before I explode in her mouth. I feel my fingers tightening against the rubber tread of the tyres, nails digging in so hard I'm surprised I don't end up with a puncture.

She lifts her head, wiping the spills from her chin and smearing them down my chest. As I go to wipe them away she snaps, 'Don't move.' I freeze, again feeling that I have no choice but to obey.

Flopping on to her back, she sprawls across the bed shamelessly, watching me through lust-lidded eyes. She hitches up her knees and lets them fall apart, exposing herself to me. My breath catches as I see how pink and wet and ripe she is. How delicious looking.

How long has it been since I last had sex? Two years? More? Too long in the wilderness, too long.

She holds my gaze, as she lets one of her hands trail between her legs.

And then, oh god, the scent of her! She smells so amazing, like candy floss. And I can imagine how she must taste, like a sweet, sticky sugar high. I'd like to climb on to the bed right now, pull myself over to her and bury my face inside her. But I understand her game by now. I know she wants to direct the action.

'I bet you'd like to fuck me,' she murmurs as she lets her hand glide over her dark, shiny pubic hair.

'Yes,' I moan, because that's a great idea too. My face, my cock, I've give anything to bury any part of me inside her right now. 'Oh god, yes.'

'Mmm,' she coos, 'but I'm afraid I can't let you right now. I'm torn but, if you come and fuck me, I won't be able to look at you. And you look so beautiful, naked in your chair, sated, with your come smeared over you. Tell me you don't mind waiting.'

There's that hypnotic tone to her voice again. I can't disobey her, even though I can hardly bear to stay where I'm sitting. But I swallow hard, trying not to shake with frustration. 'I don't ... I don't mind.'

I can scarcely believe it's possible after coming twice in quick succession, but my cock stirs as I watch her movements become more vigorous.

'Have you ever come in your chair before?'

'No, never.'

'Really?' She's panting so hard now she can barely get the words out.

'Really, I've never. I haven't done anything like this since, since I've been like this.'

'You never ... you never even made yourself come, though? You never played with yourself while you were sitting in the chair?'

I shake my head. 'No. I only do that in bed.'

'You should.' She is bucking against her hand now, squirming hard on the bed. 'I'd like to see that. I'd like to see you touch yourself. Do it now, just so I can see what you do.'

'I can't.' I hate to deny her, but there is no way I'm going to get anything further out of my cock at this moment. No matter what she does.

She smiles as if the solution is obvious. 'Just touch it. Play act for me.'

I reach down and take my very tender cock in my hand, stroking it lightly, doing what I hope will put on a good show for her.

I've never thought of myself as an exhibitionist before, but soon I'm throwing my head back, moaning and biting my lip, just because I want to make her come harder.

And she does. As I writhe and moan for her, she

does the same for real. She's getting herself off looking at me in my chair. She's arching up into her own hand, and screaming something about me being the most beautiful thing she has even seen.

She's really not bad herself.

Much later, in the middle of the night, I wake to find her rubbing herself against my legs, sliding, wet and needy, against my unfeeling thigh. When she realises I am awake she begins to kiss me roughly and, every time her mouth is free, asks me to tell her, again and again, that I can't move, that I can barely feel her wetness coating my useless, broken legs, that I can't walk.

'Again.'
'I can't walk.'
'Again.'
'I can't walk.'
'Again.'
'I. Can't. Walk.'

And she comes, screaming, twisting my nipples hard, so I scream too.

Mary

'Mary?' Carrie says from the doorway, in an are-you-awake? sort of voice.

As no other part of me protrudes from under the duvet, she is addressing my hair. My hair and a scrunchy heap of knock-off Cath Kidson florals.

'Mary?' she says again, in a slightly louder, slightly more irritated voice.

What time did I get in last night? Too late. I really don't want to be awake yet. I try to cling to sleep, ignoring Carrie's attempts to drag me into her world, and do a quick bodily functions check instead.

I seem to be, well, functioning. No hangover. Some mild and even quite pleasant soreness. Extreme tiredness. Last night, last night . . .?

I am in my own bed, right? Oh yeah, the presence of Carrie and her continued shouting makes that very likely. Oh, please shut up, Carrie. Shut up and let me sleep.

'Mary, fuck's sake,' Carrie snaps. And then we're over the edge, she's stomping across the room, her trademark hippyesque patience dissolving. She shakes me, or at least she shakes the crumpled heap of duvet and hair that currently approximates to me.

'I'm not your mum, you know,' she says in a sort of semi-shout. 'But that wanker Dr Mercury's on the phone, freaking me out. Apparently you were meant to have been there half an hour ago.'

'Huh?' I say, because ignoring Carrie is really not working anymore, not with the shaking and shouting.

'He said something like Semitics? A Semitics tutorial? Isn't that some kind of Jewish thing?'

Oh. Shit.

Suddenly realising not just where I am but where I am supposed to be, I fling back the covers in a single decisive action. 'Semiotics,' I say to Carrie, who is standing over me, her hand still outstretched for continued shaking, and looking as usual as if she has been spun entirely out of muesli. 'A semiotics tutorial.'

I'm awake.

I'm awake and I remember.

Oh. My. God.

* * *

I put my clothes on – sadly, not the all-conquering cherry dress, which looks rather anti-climactic crumpled on my bedroom floor – and stumble from bedroom to bathroom to kitchen to Carrie's sense-of-humour-vacuum.

'Sorry,' I say.

Carrie shrugs and I bustle round her to get some tea.

God, I've tried to like Carrie, I really have. But she's so earnest, and irritable, and weird. We clash in every way. Not least because she's the most un-sexually-motivated person I've ever met. I don't think she's ever *had* sex. And I'm, well, Mercury has called me over-sexed, and coming from him that's quite a lofty accolade.

Carrie also has a face that puts me in mind of a Cornish pasty, and, call me shallow, but I think that puts me off her most of all. She's just weird-looking – it creeps me out.

But, well, I'm kind of stuck with her. I needed somewhere to live. It was a short-of-notice, short-of-cash thing, and Carrie's spare room was going cheap after the previous lodger had left in a hurry. (My guess is they put some meat in the fridge, which would practically cause World War Three in this flat.)

'Yeah,' Carrie finally says in the kitchen after a characteristic uncomfortable silence, 'it was hard to wake you up. Are you OK?'

'Um, I'm fine. I just had a bit of a late one last night.'

''Kay,' Carrie says, so obviously not interested it's almost laughable. Then, thankfully, she takes her plate of toast (with far too much Marmite) and walks out of the room.

When I hear the click of her bedroom door closing I can feel myself relax. I've lived with Carrie for five months now and this is about as good as we get. The cast of *Friends* we are not.

Alone with my gently brewing tea in the quiet kitchen, I start to turn things over in my mind. Last night, and, of course, David.

Oh my god, David. I can feel myself starting to get all hot and bothered just from thinking about him. About flesh and metal and limbs and wheels.

And eventually, after much musing, all my dirty thoughts come together and centre themselves on one image, that of David's hard, bare arms and the way their muscles flexed as he wheeled himself across the bedroom, naked in his wheelchair. My mouth is dry.

I have to stop that thought right there, before I turn into a puddle on the floor and have to go back to bed, because I am already stupidly late for my tutorial with Mercury. Late enough, in fact, that fifteen minutes of fantasising really isn't going to make a lot of difference, but there's no point in taking the piss.

And anyway, I know that Dr Milo Mercury, or Mercury as he insists on being called, isn't actually going to be worried about my hour and a half (and counting) of lateness. Not when I tell him why – in unnecessary detail.

And details are forthcoming, when half an hour later, Mercury and I are not talking about semiotics, or even about English Literature in general, but about hot sexy boys and, more specifically, hot sexy David.

'I'm so happy for you, darling,' Mercury says, gushing, totally, but he is allowed to, being just the right amount of gay and just the right amount of old to get away with it. 'You know, I was starting to think your strange little obsession for having sex with the unfortunate was going to be a lost cause. I'm glad you finally found a specimen that was worth indulging your vileness for. After all, you were never really the one for turning nunwards.'

'Nunwards? You're an English professor and you happily use the word nunwards?'

Mercury makes a noise that sounds worryingly like 'Tish'.

I shrug.

'In any case, you flatter me. Professorship is still maddeningly unreachable. I am, and am likely to remain, nothing more than a humble lecturer in a ridiculously provincial university.' Mercury sighs melodramatically. I'm sure he's putting on this little poor-me performance for my amusement. Which is kind, but I'm the one with all the amusing stories today, and Mercury can't keep the floor for long – not without missing out on the best story I've had for months. And he knows it. 'So, sweetie,' he says, with a jangle of his cup and saucer, 'are you going see Mr Gorgeously-Unfortunate again?'

'Oh, I don't know.' David's elegantly muscled arms are still woefully high on my things-to-think-about agenda, but I know I can't keep going there. 'It's not really a good idea, is it?'

'It isn't?'

'Well, no. I mean, it isn't fair. I can't just have sex with him because I'm kinky for his misfortune. He is a real person, after all.' I take a big gulp of my now rather lukewarm tea.

'I would say his realness is more of a reason that you should be having sex with him than a reason that you shouldn't. I think, darling, when it comes to your kink for gorgeous young cripples, you've had more than enough sex with imaginary people.'

'But you've got to agree, it's not right.'

'Not right? Not right to have sex with someone that you find sexually attractive, and who appears to be attracted to you right back? How is that not right? Unless you have suddenly become a member of some reactionary religious sect.'

I make a sort of protesting noise here, half remembering something David might have said last night about me not being his usual type.

'Well,' say Mercury, acknowledging my objection, 'whatever you might think about that, from what you've said he certainly seemed happy to accept your kind offer of sex, so why should he complain?'

I put my cup of tea down on top of a pile of glossy hardbacks that are teetering, rather worryingly, on a small table. It is far too cold to drink now. I don't know how it got so freezing so fast. Maybe Mercury made it for the time I was meant to turn up rather than the time I actually did, for spite. (He really might have. Mercury can be a bit weird sometimes.)

As I look over at him, not knowing what to say next, Mercury smiles, a playful boyishness rippling over his worn-out old face. I feel instantly happy, all warm inside – partly because I know that Mercury has seen it all, he's cast-iron unshockable, but mostly because there is something in his manner that makes me feel so yummy I just want to hug him. (I don't though. Ever. Neither of us is the hugging kind. Well, I'm not and Mercury claims that he doesn't hug girls because they smell of perfume and that makes him cough.) Somehow, when Mercury smiles at me, the prospect of David – and, specifically, more sex with David – seems so much more real and possible than it did before.

I walk to the university library from Mercury's office. Campus looks lovely. It might still be freezing February, but through my shagadelic-coloured spectacles spring has sprung, and my night with David has left my cockles warm enough that I can't feel the nasty nippy chill in the air. The green, green grass is so bright in the sparky winter air that it's almost fluorescent, and edged with glistening dewy silver. The first little flowers are making their pastel presence felt in the dark beds. It reminds me of that super-sexually-charged lap David and I did around the park yesterday as a weird kind of foreplay. The sap is rising everywhere.

I'm also thinking about what Mercury said, about how having sex with someone who wants to have sex right back can't possibly be wrong. Turning his words over and over in my mind. Perversely, I can't help wishing Mercury hadn't said what he did. It's just confused me, frankly. I had been hoping that he would help me draw a line under the whole thing by laughing at me for being such a dreadful pervert and telling me I should leave the poor crippled boy alone.

But he (rather predictably) told me to go for it – in his own roundabout way. Which means I'm stuck, because there's no way I'm going to be able to say no with only my own willpower to rely on. After all, just what are you supposed to do when you meet someone who could be one of your most pantingly potent sexual fantasies made into flesh and blood and tubular steel and pneumatic rubber? But the problem is – oh god, what is the problem again?

Because it's not just his disability. It is a lot his disability; I'm not going to lie about that, least of all inside my own head. But there is other stuff. It's also about his ability, cringingly cheesy as that sounds. It's the whole package. The fact that he looks like a super-hero as imagined by a glam-rock-addicted comic-book artist sometime in the early 70s.

I wouldn't be tying myself up in knots if he was just any old guy in a wheelchair. It's the fact he's a fucking wet dream in a wheelchair. And he doesn't seem to realise it. Not at the moment, anyway. So why shouldn't I be the one to break the good news to him?

Also, I really like his arms. Although, when I think about his arms, I mostly think about how those toned sleek muscles would look if they were taut and stretched by the way I'd tie his wrists behind his back.

I can imagine that quite precisely, because I've tied lots of men's wrists behind their backs. I have found that, if that is the thing one wants to do, there really is no shortage of willing male wrists. Some of them even supply their own slinky rope.

I even had this boyfriend once – and he was a very big fan of being tied up by me – who knew about my disability fetish and managed to borrow a wheelchair from, well, from god knows where, really. I never asked – gift horses and all that. And anyway, as soon as I saw it I was in no real state to ask about logistics.

It was a Friday night. I had got home from work, utterly shagged and so not in the mood to be, well, utterly shagged, but then I saw this filthy great wheelchair sitting there and, frankly, I got so turned on so quick I might as well have been wired up to the mains.

Gavin (that was the wheelchair-procuring guy's name – I think) was delighted by my reaction, of course. I'd just stopped dead in the hall, staring, coat half-on, half-off, mesmerised by this wheelchair. Transfixed until Gavin winked and said, 'You like it then? Happy birthday.'

'It's not my –' I started to say, but I trailed off because whatever the calendar might have said, it might not have been my birthday five minutes ago, but it certainly was now.

So instead I just said, 'What are you doing?' My voice sounded low, more than low, more than deep, it sounded like it had just been exhumed from somewhere.

Gavin wrinkled his forehead at me. 'What do you mean? You like it, don't you? I can tell you like it.'

'I mean,' I said, the words coming out of my mouth before I could even think them, 'what are you doing standing over there when you could be sitting in that chair right now?'

'Oh.' And then Gavin smiled the smile of a man who had the key to his girlfriend's sexuality sitting within easy reach on the living-room carpet, and scooted into the chair with a wink and a smile.

Of course, during the evening of kinked-out fun that transpired, I never quite managed to forget that he could really walk. And that did spoil it a bit, because I guess my fetish is for the not-being-able-to-walk part as much as the being-sat-in-a-wheelchair bit. (And the fact that he jumped into the chair with such explosive enthusiasm didn't help my suspension of disbelief.)

But I was going to make the best of it. My god, was

I ever. And there really was a best to be made. Good old Gavin might have been – especially in retrospect – a slightly creepy, slightly over-eager guy who would do anything for a kinky shag, but, as I tied his hands, I knew that this evening was going to provide happy memories for many nights to come. The gift that keeps on giving, and all that.

I strapped his wrists to the armrests, pulling the rope hard around his left wrist, until it bit into his skin. He moaned to himself and then softly whispered, 'Tighter, oh god, tighter.'

I loved that naughty moan, so I obliged. I really shouldn't have – it was tight enough already and he'd have some nasty marks there later – but how could I resist such a greedy little pain slut?

As I wheeled the bound and blindfolded Gavin into the bedroom, I realised that wheelchair bondage had some distinct advantages all of its own – above any kink factor – because how else could someone be so helpless but so completely manoeuvrable? It was a revelation and a brilliant bonus.

A few seconds of rummaging around in the basket of kink I kept under the bed produced all the necessary equipment for a fun evening. It was actually my grandmother's old picnic basket. I don't know what she'd have thought about my using it to house a huge messy tangle of leather and chain and bondage gear.

Suitably equipped, I moved closer to Gavin. He could tell I was there, even though he couldn't see me. He was so used to being blindfolded that his senses were super-Spidermanlike.

I touched his mouth with one finger, and he parted his lips enough for me to slip it inside. He sucked. His mouth was hot and wet. And nice. His gentle rhythmic sucking seemed to communicate an urgent neediness, a kind of desperation that got me squirming as I stood there. I liked the way he needed it, the way he was so desperate for this dirty, kinky sex. The way he had to be enslaved so much that it, the desire for it, was what really enslaved him. He didn't submit to me as much as to his own desire for submission. I really loved that, because I love inescapable bondage and what could be more inescapable than one's own brain?

And then I made a snap decision. Literally. I pulled my finger out of Gavin's mouth and, with only a quick pause for a rummage in the basket, snapped a sharp, hard pair of nipple clamps on to his equally hard nipples. Ignoring his reaction, I left the room and went to make a cup of tea.

Ah, this part was always the hardest. I was so buzzy with adrenalin. It was so hard to wait on my own, to step outside it, but I knew that with Gavin it was so much better to get a little distance. One of us needed to be the one to hold back, and it was never, ever going to be him.

I tried not to think about him as I listened to the hiss of the kettle. I tried not to think about him, tied too tightly to the wheelchair. Blindfolded, so he didn't even know if I was still there or not. Helpless to remove the jagged teeth that were biting harder and harder on his nipples. This hiss of the kettle became a bubbly roar.

I had to try really hard not to squirm.

A few minutes later, before my tea was cool enough to drink, he began to call out from the bedroom.

'Mary,' he said, just loud enough for me to hear. 'Mary, please.'

Despite my distance and my attempts at calming

myself, I was still slightly shaky from the sex-adrenalin and I would have liked nothing more than to go back into the bedroom and press myself against him. But I needed to steady the pace, take it slow. I ignored him and drank some tea.

He knew I could hear him. It wasn't a big flat and he knew I'd never go out and leave him tied. So he knew I was listening to his pleas and ignoring them. I loved that. I wondered if he liked it too. If it was turning him on as much as it was me. I wondered how long I could bear to make him wait.

'Please, Mary. It hurts.'

I drank some more tea, slowly.

'Mary!'

But I made myself finish the whole cup before I went back into the bedroom.

I stood in the doorway. God, I still couldn't get over the fact he was sitting in a wheelchair. I almost couldn't bear to look. It was too sexy. So sexy it hurt.

I could tell he had been pulling at the rough ropes by the reddish marks on his wrists, and his blindfold was all askew, probably because he'd been rubbing it against his shoulder to try and make it budge. He might be able to see a little round the edges of it, but not that much, and I didn't really care. I had a plan. A bad plan. Those nipple clamps hurt. A lot. He'd be reaching his limit with them soon. And I wanted to play a little game with that.

'What?' I said, sudden and sharp enough to make him jump a little. 'What do you want, you dumb little bitch? Are you bored?'

'Mary,' he said, his voice cracking and desperate. 'Mary, please.' He was pulling at the ropes around his wrists while he talked. His legs weren't tied (that would have spoiled it), and I could see him twitch his left leg a little, even though he was probably trying not to move them. It was clearly hard, though. Hard for him to keep up the pretence when I was putting him under so much duress. Mmm, those clamps. They really did hurt.

'What?' I asked again. Pretending I didn't know what the problem was.

'Please, Mary, please take the clamps off.'

Oh dear. His poor little tortured tits. They'd gone nearly white. Those clamps were so nasty, and it had been, what? Ten minutes? Ouch. Poor baby.

I didn't answer, though. I just looked at him, tied there. He was mostly dressed. Well, he had lost his trousers somewhere along the line, but his neat white underpants were still on – with a satisfying damp patch of delicious boy-come spreading across his crotch – and his shirt was still there, just, open and pulled back, bunching down his arms, almost adding to his bondage. There was something very particular about Gavin – so neat, so clean-cut – that made me want to keep his shirt on, one way or another. He wore a shirt to work every day. Always clean, always ironed. I liked to dirty them up. Like I dirty him up. Spoil my clean-cut corporate drone. Break him down completely, but keep a little token there, a little evidence of who he used to be before I took everything away from him.

He must have been getting quite uncomfortable by now. OK, the wheelchair itself was quite comfortable, designed for hours of use, and apart from his wrists I hadn't tied him particularly tight, but those clamps, with their nasty, angry little teeth, were digging into him. Clamps and a blindfold were the combination he hated most. And so that was what he got, more often than not.

I took a step nearer, still not speaking, and stroked one of his tightly pinched nipples.

He flinched so hard he almost made the chair tip over. Then, to steady him, I put my other hand on one of the chair's tyres. When I touched it, everything seemed to liquefy.

'Does that hurt?' I said, worrying the nipple a little more, a measured, gentle inquiry.

'Y-y-yes,' he said, finding it hard to speak, forgetting to use any of the niceties that he was normally only too eager to embroider every exchange with, much to my annoyance.

I took the little piece of his flesh between my fingers and toyed with it, making him hiss and roll his head from side to side. 'Oh dear,' I commiserated, 'does it hurt that much?' And then I pinched him really hard.

He screamed out loud and then said, with a gratifying note of real panic, 'Please, please take them off.'

I laughed softly. I was close enough to him now that most of my lower body was touching the chair. The metal was cool and frighteningly real against my legs. 'Take them off? Why on earth should I do that? They look so pretty.' I ran my finger along the chain that connected the clamps until I reached the centre, and pulled gently.

Gavin yelped, struggling as far as his bondage would allow. 'Please, please, I can't stand it.'

'Well.' I paused to swallow, as if taking my time weighing up my options. 'I suppose I could consider it. What will you do for me? If I take them off?'

'Anything!' The answer came without a moment's pause.

'Really? Anything?' Thoughtfully, I placed each hand on one of the clamps, poised to remove them. 'You do realise, I suppose, how much it is going to hurt when these come off, don't you?'

'Yes, yes, I do,' Gavin said, nodding impatiently, almost angry at my constant teasing and delaying.

'And you still insist you want them off?' As I spoke I played around with the clamps some more, twisting and tugging them a little, watching the reactions.

'Yes.'

'And in return you will do anything?'

'Yes, yes, yes.'

'OK then, say when.'

Gavin was silent for a moment, letting my words sink into his endorphin-fuzzed little brain.

I smiled. Oh, yes, my darling, I thought to myself, warm fuzzies rushing all over my body, if you want them off, you are going to have to tell me exactly when to hurt you.

A few more moments passed, and then his lips moved, slowly at first. I could almost see the strain of his need to obey me wrestling with his better judgement; could almost see his mouth begin to form his safe word. But when that swollen red mouth eventually did open he said, distinctly and defiantly, 'Now.'

I squeezed quickly, both clamps at once and they came off, falling into my fingers. Almost immediately Gavin screamed, bucking forward, coming close to overturning the chair, pulling his unrestrained legs up, knees bending into his chest for comfort as best they could.

I waited a couple of seconds, then reached forward and removed his blindfold. He looked up, biting his lip, but timidly triumphant.

I smiled right back. 'You said you'd do anything?'

'Yes.'

'Good.' I held up the clamps, letting them dangle in front of Gavin's face for a moment. 'I want you to beg me to put these back on.'

Gavin looked at me, and it was like watching all the air rush out of a balloon as he said, 'Aw, god, no.' And I knew then. I knew what was coming next. His whole demeanour had suddenly changed. The dynamic I had built just drained away. 'I can't, Mary. No, I really can't. Fuck, shit, fuck, strawberry, fuck, sorry, fuck.'

Strawberry. His safe word.

I was so disappointed. It was awful to have to stop when I was so proud of what I'd created and so unbelievably turned on. I put the clamps down and waited. Waited to hear if it was a stop-altogether strawberry, or a stop-for-a-moment strawberry. Even though I kind of knew.

'Shit, sorry, that was so . . . but, no way,' Gavin said, which made a strange sense.

'Do you want to stop?'

'No, god, no, it's great. But look. I can't do any more of this. I know.' He looked up at me. 'Why don't you fuck me? I'd really like that. I really want you to fuck me.'

He meant could I fuck him up the arse with my strap on, of course. That was always his dream destination. And my Gavin, well, he wasn't afraid to ask for what he wanted.

'Well, I don't know,' I began, 'you're not really in the right position.' And, although I stayed quite calm outside, inside my brain was going, 'fuck, fuck, fuck' and 'abort, abort, abort' because the moment was suddenly so gone. Gavin was getting all pushy. And although there was this big part of me that adored his great suffocating sexual need, the flip side of that was his tendency to be *too* pushy and needy, which just ruined everything. Even when it was supposed to be all about me and my kinks, it still seemed to end up being all about him. I was pissed off about that.

I suddenly felt that this whole special night with the wheelchair had been ruined. The wheelchair, for Gavin, was just a means to an end, not the selfless gesture I'd taken it for. The plan all along was to give me a few wheelchair-centred thrills and then say the safe word and bring on one of his favourite kinks. Bastard. So much for my birthday present. Even if it wasn't actually my birthday.

The evening just went downhill from there. A little later, in bed, after some scene-finishing standard-missionary-position sex, which was probably not quite what either of us wanted (and I didn't fuck him up the arse, because, much as I do enjoy that when the time is right, the time when they've asked for it is never right), Gavin sealed his fate when he leant over me to grab a cigarette and said, 'I bet you're glad I'm not a real cripple, though. You wouldn't want to miss out.'

'Miss out on what?'

'What do you think?' he said, lighting up (even though I hate smoking in the bedroom, and had told him so several times). 'Fuckity-fuck.' He pumped his hips to make his point perfectly clear (and also to make it clear what a wanker he was.)

I played dumb, though, even though I knew what he was getting at. I wanted him to say it. To spell it out for me. 'Huh?'

'Well, you know, some poor crippled boy might turn

you on with his helplessness, but you'd miss out when he couldn't give you a good seeing-to at the end, wouldn't you?'

'Would I really?'

'Yeah. Obviously. Well, stands to reason: if he can't work his legs he isn't going to be able to work his dick, is he? I mean, it's like the same muscles and shit.'

'Oh god, Gavin. It so isn't,' I said, unable to remain aloof any longer. 'Do you have to be such an idiot? It's not like that.'

'Well, course, I haven't done extensive research like some people.' Gavin said, still joky when he shouldn't have been joky. Making me shudder.

I sighed hard enough to let him know I was pissed off. I didn't reply, though. I couldn't bear to. I just rolled over and went to sleep.

I think that was what killed it with Gavin and me. The wheelchair thing was the last straw. I had known for ages that Gavin was all wrong for me, but somehow he always seemed to sucker me back in with some kind of kinky, sexy idea for fun playtime. The wheelchair turning up in the living room was probably just another attempt to stop me realising that I didn't really like him all that much.

But it had totally backfired this time, because the games with the chair – or, at least, the way it ended up – just made me realise how much I wanted the real thing. A guy who was really disabled. And preferably not as much of an idiot as Gavin.

David

The internet – a good thing.

No matter how many 'The Internet Ate My Hamster'-

style stories appear in the media, no one can honestly say that we aren't better off now we are all connected to each other via millions and millions of miles of cable and wi-fi and cascading stylesheets. And I can talk authoritatively like that because I, like so many others of my age and technical abilities, am a web designer.

So yes, I am a little biased about the wonders of the web, because it does provide me with my bread and butter (albeit quite thinly sliced bread with just a smear of butter). But – speaking objectively, honest – the internet is wonderful. For a start it is open all hours. It's not called the World Wide Web for nothing (although it isn't called the World Wide Web that much any more, for some reason). This means that it might be eight in the morning in the arse-end-of-nowhere town where I live, but it's just struck 1 a.m. on the west coast of America, which is where I'm heading right now, hitching a ride on the back of a mouse. Surfing URL.

I'm checking in with the girlfriend. I suppose I shouldn't call her my girlfriend, mainly because she isn't my girlfriend. But last night with Mary-the-weird-student was the first time I was unfaithful to her. Not that I ever got the chance to be unfaithful to her before. I could call her my cybergirlfriend, but she isn't even that. She's more of a work-avoidance tactic, if I'm honest.

DragonSlayer666: <Hi baby, how are you>

Yeah, that's my username. Crappy isn't it? I know, but it's tough shit. I can't be bothered to go through the irritating signing-up process all over again, which

37

is what it would take to change it to something less sad.

It's actually a hangover from when I was a teenager and utterly crazy-mad for fantasy role-playing games. Which isn't to say that I don't play them any more, because I do. Just not as much as I used to. Yeah, I stop to eat and sleep now. And to talk to . . .

Slutbox04: <Hey>

Yeah. I know. And, no, I haven't asked what a nice girl like her is doing with a username like that. Not that she is a nice girl – far from it. And yeah, I know exactly what else you're thinking about her too.

DragonSlayer666: <You able to stay up for a bit?>
Slutbox04: <For you baby, always>

You're thinking: that's not a real woman. You are, aren't you? There's no way that that's a woman with a username like that. Don't bother denying it. I know. In fact, I actually agree with you. I've seen *Closer*, I know Slutbox04 could easily be some creepy guy pretending to be a woman for some kind of bizarre psychosexual kick.

DragonSlayer666: <I was hoping you'd say that>

Well, how about I tell you something right now. Something most people would never ever guess about me. Something that will kill stone-dead all those stereotypical opinions that you are forming of me, right now. I don't care if it is a man. I really don't. I fact I think that is kind of hot in a weird and fucked-up way.

Surprised?

I read in a magazine the other day that this is called being heteroflexible: essentially straight but not likely to run screaming from the room at the merest suggestion of gay sex. Don't go getting any ideas now. I'm not saying I'm desperate for a cock up my arse. Not at all. But with the right guy at the right time ... maybe it could happen. Not that it's likely to, these days. Mary the student notwithstanding, when it comes to rampant bisexuality, I've probably missed my window.

But, anyway, back to Slutbox04. Can't keep the nice lady waiting, can I?

Slutbox04: <So what are you going to do to keep me awake?>

DragonSlayer666: <I could tell you what I've got right here in my underwear>

Slutbox04: <Hmm, interesting prospect. But how about you tell me some more about the underwear first?>

DragonSlayer666: <OK. They're white briefs. A little bit tight in the back, but not uncomfortable>

Slutbox04: <You wearing anything else with those jockeys, gorgeous?>

DragonSlayer666: <Nope. I just got out of bed>

Slutbox04: <You just got out of bed? So, does the morning find you with a little wood in those shorts?>

DragonSlayer666: <Well, it does now>

Slutbox04: <Really?>

DragonSlayer666: <Oh yes. It's quite a problem. LOL. I seem to have an enormous erection and since this conversation began it's just getting worse>

I don't actually have an erection. That's just a bit of sexy talk for her benefit. I am wearing white underpants, though. And my cock does feel tingly and nice. But I'm not really there yet – which isn't all that surprising after last night. But there's no harm in letting her think that the very act of typing messages to her gets me standing to attention, all manly and virile. See, that's the whole point of my relationship with Slutbox04: I can tell her whatever I want. Whatever I want about my body.

Slutbox04: <You know what? If only you were a girl I would have the bestest present for you. It's a USB vibrator>

DragonSlayer666: <What? A what?>

Slutbox04: <A USB vibrator. It's a vibrator. You know, bzzz. And it's powered by the computer. Just plug it into the USB port>

DragonSlayer666: <And you have one?>

Slutbox04: <Wearing it right now baby>

DragonSlayer666: <You naughty girl. What have you been doing?>

Slutbox04: <Waiting all evening for you to wake up and come online. Thinking about you. Looking at porn. Looking at your picture. Getting wet>

Oh yeah. She has this picture I sent her. It's of me. But it's a couple of years old. Taken before the accident. It's actually of me on my bike. The bike that everyone assumes is the cause of my being in a wheelchair.

It isn't, actually. People always seem to think: he's in a wheelchair, he used to ride a motorbike, cause = effect. But that's not the case. I'm not saying that a motorbike on a wet night isn't a fast track to Casualty – I know the stats. But that wasn't the case with me. It happened while I was walking, and – to keep it brief

– some twat came speeding along while I was crossing the road.

In some ways it's actually lucky for me that it did happen that way, rather than in some stupid motorbike deathwish scenario, because with this accident (a) he was insured and (b) it was all his fault. Which are both big factors when it comes to getting a nice adapted bungalow, a nice adapted car, a nice adapted life.

But anyway, yes, back to Slutbox04 and her picture of me on the motorbike that did not cause my life-changing accident. I used to take a very good photograph, and it's one of my better ones, so it's a very sexy picture, even if I do say so myself.

And dear Slutbox04 is right now pleasuring him/herself with some kind of freaked-out geek-girl hardware while she flicks between assorted hardcore images on the net and a picture of photogenic old me, in my leathers, back when my legs still worked.

This can only end well.

Oh yeah, and before you ask, no, she doesn't know about the distinct difference between the me in her picture and the me of today. As far as she's concerned the person she is talking to across the electro-ether is the same fully functional human being that is straddling the silver cream machine in her picture.

DragonSlayer666: <Getting wet, there?>

Slutbox04: <Yeah, baby. Wet. Got my little USB friend cranked up to the max. I'm a naughty girl>

DragonSlayer666: <You certainly are>

Slutbox04: <So what would a big strong man like you do to a bad, bad little slutty girl like me, you know, if you were right here with me?>

DragonSlayer666: <You really want to know?>
Slutbox04: <I really want to know>

God, she is so good at this. She likes me to be quite domineering, dominant, all that. And I quite like that too. But it's not really my thing, so normally it would be hard for me to know where to start. But not with her. She tells me right where to push.

All the more reason why it's better that she doesn't know I'm not the owner of a fully functioning body.

DragonSlayer666: <Well, you have been pretty bad. All those naughty things you've been up to, touching yourself, getting wet, looking at porn>
Slutbox04: <But I was waiting for you>
DragonSlayer666: <Well, you really should have been more patient>
Slutbox04: <I'm sorry, Sir, you're right>
DragonSlayer666: <So, tell me, what do you think would be a suitable punishment?>

Ah, yes, a slight cop-out by me, but the thing is, I can just about get away with it with her, and it makes sense, because she is so much more experienced at this sort of thing than me. I've learnt so much from her about this kinky-assed stuff.

Slutbox04: <Well I guess it should be something rather humiliating. And painful. Painful and humiliating>
DragonSlayer666: <Hmm, yes. Painful and humiliating, that sounds about right>
Slutbox04: <What about my large buttplug? I could wear that all day tomorrow. I have to run masses of errands tomorrow, so that would be awful. It really turns me

on to have it in too, so that would be hard. Make things hard, I mean. I certainly wouldn't forget about it in a hurry>

DragonSlayer666: <Sounds interesting. You're sure you wouldn't enjoy that too much?>

And I have to ask, because the truth is, even though I have the full resources of Google at my disposal and it's the work of a few clicks to discover what a buttplug is and what one looks like, I really have no idea whether it would feel pleasant or not. It doesn't sound very pleasant, but with this girl you really never can tell.

I suppose I could order one and try it out myself, just so I know for future reference, you understand. I open another window on my browser, and start inputting my credit card details into a sex toy site, trying not to question my actions too much.

Slutbox04: <Oh no, Sir, the big one isn't pleasurable at all. The big one is terrible>

DragonSlayer666: <Hmm, well, that sounds OK, but I really think I need to make sure you don't enjoy it too much. How about you wear the big buttplug all day, but you also have no orgasms until further notice>

Slutbox04: <Oh no, please>

DragonSlayer666: <No complaints. And using that USB vibrator thingy counts>

See, like I say, I'm new, but I'm learning.

Mary

The basement of the university library is vast. A huge echoey dungeon, full of ominous bolted-together metal apparatus, although sadly the metalware here is just the Meccanoesque nuts and bolts of the bookshelves.

I sidle along the racks, occasionally wiping dust away with my fingers like a disapproving mother-in-law. I should be looking for obscure texts about Victorian literature (after the public library in town proved, unsurprisingly, worse than useless) but my mind is still throbbing from my night with David. And I just can't stop dwelling on the past.

David isn't the first disabled guy I've ever been with. After Gavin and the wheelchair episode that made me decide I wanted the real deal, I went out and found myself an actual, full-blown disabled boyfriend. It wasn't even that difficult. I had just what I'd always wanted. I couldn't understand why it had taken me so long to get with the programme.

I met Rich in a supermarket, in a scenario rather similar to my David pick up, except that the actual sex, when we got into the bedroom, might have been rather more A-to-B straightforward – but I'll get to that later. This was back when I lived in Bristol, and I was a career bitch then, so I was rather more cashed-up than I am now. Also, my flatmate had moved out somewhere in the middle of the Gavin-dumping farrago, which wasn't pretty. So, after I'd shagged dear little Rich into oblivion, he just never went home. He still lived with his mum when I met him – he was twenty, or something insanely young like that – and my flat was on the ground floor and just accessible enough to be viable for him. So he was a live-in sexy twenty-year-old in a wheelchair, less than a week after I'd sidled up to him next to the frozen peas.

Then – this was a quick-and-dirty rebound-from-

Gavin relationship, remember – the whole thing started to splinter and crack before my eyes in the same breathless fast-forward way it had begun.

Right from the start, I'd tried to be upfront with Rich about what I saw in him. Well, maybe I didn't say, 'I am attracted to you because you're in a wheelchair,' or talk about 'licking the footplate' as I did with David, but I didn't hide it. I certainly didn't pretend to be anything other than Little Miss Kinky. But Rich soon made it clear that while he liked the sex – though he didn't get as much as he would have liked (what twenty-year-old does!) – he wasn't too keen on all that kinky stuff I considered an essential part of a fun night in.

Yes. Call me a fool, but in my brain I had automatically equated disabled/in-a-wheelchair with kinky-as-all-hell. And Rich just wasn't into all that stuff, which in my book is a fundamental incompatibility.

But I didn't give up straight away. How could I? Rich was so perfect in so many other ways. I tried everything to get him to come round to my kinky way of thinking, believing, a little desperately, that he'd like it if he would only give it a chance. Eager to convert him sooner rather than later, I rattled my chains and manacles in Rich's face and, each and every time, he screwed up his nose and suggested some rather more vanilla diversions instead.

It was the very definition of frustration. So near, and yet . . .

But I still didn't give up. I tried to go vanilla. Consoling myself with reminders that Rich was heartbreakingly beautiful, and watching him glide around my flat in his chair like a ballerina on wheels should have been more than enough for me.

But soon I was looking longingly over his shoulder at my toy box. At my glittering icy-cold chains, my butter-soft leather cuffs, my nasty little instruments of pain. And I would find myself daydreaming about things I'd done with stupid, dumb-ass, pig-headed, needy, greedy sub-Gavin. Like how, if I didn't play dirty with him for a week or so, I'd come home to find Gavin casually wearing a leather collar, or with a pair of handcuffs dangling from one wrist.

So the relationship I had with Rich died a slow death, the slow death of no sex. And of my frustrated sexual desires for him, which were not reciprocated, well, not reciprocated in the way I wanted them to be. I think we were together for a little less than six months, and we probably stopped having sex altogether after two.

When we finally split it was nasty. Rich was vicious about my dark side, my bedroom badness. When he left me he said, 'Shit, Mary, seriously, do you really think any guy who is already disabled is going to want to get tied up? It's stupid. You're stupid. Sick and stupid.' Or something like that. Which was one of the main factors in my decision to bury my desires for disabled men deep, deep in a part of my brain where even my subconscious was scared to visit.

So then it was back to able-bodied guys. The wheelchair thing was firmly labelled a non-starter. Rich was right; I should keep my disgusting kinked-up self away from people who probably had enough to deal with.

So after Rich – for eight long years – I stuck exclusively to able-bodied guys. Until now. Until David.

And talking of now, weirdly, by the time I've finished thinking about Rich by way of David by way of Gavin and a few other chapters from the book entitled

My Shady Past, I realise I have left the university library and walked all the way from campus into the town centre and I'm right in front of the other library, the public library. The place where I met David.

Yeah, the same library I hardly ever go to.

What on earth am I doing here?

David

I leave my cyberchick to her frustrated bedtime and dreams of extra large buttplugs, in favour of a bowl of breakfast cereal, followed by a drive over to mum's house to drop off her library books.

I know, I know, my life is just thrill-a-minute, isn't it?

I live in the heart of suburbia, just off the ring road, so after only a few twists and turns I am on the dual carriageway, the open road, with only the fifty trillion roundabouts that litter it to slow me down.

I love driving my car. I love it almost as much as I used to love riding my bike. In fact, I might love it more, because now, in a way, driving makes me normal.

Some people are surprised that I can. Which is a bit ridiculous – I mean, what century is this? But every so often I meet someone who does seem to find it incredible, even when I explain that the car I use is specially adapted for disabled drivers, so I can do everything I need to do with my hands. They still look at me like I'm making it all up. Like my brain has stopped working along with my legs and I have strange delusions that I can drive a car.

I'm not scared of cars, or traffic, or anything, after what happened to me. Actually, as the driver of the car that hit me walked away from the accident practically unhurt, I find being inside the welded steel armour of a car makes me feel quite safe.

After almost a full circuit of the ring road, I pull off at one of the roundabouts and drive into the town centre.

Apparently my delightful home town is the largest place in the UK not to have its own branch of Marks and Spencer's. My mum told me that. Actually, she told me before that mini-Marks food shop opened up in the precinct, but I don't know if that counts as a Marks and Spencer's in its own right. It sells knickers, so it probably does, which means we've probably lost that biggest-place-without-a-branch-of-Marks cachet now. Shame. Now the place is even more boring than it was before.

I've lived here all my life. Well, except when I went to uni in Sheffield (Computer Science – I got a Desmond Tutu), and then I came back and got the job being a techie IT type at the uni here. Best job ever, that. Almost like still being a student. But it all went horribly wrong the night I went bumper to spine with Chitty Chitty Bang Bang. After that I didn't want to be around universities any more. Or students. Or people. So I left the job at the uni and set up my own little freelance racket, with plenty of compensation (and my mum's hearty disapproval) to smooth the transition.

And that, basically, is my life story.

Unlike me, though, this town hasn't changed much in the last twenty-six years. It's still built entirely of post-war concrete. I don't like it much. No one likes the place where they grew up, do they? Especially if they are twenty-six and still trapped there.

I roll down the high street in my car, stop-starting

to the rhythm of the pedestrian crossings and humming an old song about traffic lights I remember from playschool *('if they're red then no, no, no')* and becoming one with the one-way system *('if they're green then go, go, go')*. At one of the sets of lights I notice a sunny-looking blonde girl at the wheel of a car in the next lane. When I manage to catch her eye, I give her a smile. And she smiles back.

This is easily my favourite thing about driving. The flipside of the fact that people find it hard to believe that I can drive a car is the fact that when I'm sitting in the driving seat no one would suppose that I'm anything out of the ordinary. Even if they clock the blue badge, they probably assume a cocky young lad like me has just nicked it off his gran for the parking privileges.

After all, from the waist up I'm still the same ladykiller I ever was. My upper body's still a 99 per cent fat-free relief map of manly sexiness. My face still does the same excellent job it always did. And, as if to prove my point, sunny blonde is now biting her lip and looking coyly at me through her fringe.

I give her a little eyebrow flash and grin. And then the left filter light comes on and I have to zoom away, with my confidence raised and my blood pumping a little faster than it was before.

Leaving her for dust, I make a couple of lefts and rejoin the ring road, navigating a million-and-one more roundabouts before pulling off to end up outside my mum's house, just two doors down from my own. Yep, I live almost but not quite next door to my mum, and it isn't my favourite thing about my life right now. But it's certainly an improvement on the situation a year ago, when, immediately post-hospital, I had no choice but to move in with my mum. I would happily have given up the use of my arms, too, to save myself from that particular purgatory.

Anyway, at my mum's house, I decide to indulge her by having a cup of tea, while she bores me half senseless for about three-quarters of an hour talking about her fantastic other son, my older brother, Simon, who has four fully working limbs and is doing great things as an estate agent (read: strutting wide boy) down in London town. She also asks me briefly, and slightly disapprovingly, how my work is going, so I deliberately blind her with science, talking about flash plug-ins and browser compatibility until she shuts up again.

I don't mean to be mean, but I know she is just pretending to care. After all, she was the one who was dead against me using my compensation for my own business. Too risky, she said. Too risky! Like risk was my main concern after what had just happened. I didn't have a lot left to risk. Anyway, we can't all be sodding estate agents, can we? And, well, the whole point of my starting my own business was to give me an opportunity to indulge in my new favourite hobby of almost pathological reclusiveness.

I don't do talking to other people any more. I get out, sure. I take a drive in my car most days. But I don't get off on the idea of having to be sociable all the time.

But, having said that ... I don't know what it is about the little things I've done today, the cybersex and the in-car flirting, but it's left me feeling weird and hollow. Stuff like that is usually among my favourite things, the little pleasures that get me through the day. Being someone else. Getting off as someone else. Hiding my disability with modern technology. But (and yeah, I guess Mary has something to do with this) now I feel that's all a bit crap. I want to get off as me. All of me.

I want to have sex with Mary again.

So, while I'm sitting at my mum's kitchen table not listening to her, I hatch a plan. It's a little bit sad, but it's also a little bit necessary. I'm going to go back to the library. I'm going to see if I can run into her again.

OK, I might have totally agreed with her when we parted last night and she said that our brief moment of shag-madness should be pure one-night stuff, but maybe she was wrong. Maybe we both were. So maybe I can let fate sort that one out by going back to the library.

And if she's there, she's there.

And, god, I hope she is there.

After I leave mum's I drive back into town and park up by the public library. But I don't go in straightaway. I delay it. Maybe because I want to put off the moment when I find out she's not there. Because, deep down, I don't really expect to find her.

Or do I?

Well, either way, I do have a few errands to run as well, so I make my trundly way into town. Shopping first – madness later.

But madness seems to have other ideas, because the first thing I buy isn't on my list, which is mainly boring essentials like printer cartridges and Post-Its. The first thing I buy is something rather more decadent than supplies for my stationery cupboard. I buy aftershave. (Well, I think technically what I buy is men's fragrance.) And when the second thing I buy is condoms, I screw up my list, because sensible shopping is clearly beyond me, and head back to the library, where I know Mary isn't going to be.

But somehow I cling to the desperate hope that is burning a hole in my heart, along with the desperate need that is burning a hole in my underwear.

Sad? Well, yeah. I guess.

She isn't there. I wheel my way round every part of the smooth-floored library. I'm not lying to myself any more. I've accepted that she isn't here – wasn't ever likely to be here. I am just looking for her in the most likely place I can think of. I found her here yesterday, after all.

But she just isn't here. Nevertheless, I do three full circuits to convince myself. I even – and this is where it gets really stupid – I even make a play of reaching for something on the top shelves in the fiction section. Wondering whether that is some kind of magic spell that will make her materialise at my elbow, lifting down a bloated volume of bonking-and-bling for me.

Someone does come and help me, but it's one of the library staff, wildly apologetic about the shelves being so high. An oversight apparently – they've applied for a grant to fix it, she explains, with a please-don't-sue-us light in her eyes. She's pretty. Not like my car-driving blonde, or my mental picture of my cybersex LA babe, but still pretty in a brunette kind of a way, a librarian kind of a way, a Mary kind of a way.

As she checks out my randomly chosen six-hundred-odd pages of banality bites (and, no, I've never read this type of book before, why would I?), I give her a slightly sexy, slightly pouty, slightly winky smile.

God knows why, because these days I have rules about flirting: strictly in the car or online only. It must be what happened here yesterday that's making me behave in new and unusual ways. Because I definitely give her a bit of a come-on, and she gives me a far more blatant come-off-it. In fact she looks at me rather as she might look at someone she recognises from *Crimewatch* as a sex-crime suspect. Which just goes to show. I'm an untouchable and Mary is a pervert.

I was right all along.

Even so, I wish she was here.

Mary

Waitressing is not my ideal job by a long way. It involves far too much standing up and far, far too much smiling. And the pay is nowhere near enough to compensate. In fact, it's worse than shitty.

And it's doubly humiliating, because before I decided to answer that nagging little voice that had been whispering 'academia' to me for the last eight years or so, I was a pretty big wig in PR. I ate in places like this. For breakfast. On expenses.

However, this uniform-wearing, plate-shuffling stuff was the only thing I could find to top up my savings that fitted around my seminars, so I took it.

The place where I work, La Lucas, is an upmarket kind of establishment. It specialises in bad food; more specifically, bad overpriced food. Never a good combination. Which is why it's always half-empty. In fact this place is so lacklustre and going-down-the-pan, I'm half convinced most evenings that I can hear Gordon Ramsay in the distance, berating the kitchen staff with his delightful blend of raw sexuality and swearing.

I do usually manage to enjoy myself working here, though. But it's for such a sad reason. The saddest of the sad. The lamest of the lame. The fact is, I have a work crush.

These things can happen to anyone. That's why there are so many words for them. Crush, lust object, sex object (notice how even language can't seem to wait to objectify him), forbidden fruit, temptation, eye candy, hunk, spunk, *homme fatale*, obsession. And that last one – obsession – is the best, I think. Because that's what Thomas is. I have spent, at a rough estimate, far, far too much time thinking about him in the last few months.

It started back in October, when I'd only just begun my course and finances forced me to take this job. It was while I was eyeing up the 'Help Wanted' sign that I spotted him through the shiny plate-glass windows, and, rather predictably, started eyeing him instead.

And I don't just fancy him because he's young (he is) and fit (he is) and good looking (yep), but it's also because he waits tables with an extreme kind of sullen resentment. It's like he's having an extremely stubborn wisdom tooth pulled out for every drink he refreshes and every bill he brings. He hates it. It's beneath him.

That. Is. So. Sexy. It's that above everything else. That is so, so, I don't know. It hits the button.

It's all of this – this perfect package – stuck in tight black trousers, white shirt and little white aprony thing. And that's what gets me through every god-awful, mind-numbingly boring shift.

Oh, and I do wonder what it is he thinks he ought to be doing rather than waiting La Lucas's over-starched, over-priced tables. Fronting a rock band at Glastonbury maybe? Modelling underwear? Curing cancer? Whatever it is, fate clearly is keeping him from his calling for just a little longer, because right now he is just another waiter, albeit a cute one, with a nice line in unspoken insolence.

The only problem with using Thomas as the mind-bending drug that helps me get through never-ending shifts at La Lucas is times like tonight, when he has the night off.

But, luckily, it's yet another slow night, and I've found a way to keep myself occupied.

'And you know the really weird thing,' I'm saying to Stacey, the new waitress I've been telling the entire story of the last twenty-four hours to, 'this afternoon I found myself back at the library, no idea even why. I was thinking about something else and I just found myself standing outside it. Weird.'

'Did you go in?' says Stacey, chewing and looking bored. She is going to get into trouble when the duty manager sees that she is chewing gum on her shift.

'Nah, no point. I mean, how likely is it that he would have been in there? He told me he never goes to the library and was only there that time because he was checking out some books for his mum.'

I haven't told Stacey about the wheelchair fetish thing, by the way. We only met this evening. In fact, now I come to think of it, I haven't mentioned the wheelchair at all. Which is a good thing, surely? The wheelchair isn't relevant. There is more to David than his disability. Right?

Tell my libido that.

Stacey frowns at me. 'You should have gone in. It

was probably fate or something, bringing you back there. He could have been in there waiting for you. Like, maybe he's your soulmate or something.'

Aww, bless. Stacey is a waitressing student like me and Thomas, but she's only nineteen. It shows, doesn't it? I ask you, soulmate!

Stacey and I don't get much further with our discussion about how David and I could be writ in the stars, because things get a little busier in the restaurant after that. So Stacey doesn't have the time to draw up my astrological chart (which she honestly did offer to do). For that, at least, I can be grateful to the rude, greedy, demanding patrons of La Lucas who interrupt my daydreaming and general idling while I am at work.

Back at home I was planning to pull a late one and work on my dissertation, but I'm just too done in. Shagged, in actual fact, for the second night in a row.

But I'm pretty sure, after a whole day of turning things over in my mind, that I am going to have to try and see David again, one way or another. The whole Gavin-Rich thing might have persuaded me that disabled guys are a recipe for heartbreak and made me vow to stay away from them, and I might think, deep down, that there is something weird and wrong about this part of my sexuality, but I just don't have any choice. I can't stop thinking about David. Even thinking about the hotness that is Thomas is more an excuse to muse on how much he looks like David than a full-on perve-a-thon.

But there's a problem with tracking down David. We both agreed it was a one-nighter. We didn't exchange numbers or emails or anything like that. We shot out of each other's lives as quickly and cleanly as we'd tumbled in. Well, apart from one thing.

I know where he lives.

David

It's almost like I wake up to find myself already awake, I'm so irritable, so damn angsty. And it's a little while after I get up that I realise what it is. I want sex. I'm actually sexually frustrated. I'd thought I'd given up feeling that. I thought I'd just got used to feeling that.

I get up and, in a complete reversal of habit, don't log on to the net. Instead, I make a tentative phone call and, having struck lucky, rush out of the house without a single Rice Krispie inside me.

I have a plan, clearly a plan born of extreme frustration and the simple knowledge that I just have to do something – anything – to find Mary. But it's still a plan.

I must have made it while I was sleeping, or dreamt it, or something, because it almost feels like I woke up knowing exactly what I needed to do.

The thing is, I don't know much about Mary. I certainly don't know anything useful like her phone number or her email address, but I do know that she's a student. And I'm pretty sure she said her tutor was called something Mercury. Doctor Mercury. And that's probably enough information for someone like me. Because I am someone with contacts, proper contacts at the university, ones in the IT support department, which means I'm in a better position than most obsessives to track her down. In short, I'm going to have a word with my old workmate and partner in all things laddish, Larry.

I got my job at the university the old-fashioned way – nepotism. When I was growing up, my mum had this part-time job there, in admissions, so when I came back from Sheffield she found me a job there doing computer support. It was only meant to be a stopgap. I was supposed to be *en route* to bigger and better things, what with my university education and all that. But, well, I guess I got a bit diverted from that road to riches because I stayed in that temporary job for nearly three years.

Because I fucking loved it.

Once upon a time, back when I was a fully functioning human being, I was also a shag machine. Who could blame me? There I was, early twenties, and I was adrift in a sea of witless, clueless, shag-hungry students. A long line of interchangeable, fresh-faced eighteen-year-olds, still naive enough to be impressed by a guy with a job and a (shared) flat and a motorbike.

I had all the blow jobs behind the main servers that any guy could ever need, and if I deigned to reciprocate – which I did most times – I was a sex god. Don't think for a moment that I was a selfish git, only after my own pleasure. Sure, my pleasure came pretty high on my to-do list, but I always gave them as good as I got, and usually better.

Back then, Larry was the one other guy in the computer support department who played the game I played – after he saw just how much sex I was getting. Everyone else who worked there spent their free time rolling around in the lush, verdant hills of the internet. Larry wasn't as good-looking as me (a fact I secretly relished), but he was just about normal enough that he could easily follow in my footsteps. And his looks, like mine, were more than enhanced by the fact that we were the only normal-looking human beings in a department of ultra geeks.

It was almost as if, until I started to work at the university, Larry had never really seen the potential of his job to cherry-pick the cutest of the students (and then pick their cherries). And Larry was incredibly grateful. Actually he used to call me The Guru, which sounds pretty dumb now, but I certainly don't remember rushing to stop him doing it back in the day.

Larry, it would be fair to say, doesn't quite revere me in the same way these days. In fact, Larry is spectacularly uncomfortable with my new status as a member of the disabled community. Which is the main reason why Larry and I aren't exactly close these days. I haven't seen him since he came to visit me a couple of times in the hospital. After that, sporadic email contact has been the gossamer-thin lifeline of our friendship. He drops me three or four lines each time he makes a conquest, and I cheer from the sidelines. Pathetic, really. Really pathetic. Although, I must confess, I take heart from the fact that he isn't making anything like as many conquests now he hasn't got me to lead the way.

So Larry might not exactly be going to welcome me with open arms today, but that's just tough, because I figure that, as he has been a spectacular failure as a friend lately, he owes me a favour or two. He isn't going to like it, but one way or another I'm still Larry's Guru and I reckon he needs a little reminder of that.

*　*　*

We meet in the foyer of the Students' Union building and then have to take a lift down to the Union Bar, which is in the basement. Larry acts studiously laid-back about having to take the lift, but he makes far too much fuss about finding it – essentially making it clear that he has never had to use it before. Yeah, yeah, Larry, I get it – you can walk, I can't. You win.

Actually, on one level, I am far more weirded out by Larry than I think he could ever be by me. Looking at him, I can't help remembering how it used to be between us. We used to be so tight. And back then I thought I knew him so well. I thought he was just like me. I even used to respond to his 'The Guru' nickname by calling him Mini-me sometimes – despite the fact that he is four years older than I am, and rather different in looks, with his goatee-and-glasses geek-boy vibe even extending as far as the pot belly, bigger now than ever and quite the opposite of my own hard muscle. But, physicality aside, Larry still isn't like me at all. He's a creep.

Example: In the bar, this girl comes over almost as soon as we sit down. She's kind of weird-looking, gawky, all teeth and limp hair.

'Hey, Larry, how are you doing?' she says, breezy-cool on the surface, but I recognise that tone only too well. It's the surface breezy-cool of a woman who has been shagged and never called. Of course, hanging round a university campus and picking off the students means dealing with this kind of thing all the time.

Larry looks at the weird-but-passable girl who is standing by the table. He gives her a questioning look, a kind of do-I-know-you? which has her confidence visibly withering before he even says, 'Ella, right?'

'Yeah,' she says.

Larry doesn't say anything. He waits a moment, as if he's waiting for her to say something else, and when she doesn't he nods vaguely at her and turns back to me, about to continue our conversation.

'Hey, um,' says Ella, forced to interrupt or be ignored, 'I was just wondering. There's a party in my house on Friday. Would you and your friend...' She tails off, because she suddenly notices that I'm not sitting on a bar stool. (Really, her suddenly bulging eyeballs couldn't have made it any more obvious.) 'Oh,' she says, round a hand suddenly clapped to her mouth. 'Oh, Larry, I'm sorry. I didn't mean to interrupt.'

Larry smiles. 'Hey,' he says, 'no problem. Look, I'll try and make your party. Put the address down here.' And he hands her a slightly sticky cigarette paper and a biro from his top pocket. That move reminds me of the old days, because one of my rules – one of the rules I taught Larry – was always to carry a pen, for writing down phone numbers, but not to carry paper – or, god forbid, an address book – because that looked too obvious. It's never that hard to find something to jot on. Larry complained about this rule at first, calling me a Luddite for not using a palm pilot to collect addresses and other useful details. But it looks like he's finally come round to my way of thinking, which is that nothing looks wankier than standing typing a girl's number into a fiddly lump of plastic. A little pen in the pocket – so the dashing way to go.

While she's writing her address on Larry's fag paper with her head down, Larry flashes me a distinctly pleased sort of look. A party invite was always a good score. Always rich pickings at a student party.

After she's gone, shooed away by Larry's promises of an imminent phone call, Larry's smug look cranks up at least ten notches. 'Did you see that?'

'What, you playing that poor girl who was all of, what, nineteen?'

Larry pulls a face. 'Since when did you care about birth certificate details? Aren't you the guy who used to say "legal is legal"? Anyway, what I meant was: did you see the way she clocked you? She was interested. Very interested.'

'In me?' I say, wondering if suddenly all women have become kinked-up sickos and I am very hot property.

'No, dumbass, in me. Did you see the way she looked at me when she realised I was having a drink with a disabled guy? Mucho de Brownie Pointas. You're better than a puppy, dude.'

'Right,' I say, irritated to fuck, but I suppose, as I am here trying to get Larry to do me a favour, I'm just going to have to put up with his particular brand of creep-chic for a little bit longer. And try not to remember that that was exactly how I used to be too.

'Anyway, this favour you wanted,' says Larry, suddenly reading my mind.

'Well there's this girl . . .' I begin but that's as far as I get.

'Oh my god, man, there's that fucking ponce Thomas.' Larry almost spills my Coke as he points a vicious finger at a tall guy standing by the bar.

'What?' I say, completely thrown. What has happened to Larry? He has the attention span of a three-year-old.

'Thomas. God, I hate him. He thinks he's fucking god's gift. Just look at him. All the bloody girls seem to fancy him and it's so obvious he's gay. So fucking obvious.'

I glance over at the guy Larry is pointing at. This Thomas is very good-looking. Tall, dark curly hair, Angelina Jolie lips. There is nothing about him that screams 'raging poofter' to me, but Larry has that thing that a lot of so-heterosexual-it-hurts guys have, whereby any bloke who is good-looking is automatically defused as competition by being pronounced gay.

Another, slightly weird thing about this Thomas – and this is going to sound a bit I-love-myself after what I've just said – is he looks quite a lot like me. (Except he is standing up.) So, by that logic, Larry would probably think I was gay, despite the fact that he has been witness to masses and masses of evidence to the contrary – except that he currently thinks I have no cock at all.

'Larry,' I say, slowly, realising I'd better take charge of this conversation before it goes off on another wild tangent, 'I'm a bit pressed for time, mate, sorry, so can I just tell you about Mary?'

'Heh. There's something about Mary, eh?'

Well, quite.

After I've explained the situation to Larry, he is distinctly unhelpful. Well, up to a point. He does do what I ask – mostly as an opportunity to show off the fact that he can access databases he probably shouldn't be accessing via his palmtop. But then he stops being so helpful.

'Well, look, mate,' Larry says, hiding the screen so I can't see the info he's found. 'I've got her details here.

Mary Taylor, Victorian Literature MA, address, phone number, etc, but I can't just give this stuff out, even to you.'

'What the fuck? Larry, since when did you have scruples?'

'Since I got a written warning for misconduct, that's when,' Larry mutters, not looking at me. 'But, look, I know you're in a fix. So, as it's you, how about I just give you her address?'

'How about you give me her phone number?'

'Mate, I can't. I can't give you her number!'

'And yet you can give me her address. Surely giving out her address is way dodgier.'

'You don't want me to give you her address?'

'No. Oh god. OK, shoot.'

I note down the flat number and my heart sinks a little. A little bell rings as I remember Mary in the park café a million years ago saying something about her place having lots of stairs. One more obstacle to overcome.

'Come with me,' I say, once I have made a note of Mary's address (because, yes, I do follow my own advice and I do, still, always carry a pen).

'Oh, mate, I can't. I'm meant to be working.'

'Yeah, but you're not, are you? You're in the pub,' I say, gesturing at the smoky surroundings.

'Ah, well, it might look like I'm in the pub to your untrained eyes, mate, but I'm actually checking the terminals in the psychology lab right now. And I can stretch that a bit, like as far as the bar here, but actually leaving campus – well, that's taking the piss.'

'Oh, come on, Larry, is there really any piss left to take? Come with me. I have a feeling I might need you.'

'Well, maybe I could be persuaded . . .'

'What do you want, Larry?'

'Come with me to Ella's party. Be my girl-bait puppy dog.'

Mary – bless her – lives on the third bloody floor. And never mind getting up to her flat, I can't even get up the three huge stone steps from street level to ring the buzzer on her entryphone. If Mary really does have this huge kink for disabled guys you'd think she might have chosen where she was going to live a little more carefully.

But luckily, as Larry wants to strut about with his I-have-a-disabled-friend cachet and so get to be a sex god by standing next to me at this stupid party (what-ever happened to my semi-hermit status?), he can bloody well climb up and press the buzzer for me.

A few seconds later a window is thrown open high above our heads. I hold my breath in anticipation, but the crazily frizzed head that pops out is a long, long way from Mary's sleek bob.

'Yeah?' shouts the frizz.

'Um, does Mary Taylor live here?' Larry shouts, taking a big step backwards and craning to make eye contact.

'Yes, but she isn't here.'

'Oh, er.' Larry looks at me. 'Do you want to leave a message or something, mate?'

'Um.'

'Hey,' says the frizz, looking at me and then back at Larry, 'is your friend, like, all right?'

'I'm fine,' I reply, wishing I had something more withering up my sleeve. The fact that I'm in a wheel-chair doesn't mean I shouldn't be allowed as much eccentric lovesick behaviour as an able-bodied nutcase. But I can't think of anything. (And forget I used the word 'love' then – it doesn't mean anything.)

'What do you want me to tell Mary?' she shouts. I feel suddenly very shy. Some people from the hairdresser's over the road are looking.

'Nothing,' I shout back.

And then Larry, who appears to be interpreting for me, shouts, 'Nothing, forget it.'

The frizz shrugs and closes the window, leaving us back on the street and no further forward.

'Fuck,' I say, turning away and starting to wheel back to where I parked the car.

Larry comes up behind me and puts his hands out towards my chair, as if he's going to push me. 'Don't,' I say, almost subliminally quietly but Larry picks it up and takes his hands away.

'Why didn't you leave her a message, mate?' Larry says, once we're in the car heading back to the university.

'Because it looks so lame, that's why. A message is trying too hard. A message says, ooh look, I managed to find out where you live. A message says bunny-boiler.'

Larry laughs. 'Don't be a dumbass, dude-mate, only chicks can be bunny-boilers.'

'Oh, don't be so damn sure.'

Mary

I don't have a driving licence. Never a problem when I lived slap-bang in the middle of Bristol. In fact, as there was nowhere to park there anyway, a car would have been a hindrance. But, now I live in the middle of East Midlands Nowheresville, not having access to a car makes certain things very difficult. Things like tracking down suburb-dwelling disabled sex gods like David.

God, to be more mobile. This part of town is so inaccessible by foot. Vast and sprawling and stupid. And there are bloody roundabouts everywhere, which means to get from A to B I am obliged to go via X, Y and Z – which translates into three pedestrian crossings and a scary subway. None of that would be much of a problem if I knew where I was going. But I don't – not really.

When David drove me to his house my mind was on other things for the best part of the journey. I probably looked at him more than I looked at the landmarks or noted the route we were taking. And as for the journey back, in the taxi I called at god-knows-what-hour-of-the-morning, it was dark and I was more than a little sex-drunk.

About midday I start to get hungry and give up. I'm having lunch with Mercury and, if I can't find David, at least I can spend a bottle and a half of wine and twenty cigarettes talking about the miserable fact that I can't find David.

Monroe is a new and really not at all bad gayish café/bistro near the centre of town. In fact, by this town's standards, Monroe is quite a revelation. Not that it's perfect. The décor leaves a lot to be desired, for a start. Basically, the inside is a riot of floor-to-ceiling wood, with tables and chairs so rough-hewn they might have been gnawed into shape by beavers. It's so like being inside the Faraway Tree that I'm fully expecting Moonface to show me to my table.

I make for a cosy corner where Mercury is already plonked, waiting for me with a glass of sticky-looking red in his hand and a talcum-powder cloud of Gauloise around his head.

'Hello, darling,' he says, standing and greeting me with a whiskery air-kiss. 'How are you?'

'Not great,' I say, managing to make a 'mwah-mwah' noise, sit down with a bump and simultaneously slosh a generous helping of the wine into my glass.

Once lubricated by a few glorious gulps, and with one of Mercury's fags lit and dancing in my hand, I explain all about my current preoccupation with, and quest for, David. Ignoring the fact that my disappointment at not finding him is a complete reversal of the shagging-poor-David-is-bad-and-wrong line that I was touting last time I talked to Mercury about him.

I trot all it out, anyway, along with a big side order of talk about how sexy David is. Most of which Mercury heard yesterday, when we were meant to be having a tutorial, but that's tough on him, because I am too obsessed, in too deep, to think or talk about anything else.

Mercury listens patiently, pausing only to order a Welsh Rarebit from a cute waiter, and it turns out that my change of heart has not escaped him. He says, 'Well, darling, so, since I last saw you, a little over twenty-four hours ago, you have decided that you are in fact obsessed with this boy. This boy who, you assured me, was nothing but a "one night shag sort of thing."' He says that as if it's a direct quote, but I don't think I said those words. Doesn't sound like me. But I don't get the chance to question it, because Mercury keeps right on talking. 'And you are obsessed to the point that you are now stalking him cross-country with an almost pathological gleam in your eyes.'

I laugh a bit at that. 'Well, not really. I haven't managed to catch sight of him. So I'm not a stalker, or at least not a very successful stalker.'

Mercury nods encouragingly and takes a long glug from his glass. 'I see. Well, you seem a little stuck there, darling, all het up with nowhere to go . . .' Mercury lets his words fade away into his glass. I know my dead-end talk is starting to bore him now. There really is nothing much else to be said about my David obsession. So I know what's coming. Mercury waits a couple of beats before launching a new conversational attack. 'So, incidentally, and I meant to ask this yesterday, but somehow I couldn't get a word in: how does our lovely waiter-boy fit into all this?'

Mercury knows all about my Thomas-crushing of course. And he heartily approves. In fact, I think he has something of a soft spot for Thomas himself, ever since the time I took him to La Lucas on my night off and arranged things so we had Thomas pouting and sulking sexily over our table as he took our orders and refreshed our drinks. Actually, Mercury brings up the subject of Thomas a little too often in our conversations. He even gets impatient with me sometimes about the fact that, when it comes to my Thomas-crushing, I have been happy just to look and not touch. I think he likes to think that if he were me he would have been far more proactive in that department.

Sometimes I wonder about the root of Mercury's continuing interest in every twist and turn of my love life. He has followed it like a soap opera since we met and hit it off back in October. I suspect he would quite like to be a rather kinky thirty-three-year-old heterosexual woman, and through me he is living his vicarious dreams.

I screw up my forehead, not sure for a moment how to answer his Thomas query. I'm so hooked on David I've all but forgotten who Thomas is for a moment. But, eventually, I get with it. 'Thomas? Well, he doesn't really fit in. I don't really know where I am with Thomas. Well, I do, I suppose – I'm nowhere. He's so damn pretty. So pretty he makes me all tongue-tied. I can't really seem to get it together to hold more than a casual conversation with him. It's totally different to David. I mean, maybe before I met David I thought Thomas was worth thinking about, or, at least, dreaming about. But not now. Not now there's David, because David is in a different league, really. Just the thought of him. Just the thought of the wheelchair. The fact he can't walk. It just does it for me. It does it right down to my bone marrow. Thomas is history. The only thing I am interested in him for now is the fact that he looks a bit like David.'

Mercury looks rather disappointed. 'Yes, except we must remember that at least with waiter-boy you know where he is, whereas with wheelchair-boy, well, we have something of an impasse.' Mercury – ever the sexual reductionist.

'True,' I say, looking sadly down at the plate of smoked salmon which has appeared in front of me magically, as if brought by elves.

Mercury clearly picks up on my melancholia, because he says, 'Oh darling, I'm sorry. But it does look as if Tiny Tim has slipped through your fingers. Why on earth didn't you think to get his telephone number whilst he was still dazed from your expertise in the bedroom department?'

'Well, I suppose because I just thought it was a one-night thing.'

'Or you wanted it to be a one-night thing, because having sex with poor cripples is so bad and wrong?'

I blow out a long plume of smoke before I say anything. And then what I say is, 'Oh. Oh, fuck.' I guess this is what comes of letting seen-it-all, done-it-all gay guys know all about your sex life. They do tend to be rather astute.

Back at home and in my lonely bedroom, my laptop sits unopened on my desk. Just the sight of it makes me feel sick with guilt. Two 'meetings' with Mercury in two days and neither of us so much as mentioned my dissertation.

My plan for today was supposed to be: track down David and make a date with him for later, have lunch with Mercury, work on dissertation for a couple of hours, go round to David's, and make the most of my evening off from La Lucas by tying him down on his bed and fucking him into the mattress with a strap-on. And from that to do list, I have managed to have some lunch. To think that this morning the likelihood of me keeping that date with Mercury seemed slim to none.

I'm drying my hair after a productivity-avoiding bath when Carrie appears in the doorway.

Her lips are moving but I can't hear a thing over the buzzy roar of the hot air baking my Louise Brookes bob into place.

'What?' I say, yelling as I slide the switch on the dryer to off and the droning subsides through various pitches of humming and whining into silence.

'I said, "some blokes called round after you",' says Carrie, clearly irritated at having to repeat herself.

'Oh. Who?'

'Well, they didn't say.' She shrugs as if that was obvious.

I hold the hairdryer in my hands, feeling the weight of it. God, Carrie is annoying me right now. The urge to throw the hairdryer at her is very strong. 'Oh,' I say, not caring, but wanting to get rid of her, 'did they say anything interesting?'

'Not really. Just that they were looking for you.'

'Oh.' I shrug and turn back to the mirror.

Carrie looks at my reflection and gives a sort of shifty smile. 'Sorry,' she says, sounding sincere. 'Actually, though it's a shame because one of them was really quite nice-looking, not the one in the wheelchair, the other one.'

'Not the one in the ... what?' I drop the drier. I do a sudden about-face, from giving off powerful leave-me-alone vibes to practically wrestling Carrie to the floor so I can pump her for details.

Of course, when Carrie has filled the suddenly very interested me in with every last detail of my gentlemen callers I'm jubilant. Over the moon, even. Well, up to a point, because what can I do now? David came looking for me. Got my address somehow. So far, so strike up the band, but where does it get me? He's not here now and for some reason the bloody weird idiot didn't leave a message, or a number, or the slightest hint as to which of the many suburban sprawls on the outskirts of town is the one he drove me to a few days ago.

* * *

So I end up doing something rather sad. I stay at home, confined to barracks in the dumb hope that he calls back.

But I'm still waiting, all forlorn and Rapunzel-like, over twenty-four hours later, when Thursday evening rolls round and I have to leave the house for work. I'm pretty down by this point, pretty flat from pining after David. Even the promise of a shift with pretty, sparkly Thomas can't lift my sunken spirits.

The only slight consolation in this misery pit is the fact that my enforced twenty-four hours of home-alone time have done wonders for the word count on my dissertation.

'Are you working tomorrow night?' Stacey barks suddenly, as she pokes her head out of the back door, making me jump out of my illicit cigarette break. (And why exactly am I smoking out by the bins? I'm meant to be a social smoker and last time I looked La Lucas's dustbins weren't exactly world-class raconteurs.)

'Huh?' I say, in a smoky croak that gives me time to figure out what she said and process an answer. 'Um, yeah, actually.' Because I am, even though I'd much rather be at home waiting for David to call.

'Oh, that's a shame. There's a party at my place.'

'Oh, um, ah, well,' I say, with what I hope is a convincing note of disappointment in my voice, enough to mask the fact that, really and truly, the last thing I want to do is interrupt my David-obsessing time to watch second-year biology students being sick after too much cheap vinegary wine.

'Well, if you want you could always come after. It'll

still be buzzing then. Thomas could probably give you a lift; he's coming after work too.'

'Oh. Right.' And suddenly I'm torn. What I want, what I really, really want is to go home straight after work tomorrow night and every night for the rest of my life, in case David calls back. But somehow Mercury's remark that at least I know where I can find Thomas floats to the top of my consciousness. And a lift to the party with the beautiful Thomas is so, so tempting.

Mary Taylor, you fickle, fickle woman.

Friday then becomes, in my mind at least, David's last chance. I have to draw the line somewhere. Even if I am almost paralysed with lust when I think about the way his legs felt slightly cooler than they should have done. That alone is enough to make me feel slightly wobbly and melting inside.

And then, crushingly, despite my wishing and even, at one rather desperate stage, praying, David doesn't show up on Friday, although I've waited in for him all day. So I pack my David-related fantasies up in a big old mental box, slip it under the bed in my brain's spare bedroom, and set a course for Operation Flirt-with-Thomas.

The trouble with Thomas, though – something I'd almost forgotten as I pitted him against David in my lust-addled brain – is he's a little bit too pretty, a shade too good for me, just ever so slightly – whisper it – out of my league. Admittedly he is very similar looking to David, but the rough and nasty fact is that, my predilections aside, David's disability does make him a more accessible proposition. More available. But then, I wouldn't stand a chance of seducing a fully functioning David. I know for a fact he wouldn't look twice at a girl like me.

Maybe because it's party time, Thomas seems slightly less aloof and Mr Untouchable this evening. Although, perversely, his aloofness is a big part of his attraction. I have an occasional delicious fantasy of breaking that ice-prince façade with a well-tested mixture of sensory deprivation and cock-teasing. Mmmhmm. I'm pretty sure that chilly mask would slip if I had him tied down on my bed and blindfolded, while I grazed his aching cock with my lips until it was screaming for release – and so was he. But that fantasy is just a remnant of the way I used to keep my home fires burning before I devised my endless David fantasies.

So I'm missing the sneer, but even in a slightly more friendly mode Thomas is still the hottest dish on La Lucas's menu, or probably on any menu within a twenty-mile radius. So I shouldn't complain. And his being a little more approachable is quite useful if I am going to be sharing a car with him later.

Maybe the real reason I am finding him less intimidating is simply that, since David, I just don't fancy him so stupidly, achingly much. Or perhaps I don't fancy him so much because I am finding him less intimidating. But I don't have enough lifetimes to try and unravel that conundrum, so I just shove it to the back of my mind while I get on with waiting tables and ferrying plates of overpriced slop.

Either way, the upshot is that I can cheerfully confirm that I still want that lift to Stacey's party and even playfully bump elbows with him once or twice over the counter without losing the ability to breathe or stand upright.

And it must be our lucky night, because even though it is a Friday, it's a quietish one, so before the clock strikes twelve we are both out of the kitchen, out of our uniforms and driving towards the seething student heartland and Stacey's shabby shared house.

David

I've driven past Mary's house, what, five times? Six? More than twice a day since Wednesday, anyway. I haven't stopped. What would be the point? I'd have to get someone to ring the bell for me and how fucking lame would that look? Yeah, that's right, about as lame as driving past her house over and over again without stopping. But, well, I guess I was hoping I'd see her on the street or something. But no show. Either she doesn't actually live there or she's become a recluse.

So I'm back to square Larry, picking him up to drive him to mindless-girl's party in the hope that I can persuade him to give me Mary's number. I reckon I've got a good chance, especially if the pulling power of having a crippled mate is as potent as Larry seems to think. So I'm basically prostituting my misfortune in order to get Mary's number out of Larry. Well, why ever not? It's about time this fucking disability found a way to earn its keep.

Larry doesn't pick me up until really late. He has some geeky appointments in the virtual world of EverQuest to attend to first. And he also claims that being too early would look lame. I get his point, but even an internet-loving freak like me finds it hard to understand why Larry wants to spend time online rather than at a party full of potential conquests.

So it's past ten by the time we arrive. Not that I'm complaining, being here under duress and all that.

Although, really, the party isn't so bad. The student house it's being held in is reasonably flush to the street, so I could get over the threshold with just a bit of a bump from Larry, and inside it's only mildly annoying in a non-fitted-fluffy-carpets-rucking-up-under-wheels kind of way. I settle myself in a corner of the sitting room. The kitchen is a non-starter because everyone is standing up, and there's only so much staring at people's groins I can take.

This is the first time since the accident that I've been to anything like this, apart from my cousin's wedding, so I feel a bit awkward and spacey. But it's OK. My expectations are pretty low. However, that might well be no bad thing, I realise, as I am open to being pleasantly surprised.

A nice if slightly dazed-looking girl offers to fetch me a can of lager, and I accept, taking it smilingly as she perches on a stool next to me. We haven't made small talk for more than about ten minutes – so we haven't progressed much past 'so, what do you do?' – when she says, 'Do you think this outfit is too tarty?'

'Um.' I look at her. She's wearing very, very tight jeans tucked into brown boots and a sparkly red top. The top is very low cut, very hello, here are my tits.

'My boyfriend thinks it is,' dazed girl continues. 'He actually said if I wore it he wouldn't come with me, and he hasn't come, can you believe that?'

'Er, well.' I stop talking and cough to clear my throat. Is this girl flirting with me? 'Well, I suppose it depends what look you're going for. If you're asking me then, yeah, it's sexy.'

'See, right,' says dolly daydream, 'it's sexy. That's what I said.'

'Well, your boyfriend sounds like an idiot to me.' Wow. This is weird. First Mary, then Larry's assertion that I am a good pulling accessory – which might not exactly be a direct sex-link but at least links me to some kind of sexuality in a sideways sort of way – and now this.

Then dizzy-daydream-believer stops my rather excitable train of thought dead when she says, 'God, thanks. You are so useful. It's like my roommate, Rosy. She's got this gay friend back at home and she asks him everything, like advice on clothes and stuff, and it's really useful being able to get a male perspective without having to worry.'

I open and shut my mouth several times while she says all this, becoming more and more incredulous, until eventually I can get a word in. 'Hang on. Hang on, what? I'm not gay. Did someone tell you I was gay?'

She looks quite shocked. I'm not shouting but I'm maybe slightly on the assertive side, certainly more assertive than Miss-completely-unworldlywise expected some crippled boy in a wheelchair to be.

'Uh, sorry, no. I didn't mean that, exactly. I just meant, well, you know.'

And then, and I can hardly believe this is happening, even though it *is* happening, right here, right now, to me, she looks at my groin. She stares right at it. And continues, 'With you being well, what do they call it? Is it just impotent, or is there a special name for men who can't do it, when they're like you?'

'What?' I probably seem confused, but I'm not. This situation is very, very non-confusing.

And then her jaw just drops. As she realises her mistake, I don't know which one of us is more embarrassed. I'm pretty mortified by the whole situation, but I'm staring into the befuddled eyes of a pretty, if pretty gormless, twenty-two-year-old, who has chosen to presume I am a eunuch and is clearly panicking behind her pupils as she tries to figure a way to climb out of the almighty pit she is stuck at the bottom of. And while I'm weighing up whether or not to haul her out myself, I hear a voice that owns my soul say, 'David?'

I look up. I look across the room at her. She's right there, frozen in the doorway. And her face. My god.

She just . . . she can hardly move, she wants me so much. I didn't think I could still do that to people.

Mary

There's a lot we could say to each other. A lot I could ask. But questions float away – feathers in the wind, never quite coming to land.

Questions like: 'What are you doing here?' 'Why didn't we exchange numbers?' 'Why did you come to my house?' 'Why didn't you come to my house again?' I find I don't need to say any of these things. I find I don't care. All I need to say is one question: 'Where's your car?'

'Right outside.'

And just as we are leaving I bump into Thomas. And I barely even look at him. He's nothing more than the most minor of minor distractions. He just can't compete.

* * *

The car journey is hard. I don't want to talk too much. I don't want to break the spell. I just want to be fucking David immediately. But it's hard to sit in silence, so in the end I say, 'How are you?'

'Fine.'

'Have you, uh, have you been thinking about me?'

'Nothing. Um. Nothing else.' He swallows. Hard. God, that nervous swallow is so sexy. It makes me want him even more.

And maybe it's that that makes me take a chance, that makes me spill what might be much too much. I say something. Something big. 'I don't think this is going to be a one-night thing. Or even a two-night thing. I hope you agree but I just, oh god, David, I want you so much.'

David doesn't reply, he keeps his eyes fixed on the road. But I can see it in his face. He agrees with every word. Relief floods through me. 'What,' he says after a short pause, 'what are you going to do?'

'To you?'

'Yes. What are you going to do to me?' And, god, when he says that my hair seems to stand on end. He so wants it.

'Well, my eager little bitch-boy, I haven't really decided yet, but I think for starters I'm going to tie you up.'

David almost crashes the car.

In David's house I keep my promise, pushing him down on the bed and tying his wrists to the headboard with the thin cords of nylon fabric that started life as part of my top – until I ripped them off, desperate for bondage material. David's house is really not kitted out for kinky sex.

'We should have gone to my place. I have all my stuff,' I mutter as I fiddle with the cords, trying to get the restrictions just right.

'What stuff?'

'Sex stuff.'

'Well, the trouble with your place is it isn't very accessible, is it? Unless you have a lift stashed away somewhere round the back.'

I laugh a little and then shut him up by pushing my fingers into his mouth and twisting them around. He gasps and then sucks, wetting them and making them slide more easily. I pump in and out, thinking about what he would be like sucking cock. Tied down like this and having a massive erection jammed into his helpless, saliva-sticky mouth. I wish with all my heart I had come prepared with a delicious ring gag, so I could strap his pretty, pouty mouth open in a permanent surprised O, like a blow-up doll. But, without my much-loved equipment to fall back on, I just have to rely on my improvised wrist ties and the extra-delicious bondage-substitute of David's own bodily limitations.

I take my fingers out of his mouth and climb on to the bed, then dip my head and run my teeth down his chest. I do it slowly, over and again until he starts to keen lightly. Not talking back to me any more, no small talk or bratty backchat, just making the sounds of pure, frustrated lust. I know his cock is hard, just from feeling it against my leg once or twice. And I know how much it is straining and begging for me to touch it, too.

'Missed me,' I whisper as I glide back up his torso and let my lips float next to his ear.

'Just a bit,' he manages. And that's just a tiny bit

too flippant for my liking. I thought I'd got rid of that with the bondage and teasing, but it seems he still has a bit of zing left, which is nice, actually, especially as I have a little something in mind to bring him down a notch.

Keeping my mouth pressed lick-close to his ear, I form soft private words out of the lightest breath. 'Did you touch yourself? Did you touch yourself and think of me?'

'Actually, no. I wanted to, but I was waiting. I thought I'd find you. My friend Larry has your number. So I saved it all for you.'

I sit back on my heels, straddling his chest and let him babble all of this out. I feel wonderful as I watch him, talking rubbish, but burning with a kind of vicious ravenous need at the same time. I am like a different person when I am with him. Not a nurturing thing. Pure animal. When he's finished his explanation, I say, 'Do it now.'

'Do what now?'

'Touch your cock. Hang on, I'll just unhitch.' I lean forward, my body brushing against his face, undo a knot and free his right wrist.

'What? Do what?' He's frowning.

I climb off him and reposition so I'm lying next to him, my body curled around his, my head on his chest. 'Go on. I want to see you do it.'

'Sorry, I, well. I'm sorry. This isn't quite what I expected.'

'Well, if you want to come tonight, that's what you're going to have to do.'

I run my fingernails over his chest, digging hard into the vulnerable flesh around his nipples. He groans, pushing his head back and showing me his white swanlike throat. He is so magnificent. His body is truly wet-dream perfection. A dizzying blend of sculpted and damaged that seems to flood my senses, leaving me almost as helpless as he is right now. I push his right hand down his stomach to brush against the head of his hard cock, which is rigid and tight against his ironing-board belly, and he moans again, turning his head to the side, away from me. More dazzling white neck. I stretch up and lick it. It's as smooth as soap, but it tastes of musk and dark sweat, sour and sweet.

He starts to touch himself, pushed over the edge by my tongue and teeth making cobweb patterns. I keep pinching and toying with his nipples too, thinking of my clamps at home (although they might be a little too much right now) and twisting his delicate flesh extra hard every time I want to hear that pained little cry that gets me a little closer to my own personal goal for the evening.

When his right arm starts to move a little faster, I stop playing with his nipples and reach down between his legs, finding that soft secret place behind his balls. A little tiny piece of tenderness that holds any number of very satisfying secrets. I press gently. David inhales sharply when I do that. So close.

And then it just takes a little more pressure from me on that tight little half square inch of skin, and he's off, squirming and screaming and coming hard into his hand. I watch his face, the pink blush over his pale cheeks, the long sharp line of his elegant nose, his firm, over-sized pout, his tight-squeezed eyes.

I try to make myself remember it all.

David

When I open my eyes she's looking at me and smiling. It's like a dream. My bedside lamp is on behind her – the only light in the room – and she's backlit, stray strands of her otherwise immaculate bob creating a fuzzy frizz halo. She looks like an Eastern European religious painting, and I feel suitably blessed.

I'm still pretty buzzy post-come, but I'm aware that I need to reciprocate and wonder where I should start. My left wrist is still tied to the bed frame, so I'm not in a great position to start directing the action. Nevertheless, I feel I ought to offer my services.

But before my mouth is even a tiny way open, she decides that it is – as it always seems to be – her move. And move she does, flipping from lying next to me on the bed to straddling me again, but this time right over my face.

My world goes dark. Dark and hot and heavy with the scent of night-blooming pheromones. My world is nothing but Moonflowers and Jasmine. I push my tongue out between my lips and I find her, right there. Closer than close. It would be just too, too easy, if it weren't for the fact that I can barely breathe.

I put my right hand against her thigh. But she grabs it, pulling it up and pushing my fingers into her mouth, biting on them. My cock's getting hard again, swelling gently, even though I know it knows better.

I find new paths with my tongue, bumping up against one of her hands, which is here too. We work together, her hand and I, a team with a common goal – to get Mary to come before I suffocate.

It's mercifully quick. I don't know if it's my tongue or her hand or her own bizarre kinkiness that does it, but we're there before I know it. Suddenly, suddenly, she's collapsing, her weight falling against the wall behind me. She moves her legs a little as she relaxes, and delicious light and air rush in to find me. I can hear her moans and sobs properly now, and my own rushed panting.

She shifts, moving down my body and lowering herself back on to the bed, leaning over to crush her lips against mine, which are still wet and swollen. Bruised with her.

She kisses me for a long time.

Mary

I can't let the evening end without a proper shag. For some reason we never got around to that on our first night together. So this is our first time – which is worth noting.

We give it half an hour. I make some tea in David's kitchen first. Everything is surprisingly clean for the home of a bloke who lives alone. When I mention this to David he looks a bit bashful and mentions something about his mum living really nearby.

Too cute.

And then, once our tea is drunk, we do it. I climb on top of him. Pure Madagascan vanilla. No bondage or anything. Just me and him. I'm so wet. I practically glide on to his hard cock. It feels perfect, like it's replacing a lost part of me. I move up and down. Slower. Faster. Wanting it to last forever and yet not being able to wait for the climax. I use my hand to tease my clit at the same time, because I really want to come when he does. I really want to be right there with him.

His swollen lips are parted a little. His cheekbones are dusty with pinky blush. His eyes are closed. He is so beautiful.

'David,' I whisper, 'do you like fucking me?'

'I . . .' David opens his eyes.

'How long has it been since you fucked a girl, David?'

'I don't know. Two years. Bit more.'

I don't know why it turns me on that David hasn't had sex for so long, but it does. It immediately turns up the heat.

I slow down my movements on David's cock, until I am barely twitching.

David stares imploringly at me, but I keep very still.

'Please,' he whispers, 'please don't stop.'

I laugh. And even though I feel slightly power-crazed, even though my mind is racing with images of climbing off David right now, tying him up again, teasing him back to his peak, over and over, making him wait all night, begging and pleading – I can't. I can't do it. Because I just want to come with David's cock inside me too much. So I start to move again. Faster and faster. Until there is no way back.

Part Two: **March**

David

Getting serious with Mary is too fast, too easy. It's all down to the sex, of course. I want to have sex with her all the time; I can't seem to control myself. And in order to facilitate this all-sex-all-the-time lifestyle, I need Mary to be around all the time, which means within a couple of weeks she's practically moved into my bungalow.

It's weird, because I used to be the kind of guy who would try to avoid even letting a girl know my address, let alone clear out a drawer for one. But now look at me. Here I am with a semi-live-in girlfriend. Mary's met my mum – my mum's round a lot – she has a packet of tampons in my bathroom cabinet, a lipstick on my mantelpiece and, best of all, a basket full of sex toys tucked under my bed.

So I've compromised. And it is so very worth it. I have never had so much sex in my life. Why didn't anyone tell me how much fun this whole committed relationship thing could be?

It takes about three weeks for Mary to get around to tying me to my wheelchair, after hours, days and weeks of incessant talking about it. Not that I should complain about that, because the way Mary talks about these things would be more than enough to keep me sated even if she never acted on any of it.

Strangely, she doesn't use any of the old equipment from her basket, which I now know from experience contains all manner of soft ropes and cuffs, even chains. This time she talks about wanting the perfect look and liking things to be all new and shiny for this special occasion.

In the end, after masses of deliberation, she straps my wrists to my armrests with two pieces of emerald-green ribbon that she unravels from her hair. As she winds the satiny strips around and around, and her hair falls out of its stubby pony-tail into that familiar chin-length bob, she whispers to me not to struggle or tug at the ties too much or the ribbons will tighten and dig into my flesh.

I don't reply. I can't speak anyway, I'm too turned on. But Mary has this way of talking to me sometimes that just makes me meek as a kitten. She seems to make it clear that she owns me, and I don't have any say in the matter.

Maybe it's because she is so precise when she does these things to me. I know she plans every detail, even when things seem impromptu. And when she takes control, she seems cool, almost distant. In contrast, I feel dirty and wanton as I find my breath quickening and my flesh flushing. And it feels so wrong to get turned on by her nastiness, her cruelty, her abuse. It's wrong. I'm wrong. And all those wrong feelings make me so hot. They are what make her better than anything. Anything I've ever had.

Mary is still acting super cool. She doesn't know what's happening in my head – well, I don't think she does. At any rate she shows no signs of knowing about my inner battle with the contradictions she has unearthed in me. She pulls her knickers off, which are also green – bottle-green – and puts them over my head, pulling them down so they cover my eyes. The world goes dark and greenish.

And then she leaves the room. I don't know how long she's gone for, and I don't think she goes far away – I only know she's left the room because I hear the click of the door.

But when she comes back, I am about twenty times more desperate for her than I was before she went away.

She straddles me and licks my cheek. I'm panting, but I don't want to be. I'm embarrassed by how turned on I am by being left like this. Being controlled like this.

'Admit it,' she says, her mouth by my ear, 'you love this, and you're hard as a rock, aren't you?'

'Uh.'

'You love it, you little bitch. You love being like this.'

'Being like what?' I say, trying to keep some kind of control.

'Being helpless like this. I love making you helpless. I know you think it's kind of sick. But I'm not going to lie to you. I am turned on by the fact that you are helpless. Well, maybe I shouldn't say that, exactly, but you seem helpless. At least, you are easily *made* more helpless. Oh, I know what you are day-to-day is different. I've seen you driving your car and being all Mr In-Control, but behind bedroom doors, with me, this is what I like. Seeing you tied up. Blind. And the thing is, I think you like this too. I see it in you. This goes beyond the accident, beyond your disability. This is something deep down in your bones. You love this.'

Having whipped up a bizarre torrent of emotions with her little speech, she reaches between my legs and finds my hard cock, aching and thrusting into her hand.

I'm keening and mewing as she slides back off my lap and crouches between my legs. I hear the low sound as she opens my flies, feel her soft, smooth, breath for a moment, and then feel her envelop me in sudden wet heat.

I can't move. I can't see. I can't do anything. All I can do is come for her. Over and over. Screaming and sobbing.

Mary

It takes – what – a month before I feel normal with David. Up until then it's almost like I'm in awe of him. That's the exact word for how I feel. Awe. I worship him. Seriously. He is my religion. Everything I've ever wanted. I look at him when he doesn't realise, and my mouth goes dry. I just cannot believe he's here. He's with me. I spend whole days smiling like a goon.

I don't think he knows how extreme my feelings are, and it really is better, for so many reasons, that he doesn't.

It does start to fade away eventually, that feeling that he is just too perfect. I don't let his godlike status stop me from having sex with him. Oh, do I ever have sex with him. But maybe my feelings make me a little more, I don't know what, maybe a little more aloof than I would normally be with him. But in a way that works quite well. Makes it easy for me to play the icy dominatrix, which is pretty fun.

I've kind of moved into his place. Well, halfway. Put

it like this: I spend more time at his place than Carrie's, which might be a bit premature, but is such a relief.

Carrie knows all about David. Obviously there was the time he came round with the mysterious Larry. And then there was the conversation I had with her when I finally unearthed myself from David's place, three days after our reunion at the party.

She cornered me in the kitchen – caring enough, I ought to note, to ask me where I'd been all this time. And I was on such a ridiculous high I told all.

And then she said, 'So this David, he was the guy that came around here. The one with the friend in the wheelchair?'

'No. David is the one in the wheelchair,' I said. I was modging together a rather half-arsed tuna sandwich as I spoke, so kind of distracted. In fact I was feeling like I hadn't eaten properly for days and I was so desperate for protein I would have happily shovelled the tuna into my mouth straight from the tin. So I was preoccupied with the much-needed sandwich and didn't catch her slightly off-beat expression, until I finally looked up and saw that she was staring at me, her mouth a little open.

Then she said, 'And that's who you've been with?'

'Yes.'

'All this time?'

'Yes.'

'That guy in the wheelchair?'

'Yes.'

'Having sex?'

'Yes.'

'All this time?'

'Yes. Didn't we already do that one?'

'Yes.' She laughed. And then she frowned again. 'But is that OK? To have sex with him? Like that? Like for several days?'

'Well, yes. I mean, I think so. I didn't break him.' I smirked. 'He was like that when I found him.'

And that was so David talking. That was the kind of thing he would have said and then laughed and looked round, hoping to find a shocked expression on a nearby face. Carrie did indeed have a shocked expression on her face, but I wasn't nearly so comfortable with it in the cold light of the kitchen.

'Sorry,' I said, quickly, 'just a joke.' And after that moment of discomfort, Carrie disappeared to her bedroom.

And that was really the last time I saw her properly. To speak to.

Yeah. I feel a bit guilty about that. I have popped in, to pick up books and stuff, but managed to avoid anything more than nodding in the hall. I suppose she knows, has guessed, where I am spending most of my time.

But I don't spend very much time thinking about Carrie and whether she wonders why I'm never home. I'm far too busy thinking about other things.

After a while I do manage to shake the notion that David is a figment of my imagination, but my passion doesn't dim one bit. I can't see that ever happening. I honestly think I will never get tired of David. But if I do, well, after I've tied him to his chair and had his cock inside me, I feel I could exit this world with everything ticked off my personal Things To Do Before You Die list.

But another week passes and I have to think of

another little cruelty to inflict on him. Well, I don't, strictly speaking, have to do so. In fact, sometimes I wonder if I should hold back. Give him a break. But all I want to do is find new ways to torment him – he suffers so very beautifully. And something in the way he writhes tells me that slowing down is the last thing he wants me to do. No matter how much he might sometimes protest.

It's wrong, sure, on one level, but it's so right on every other level that that isn't worth worrying about.

So tonight, when I tie him to the bed – which has become such a regular occurrence it is practically part of our nightly routine – I have yet another new twist waiting in the wings. I stroke his beautiful cock with my hand until he's nearly there, then I stop and kiss him.

'Uh,' he gasps when I pull my mouth away, 'what are you doing?' He pulls at his wrist cuffs a bit, struggling prettily, but he knows he isn't going to get anywhere.

After a little more teasing and kissing, I take him back to that same point, stroking his hot velvet cock and pulling my hand away just before his big moment. David cries out when I stop this time, 'Mary!'

'Shh,' I say, putting a finger to his big soft lips. 'Don't worry. I know what I'm doing. This way, when you do come, it will be amazing.'

David seems to relax a little bit then. He trusts me. He shouldn't.

I spend a long time on his body, stroking his slender legs, sliding my hands underneath him to stroke his hidden arse, toying with his nipples. I caress every part of him, except one. The one part that is really trying to get my attention. David twists at the manacles making the leather creak with his desperation. I love that sound.

Eventually, deciding that maybe David has suffered enough, I take hold of his cock again. He seems to melt the second my fist is tight around it. He's liquid with need. Incoherent. I pump slowly and he's desperate straight away, moaning and squirming.

And then, again, just before he's going to come. I stop again.

David squirms again. 'No,' he says, sounding almost annoyed, on the edge of anger. 'Please. I can't. Can't wait.'

I press my mouth close to David's ear. 'Baby,' I say, making my words sound like sweet nothings, 'you're not going to come now. In fact, oh, I'm so sorry, but you're not going to come at all, not until this time tomorrow.'

David shakes his head. In fact, his whole body seems to shake. But I can tell he understands.

And I trust him. A few moments later, when I free his wrists, he doesn't even try and reach for his cock. Despite his desperation, he doesn't even think to.

I kiss him and I smile.

David

Today is a physiotherapy day – I go on a Tuesday and a Friday. I don't want to go, of course. In fact, what I really want to do is spend the day trying to find a way to get Mary to let me come before curfew. My cock is so not happy about what went down last night. But, as she so often points out, I'm a good boy.

So it's going to be a weird one. But then, physio is always sort of weird.

When I was in hospital after the accident I always looked forward to physio, mostly because it was a distraction from my new life of misery and depression, but it wasn't exactly fun. In fact, it was often painful, usually boring and, worst of all, seemed to revolve around me failing to do things that would hardly be thought of as achievements in the real world. Not that anyone ever mentioned that.

Actually, there'd just be this weird optimism about it all. For example, the first time they got me to stand and take some of my own weight everyone was so excited, even I got excited. But much later that night when I was in bed, I kept thinking of my old mates, Larry and the others, and how I used to impress them by getting ten different girls' phone numbers in one night, or dating a girl who supplemented her studies by modelling. Now that was impressive.

And then about a week after this particular great achievement, I was talking to one of the doctors who offhandly told me that being able to stand up didn't really mean anything, certainly didn't mean I was going to walk again or anything like that, and I shouldn't get my hopes up.

Physio was a lot like that. One person would be cheering me on, practically telling me I would be breakdancing on the moon by teatime, and then another – usually some gruff old school doc who'd seen it all – would shrug and tell me that I could probably start turning cartwheels in physio and it would be 'no guarantee of anything because with your sort of injury healing patterns are unpredictable.'

And now physio is going to be extra surreal because of that little trick Mary pulled last night. I feel like I've been semi-hard all day, my poor cock teased half to death.

Last night, when Mary gently told me I was going to have to wait twenty-four hours before I could come, it was so sexy I thought I was going to die. I know, it's so perverse, so bizarre, why does the idea of not being able to come get me off? It makes no sense, and yet ... I knew I'd face a whole day of delicious agony. But I reckoned without physio.

Now, I did think I might be OK, because this place doesn't normally make me feel in the least bit sexy. But things don't exactly work out like that.

It surprised me at first that physio isn't very sexy. If someone had asked me, a couple of years ago, before the accident, what I thought it might be like going to physiotherapy, I don't really know what I would have said, but I think I might have thought that it would be a bit, sort of, sexier. OK, not girls-boarding-school-senior-dorm-after-lights-out sexy, or women's-prison sexy, but I definitely would have thought there would be something sexy about the place, in that institutional-sexy way. You know what I mean, gymnasium equipment, uniforms, stuff.

But some days here every woman in the place seems like she might have another job moonlighting as a body double for an Eastern European shot-putter. Some days, most days in fact, it's as grey and depressing here as a pre-Jamie-Oliver school dinner.

So, like I said, I thought I'd be OK – or as OK here as

anywhere – but I'd reckoned without this new girl, Eleanor. She's what they call a breath of fresh air. In this wasteland of sheer unsexiness, Eleanor is pure totty. It's like she's tumbled off the set of the Benny Hill show and landed on this unworthy stretch of lino. OK, that's too much. She's not quite Benny Hill material, but it's all relative. And she is a trainee physiotherapist, which in anyone's mind approximates to nurse, which, of course, when it's a girl like Eleanor, approximates to sexilicious.

And guess what I so don't need right now! Yup, sexilicious.

No matter that Eleanor is makeup-free and has her hair screwed up in an ugly purple butterfly clip. No matter that her uniform is at least two sizes too big and bags and sags around her little waist, looking as grey and greasy as old fish and chip paper. No matter that her shoes are scuffed-up cheap trainers rather than *Carry On Matron*-style stilettos. Today, and in my tortured state, Eleanor looks fucking hot. And, what's more, underneath her function-over-form work togs Eleanor is totally my type, from her honey-coloured highlights to her neat, petite ankles. She even has the kind of mouth I like, a pink permanent moue.

She has a cocksucker's mouth. And the funny thing is, I have a cocksucker's cock.

Oh shit. I really wish I hadn't just thought that.

So, five seconds after meeting her, I fancy Eleanor. And it doesn't take a body language expert to notice that fancying Eleanor has suddenly become a pretty popular occupation around here. Every bloke in the room is practically foaming at the mouth. Which means that I must be the only guy in here who isn't actively trying to get themselves partnered with her.

Which means the fact that I end up working with her is sure and certain proof of Sod's Law.

And I really don't need this right now.

Even under normal circumstances I can be a bit funny about being touched. Because, well, here's the thing, if you're a man like me, i.e. a man who knows what it is to be the filling in a tyre-and-tarmac sandwich, something happens to your body. Not something physical. Take all that as read, obviously. But something else. Something social.

People touch you. People touch me in a way that they wouldn't normally touch an adult man. People touch me like they'd touch a child or a pregnant woman.

And even at the best of times, that pisses me off. I get all grouchy when I feel like the shot-putters are touching me too much. Of course they have to, a bit. But I don't like it, because I know they're touching me because of what's happened to me. Maybe, under other circumstances, I would have made an exception for Eleanor, but not today. Not the state I'm in.

I don't want Eleanor to touch me right now, not for any highfalutin quasi-political reasons, but simply because I'm so fucking horny it isn't even funny. But, for so many reasons, it's tricky to avoid. Especially with fate feeling in a particularly cruel mood.

So I'm doing some stuff on the bars, and Eleanor touches me, right now, right here. Just a hand on my waist to steady me, stop me from falling. But her hand is so warm I can feel it through my T-shirt. And it's then that I really wish I hadn't worn such comfortable, loose-fitting clothing today. Eleanor has an effect on me. And although a small, faithless part of me is glad that I am getting this opportunity to show her that my cock isn't as useless and pointless as my currently very uncooperative legs, most of me is so mortified.

Eleanor – the professional – ignores my humiliating case of Eiffel Tower smuggling. At least she does at first. But then, as she rights me and takes her hand away she pauses and lets her hand trail over my stomach. And when I look at her, she gives me a smile that might as well be a written invitation.

What the fuck?

I put it out of my mind, though. I have to. I grit my teeth and get through my session mostly without even looking at her. And then I skedaddle to the social club as fast as my wheels will carry me.

Oh yes, the social club. This is pretty new for me: up until about a month ago not many of my activities had the word 'social' or, indeed, the word 'club' in the title. This is very much a new thing.

But lately I have been going to this social club after physio, which is also run in the spinal injuries unit. Actually I did go to this place for a bit after I left hospital, but I drifted away as soon as I got my bungalow sorted and wasn't living at my mum's any more.

Really, though, I don't know why I was so keen to drop this place before, throwing it over in favour of jacking into the net (and jacking off on the net). It's so much better than I remember. It's actually pretty OK. Hanging out with other guys in chairs is not that bad. Not that depressing at all. I didn't know. I haven't hung out with other disabled people that much.

I suppose that's because I never felt that comfortable with the whole disability thing itself, despite being a member. However lame that sounds. Probably a lot of that was because of Larry.

After my accident Larry visited me in hospital twice. I suppose I should have been surprised that he even did that. His first visit started off OK. He bounced around with a kind of hyperactive bumptiousness and made lots of comments about nurses – really, lots – like every other thing that came out of his mouth was a comment about *Carry On* films or bed baths or *The Singing Detective*. But he couldn't keep it up. He quickly relocated to the land of downcast gazes and shuffling feet, as the conversation got inevitably more serious and the extent of my injuries became clear to him. When it came to facing the real facts, rather than just messing about with the curtains around my bed, he couldn't deal. He found an excuse to leave as soon as it was polite. In fact, even slightly before it was polite.

I was very surprised when he came back to the hospital a week later. Even though it was just to tell me to my face that this was 'too heavy for me, dude.'

I never thought I'd see him again after that. I never *wanted* to see him again after that. He didn't even hang around long enough for me to tell him how I was going to get myself walking again within a year.

So, yeah, Larry made it clear he was uncomfortable with it – my disability, the hospital, everything – and that made me decide I was going to be uncomfortable with it too. Course, buying in to Larry's philosophy was a pretty dumb thing to do because, as Larry was uncomfortable with me along with everything else, siding with him left me completely on my own.

So, hey, you know what? I might just be better off hanging out with people who don't completely crap themselves at the very idea of me. Yeah, just starting to see that now.

So I go along to the social club twice a week and get something of a self-esteem boost as a result. And it's really all down to Mary.

Not just that her acceptance and validation have made me happier. I mean, they have. A bit. But that's not the main reason why being with Mary has made me want to come here. It's a lot more mundane than that. The real reason was that I needed to get an off-the-peg social life, quickly, so Mary wouldn't think I was an utter saddo. I couldn't let her know that all I do for kicks is go round my mum's and chat to other weirdos on the interweb.

I mean, my best real-life friend is still Larry. And most of our contact is limited to his boastful emails.

More or less. Actually things have changed a bit since Operation Track Down Mary. For the last month he has even been pestering me. He texts me a lot, about once a day, which is a big leap from not at all. Although that is mostly because of the crippled mate = girl bait thing (which was a real text he sent me, believe it or not).

And I think he's also keen to meet up again because, somewhere along the line (and I'm not sure exactly where or when), I gave him the impression Mary was something of a babe, something like the girls I used to date. So he might have thought the game was back on. Maybe he's got over his cripple phobia, or maybe he's forgotten I'm disabled.

But it isn't. She isn't. She's much more ... oh god, how to put it. Mary just isn't like the girls I used to date; she's much more mature, in every way. Good ways and bad ways.

She's really not what Larry would expect of me. And, now I come to think of it, that shame goes both ways. I don't want Mary to know what I was, just as much as I don't want Larry to see what I've become.

But whatever point on the graph my friendship with Larry might be on, I certainly don't want to let Mary think he represents my social life.

So the social club is my new social life. A good thing. I even come here when Mary is too busy to come with me. Like today.

It's basically just cripples and their hangers-on, being social, drinking tea and competing over who can tell the most gruesome injury/disease/botched-operation story, which I always give a good go, even though my story is pretty unsensational around here. So long as I can avoid getting talked into joining a basketball squad, I'm pretty happy. Although avoiding the sporting evangelists is easier said than done. Just because I'm a young guy and reasonably worked out, everyone seems to assume I am desperate for a place on their wannabe paralympic squad. Course, I don't mind them asking. It's flattering and it does give me a chance to explain that I am getting more than enough physical exercise these days. Heh!

Yeah. Boasting about the fact I am getting some. Not the most honourable pursuit, but that is what I spend a lot of my time doing with my new friends when Mary's not around. I can't really help it; if she's not here, all I want to do is talk about her.

Obsessed, much? Who? Me?

Andy's probably my best mate here. He's a wheelie too. (That's what he calls being in a wheelchair: being a wheelie. I'd never heard that one before I came here.) He's a really good guy. We get on great. He probably gets on great with everyone who comes here. He's one of those people who just get socialising, who can just do it. In the beginning, I didn't so much make friends with Andy as not fend off his garrulous advances. Not that I don't like him. I *do* like him.

I'm in a corner with Andy right now, huddled and tight, bumper to bumper. And, yeah, I'm boasting about Mary. But I just can't help it. She's at the forefront of my mind even more than usual today. I even end up telling Andy about last night. About how Mary told me I couldn't come for twenty-four hours, and how that made me get hard when Eleanor touched me.

'Are you going to tell her?' Andy says, laughing a bit. Clearly loving my confessional mood.

'Tell who? Eleanor?'

Andy laughs again. 'No. Mary. You should tell her about your little humiliation. She'd love it, the kinky devil.'

Oh yeah, Andy has met Mary. In fact they get on well. He knows all about her kinky predilections. Her kinks for bondage and badness, that is: I'd be very surprised if he knows about her disability fetish. She is very cagey about people knowing about that, especially other disabled people. She had a mini-crisis about coming here with me for the first time, in case they had some kind of sicko-detector switched on and decided to give her a hard time about her disgusting-ness – being all super kinky for men who can't walk. But, as I pointed out to her, who's to know?

I think Andy is quite kinky himself, because he loves hearing all about my escapades with Mary. Every time I'm here on my own, he seems to corner me and ask questions, lots of questions. Maybe he fancies Mary or something. Well, his luck's out. He might have the wheels but I know she's not interested. I checked.

After the first couple of visits to the social club with Mary I found I was getting a bit paranoid every time she looked at or spoke to another guy in a chair. Especially Andy, because she and he were particularly chummy. I ended up taking Mary to one side and making her promise me that she didn't fancy him. She said she didn't and then told me off for assuming she would be interested in any guy who rolls rather than strolls. It doesn't work like that, apparently.

But anyway, for whatever reason, Andy does like to talk about my sex life. And that's what he's doing right now.

'You don't have any problems, then? You've got full feeling?' he says suddenly, causing me to open my eyes very wide in surprise. He says it in a very matter-of-fact way as if he's talking about, I don't know, biscuits or something.

'Yeah,' I say, trying to match him with equal bravado. Deep down I'm terrified that he'll expect me to get my fully functioning dick out and show it to him.

'And sex, that's normal too, you can get an erection and come? The works? It's all there?'

'Yeah.'

'Heh. Well, that's good.' He scratches the side of his nose. 'I think that's pretty much usual for your type of injury, although it varies a lot. Was she surprised by that, Mary? Delighted to find you in full working order?'

'Um. Maybe, I guess.' And that's more than a little weird because I never thought about what Mary expected to find in my underpants. A strange, hollow feeling creeps into my brain then, as I consider the possibility that Mary was disappointed that I was the Full Monty in that department. Maybe it would have turned her on even more if my dick was as useless as my legs. I squish that nasty feeling away.

I end up saying, softly, 'Actually, sometimes I feel like it's a bit harder to get, well, hard, like my erection isn't as strong. But that happens more when I'm on my own than when I'm with Mary.' (And it certainly isn't a problem right now. Right now I'm in a serious tent-pole situation if I so much as think about it!)

Andy reads my mind. 'Yeah? I bet you wish you'd had a bit more of that problem earlier today when Eleanor was squeezing your arse.' And he laughs a lot.

I laugh with Andy. And I can't help wondering if maybe I got him wrong, maybe he doesn't fancy Mary at all, maybe he likes me.

Mary

David's got physio and stuff today, so I'm at the university library, working. I'm to and fro from the stacks, bringing up obscure articles and texts, ploughing through endless desert-dry, long-forgotten Victorian novels. I love this. Sex with David is wonderful, but this is every bit as fulfilling. This is the other side of me. I'm in academic heaven.

The library is fairly empty today – a lonely Tuesday – so I've had my pick of the very best study spots. Right now, I'm sitting at this nice big window table, with piles of books and paper all over it and my glasses sliding down my nose. I feel satisfyingly like a character in an 80s college movie, one of those scenes where the character has to suddenly start studying hard to pass their exams, after 90 minutes' worth of partying down. This, just this, is exactly how I used to fantasise that academia would be when I was hard at work at the grimy PR coal face.

After this wonderful morning-long wallow in the cerebral, I head off to meet Mercury for a quick update on my dissertation followed by another wallow – this time in the rather more carnal. I'm so ridiculously high, I all but skip down the street, with my head so full of facts I keep thinking that they're going to start spilling out and splashing on the pavement in great luminous puddles.

As expected, our dissertation update meeting quickly becomes more of an update on my sex life. In fact, after less than ten minutes, we've abandoned the austere (and smoke- and alcohol-free) surroundings of Mercury's office for our usual table at Monroe. Before we know it, it's more mid-afternoon than lunchtime and we're both perfectly pissed and lusciously lush. I'm even cocktail-goggled enough to reflect that although this place still looks like it was hollowed out of oak by a bunch of particularly determined termites, it may be starting to grow on me.

Mercury suggests we eat something (a very timely idea) and orders himself a plate of hummus and olives, accompanied by some jaw-challenging bread that claims to be wrought by artisans. I go for soup – the ubiquitous carrot and coriander – and yet more salacious updates on my sexual adventures.

Although, really, there is nothing about my relationship with David that Mercury doesn't know. Every up and every down. Every position. Every room. He could probably recite my description of the time David and I glided from room to room, like a porno Torville and Dean, David naked in his chair, all steely muscles and steely steel, me with my warm smooth legs pressing against slightly cooler, slightly hairier ones. Close and connected. He was so hard inside me the entire time. So cool and in control as his muscles flexed, hands on the wheels, moving us around, pirouetting and gliding and fucking all at once, like something from a delicious dream. Mercury has heard it all.

'So things are good, then?' says Mercury when I've finished my salacious storytelling with an update on last night's David-tormenting session, and how he is at his social club for wheelchair users with a cock that springs to attention if it so much as feels a draught. Mercury laughs heartily at this. He is always very appreciative of my more imaginative stunts.

'Oh yes,' I babble, happily, 'it couldn't be better. It really is refreshing, because David knows exactly why I find him so attractive. I told him upfront. It turns me on. His helplessness. Or maybe his perceived helplessness, because he isn't all that helpless. Not really. And I know he doesn't like to think of himself as helpless – he's incredibly proud. But he can give the illusion of being helpless so easily . . .'

I tail off and look at Mercury, but he doesn't meet my gaze at first. He's got his head down, busy carving a swooping groove in his hummus with a crust of his bread, chuckling lightly to himself. Then, after a few moments' silence, he seems to lose interest in his pretty patterns and pops a luscious and lustrous olive into his mouth instead, finally looking over at me.

But he still doesn't say anything, just flashes his eyebrows, so I keep going with my garbled rationalisation of my relationship. 'I don't know. But there's just something to be said about being able to be this honest about what I like. What I like and what I want. It's just, just wonderful.'

'Well,' Mercury says, with a rather sarcastic smile, 'I'm glad things are so sunny in Mary-land. You're shagging away merrily and all your little dreams are coming true.' I can tell Mercury is patronising me, amusing himself because I'm starting to bore him. Normally I'd read these signs almost unconsciously and segue into another depraved topic, but I have a one-track mind these days. I want to keep talking David. I'm all fired up now from reliving my most recent David sex-capades, and there's still an hour or so until he picks me up from the library, so in lieu of real David, I want filthy David talk. I like talking about him, it turns me on. I like talking about him almost as much as I like being with him. But as Mercury is getting bored, I decide to settle for thinking about David. And have a change of scene. So I wrap up, plead that my books are calling and get back to the library.

And off I skip, back to my books and pens and papers, and my occasional breaks fantasising about David and his poor frustrated cock.

David

When the social club starts to wind down, I get going to pick Mary up from the university library.

I'm feeling a little het up because she's sent me a couple of teasing texts during the afternoon, asking how I'm feeling, so I know she's starting to get frisky. She misses me. I like that. But I'm being cool. Although I knew exactly what she was referring to in her texts, I didn't play along. I didn't tell her how I was feeling –

frustrated, horny and completely unable to stop thinking about sex, about her, and about what she might do to me when we get home tonight. How could I possibly condense all that into txt-speak? So I just sent her a one-word message in reply, 'fine'.

I try not to think about these things as I drive to meet her. I don't want to have an accident. Another accident.

Maybe I drive a little faster than normal, though, because I arrive early and Mary isn't there. So I'm sitting in the car outside the university library, squatting on the double yellows waiting for her, when someone raps on the car window. It's not Mary. And it's kind of awkward.

It's awkward because it's Larry.

And I've been ignoring Larry. Now it might have been an easy enough job to ignore Larry, when Larry was personified by a bunch of irritatingly laddish texts, but now we're face to face – give or take a bit of toughened glass – I can hardly blank him and drive off, can I?

I push the button and the window hums down.

'Hey,' I say.

'Hey, dude. What you doing here?'

'Um.' I don't want to tell him I'm waiting for Mary, because then he might wait with me. She could be here any minute. And the last thing I want is for the dreaded Mary–Larry interface to happen right when I so desperately need Mary's assistance with a little problem in my pants.

I can think of only one way out. It'll make me late meeting Mary, but this is a very devil/deep-blue-sea conundrum.

'I was looking for you, actually, mate,' I say, as brightly as I can. 'Fancy a quick one?'

We end up in the Union Bar, just like before, with awkward pints of lager and fidgety packets of crisps.

But after a little small talk, something truly unexpected happens. Larry leans forward and fixes me with a slightly shifty look. 'It's nice to do this again, mate. It was really excellent before wasn't it?'

'Before, what, before the accident?'

'Nah, shit, dude, not that. I meant you and me, tracking down that chick. Just us boys. Just like old days. Didn't you just love it?'

'Er, well, yeah, kind of.' God, did I? I haven't thought about it, except when deleting Larry's increasingly frequent texts.

'Now, can I just get something straight?' he says next, not even pausing to let me come to terms with the last thing he said. (What *was* that exactly? Larry declaring his undying love?) 'Mary, the girl you are now shacked up with, she isn't the one we saw, right, the one who leant out the window with the hair?'

God, is Larry thick? I don't think I ever noticed Larry was thick before. An ignorant, reactionary idiot, sure, but not thick. Surely the fact that the girl who leant out of the window wasn't the right girl was obvious from the conversation? But I don't mention any of that. I just say, 'You mean Carrie, she's Mary's flatmate.'

'Ri – ight,' says Larry, cool as, but clearly going somewhere. 'So this Carrie, she's available?'

'Well, as far as I know. I haven't met her.'

'You haven't met her? You're going out with her flatmate!'

'Yeah, but I don't go to Mary's place. It's up three flights of stairs, which is kind of a pain. Anyway, why are you so interested in Carrie all of a sudden? Don't you like to aim a bit higher than a crazy wholemeal hippy?' Because I might not have met Carrie, but I certainly have heard a lot about her – she is the second biggest reason why Mary now practically lives in my bungalow.

Larry gives me a look that I haven't seen for a long, long time. It's a bit like the way he used to look at me when I first met him, before I taught him how to be a player.

'That's not quite true, David. You used to aim a lot higher than that. And I was often lucky enough to get the ones you didn't want. But now I haven't got you around, things are different. When I said I needed you as bait, well, truth is, I always needed you as bait. Look in the mirror, David. There's a reason why you used to have to beat them off with a stick, and it wasn't your dazzling wit.'

This is a rather uncharacteristic outburst for Larry. He's not usually one to express himself. So I guess he must be feeling desperate. 'But what about that girl, the one who came up to us before? The one who had the party?'

'Yeah, there is her. Emma? Ella? She's completely mad, though. But yeah, OK, I didn't say it was a complete drought, I'm just saying I might not be able to complete with your all-dolly-birds-all-the-time standards.'

'Oh. Right.'

And my first thought, all the time this weirdness is going on, is – rather treacherously – that Mary herself isn't up to my old self-imposed 'dolly bird' standards.

The ones Larry is going on about. The ones I really did used to have. And my second thought, even more treacherously, is that how Eleanor, the physiotherapist totty, does meet the standard. Oh yes, Eleanor is the kind of girl I would have set my sights on, way back when.

Larry sighs, a deep and heavy end-of-the-world sigh, into his pint. 'And it's not just that, David. I'm kind of bored of all this dogging around, anyway. It's a lot less fun than it used to be when it was you and me, young lads. But I'm turning thirty next month and I just don't know if I can keep it up anymore.'

Oh shit. First I'm a girl-bait puppy, then I'm an advice-dispensing eunuch for that party-girl and now I'm a fucking therapist. Can't I just be a normal bloke? There was a reason I used to try and avoid people.

I roll my eyes and start scrabbling around for a way out of this conversation.

I finally manage to get a goodbye in edgeways, and escape from the Union Bar. I get back to the library and my heart leaps when I see Mary standing outside, wearing a light-brown raincoat and clutching a huge pile of dark-brown books. She looks a bit tired, but seems to brighten as I pull up. She doesn't ask where I've been, which is good because I don't want to tell her about my encounter with Larry, in case it leads to me telling her about the old me and the sexy type of girls I used to date.

When we are both in the car, Mary reaches over and squeezes my thigh. I find myself flushing a little. I know it's from guilt. But those feelings melt away as she slides her hand up my leg until it grazes my crotch and squeezes there, ever so gently. 'I missed you today,' she half whispers. 'I went for lunch with Mercury and bored him half to death talking about you.'

I gulp and try desperately to make some less squirmy conversation, telling Mary about my time at the social club, and how Andy asked me a million questions about my sex life again and seemed very amused by my twenty-four-hour delayed gratification. But I don't mention anything about a new assistant physio, or about the incident that followed when I worked with her. I feel more guilty about that than anything else, despite the fact that, really, it was all Mary's fault. More to the point, I don't like feeling guilty about stuff. It's new to me.

But, luckily, there are some more pressing matters to attend to. Like the fact that I am in danger of spearing a hole right through the crotch of my trousers if she doesn't let me come pretty soon. So I end my tale of physio and social club and Andy by pressing that point. 'So, anyway, I told him I would be getting it tonight, I've been waiting all day.'

She laughs, half to herself. 'I was wondering how long it would take you to remind me about that. Well, actually, I did half suspect it would take you no time at all.' She smiles, like she's said something really clever. 'Anyway, don't worry, I haven't forgotten. In fact, I'm looking forward to it almost as much as you are, you greedy eager little bitch.' It sounds a bit like a threat and a lot like a promise.

My breath comes a little quicker.

She's noticed, of course, even though I haven't said a word, even though my breath is whisper-soft, even though she is looking out of the window and not at me, as if her mind is elsewhere. She always notices. And I always know.

I try not to think about that. I try to concentrate on the road. In fact, I'm concentrating on the road more than I really need to; it's not a particularly complicated bit of road. And then she says, 'Well, not long now.'

'No,' I say, not daring to say more, because I feel sure she's about to twist things around somehow to tell me that I can't come tonight either.

'Has it been very, ahem, very hard?' she says, trying not to laugh at her very obvious, very deliberate double entendre.

'Yes,' I say blankly, answering the question both ways, giving everything away with the way my voice half cracks in the middle of this confession.

I can tell without looking at her that she's grinning broadly. I can practically hear it. 'Well, I am glad, actually. I didn't really think you'd do it.'

'Do what?'

'Hold out for me. Wait all day. After all, I couldn't have prevented you from nipping off to the loo at any time today and sorting yourself out. I wasn't watching. I wasn't there. I wouldn't even have known. But it never occurred to you to do that, did it?'

I don't reply. But she's right. It never did.

It's not long after we get home that I get my reward for my good behaviour, for which I am truly grateful. I wasn't in the mood for waiting around.

I don't know what it's all about at first, this evening's diversion. It isn't what I thought it would be. At least, I thought it would be something more straightforward, more of a quick release. I have another thing coming.

My arms are tied tightly down to the armrests again with those same jewel-bright green ribbons. A fact that has added to my discomfort in more ways than just the obvious, because when she ties me down my cock starts to feel like it is going to explode.

Mary plays with me a bit once I am helpless, manoeuvring me from room to room.

In the hall she toys with me, stroking my face and then pulling my hair, hard. Making me beg for her mouth on my cock, only to have her refuse and slap my face.

In the bathroom she runs the taps, smiling sinisterly, before suddenly scooping handfuls of icy cold water over my head and my crotch, which does nothing to cool me down, and has her leaning up against the wall for a long time, panting, staring at my wet hair stuck to my face, the drips running off my chin, and clearly having a hard time not peaking too soon herself.

We end up in the kitchen.

At first I just sit and watch her. She looks sideways at me, peering around the shiny brown curtain of her hair. She's mixing something up on the stove. I'm not really paying attention, choosing instead to concentrate on my confusingly delicious feelings of exposure and helplessness. But I do notice that something in the warming air smells like chocolate.

She's in another world. Her head full of her plans, plans for me, whatever they might be. Meanwhile I'm wet and I'm cold.

My kitchen has always been a little cooler than the rest of my house, for some reason. So, even though the combi-boiler is roaring away in the corner, and the thermostat is cranked up to keep the March winds out, there's enough of a chill in the air to make me shiver as water continues to drip from my hair down on to my chest and my nipples grow stiff and sensitised.

I'm half-naked, just wearing my jeans. No shirt, no shoes. I feel incredibly vulnerable like this, and almost doped up with frustrated arousal.

The big window above the sink shows nothing but black sky and silent garden, but I still wish Mary would pull the blind down – someone might look in and see me. My paltry, untended garden isn't over-looked, but I can't quite shift the idea that if someone were standing out there, lurking on my lawn for some reason or other, they would be able to see me, squirm-ing with arousal, dripping-wet, half-naked and tied to my wheelchair with emerald ribbons.

So here I am, feeling extremely vulnerable in the echoey kitchen, which (for reasons I absolutely refuse to examine any more closely right now) I appear to quite like. My cock quite likes it anyhow – it's viciously hard and eager, and that isn't just the result of twenty-four hours of understimulation.

'You weren't there when I came out of the library,' Mary says in an inexpressive voice, turning away from the stove slightly.

'No,' I say. 'Sorry.'

'That's OK. You're not my chauffeur. But, you see, when you weren't there I went to the Student Union shop while I was waiting. Just for something to do, really. And they didn't have anything I wanted to buy. So I bought a couple of bars of chocolate. I mean, at the time I just thought it might be nice to eat them this evening, if we were watching the telly or some-thing. But then I thought, on the way home, that you probably wouldn't want to eat too much chocolate because you like to watch your weight and everything.

And I also thought, well, how often do we sit and just watch telly?' She sighs, as if wistfully imagining a different kind of life, one where she and I sit and watch TV of an evening, rather than shag each other half-conscious every chance we get. Then she turns away to stir the confection on the hob, still speaking.

'You reminded me in the car what a good boy you'd been, waiting all day with your cock all tender and needing, and, well, I had this other idea. A little reward – fun for both of us. A sweet treat.' Her brow is furrowed as she keeps on stirring the pan. 'But it doesn't seem to be working quite the way I wanted it to.'

She turns back to face me, looking partly peeved and partly amused. Whatever she's making smells really wonderful now. I'm feeling hungry. Hungry and quite confused. Is Mary cooking something for me? If so, why am I tied up?

'It's still a bit too thick,' Mary says, distractedly, 'I'm not quite sure what to do ...' She looks around my kitchen as if searching for some assistance. I can do nothing but stare dumbly at her, as I don't have a clue what she is talking about. This is getting annoying.

Then she suddenly brightens and says, 'Do you have a cookery book?'

'What?' I might be starting to feel peckish, but this blend of cookery and kinkery isn't my idea of fun. I thought I was going to get a mind-melting orgasm, not dessert. Unless, of course, the two are somehow connected. If so I'd like the connection revealed sooner rather than later.

A curious expression flashes across Mary's face, half confused, half conciliatory. She's realised she's losing me, so she steps it up.

She comes towards me slowly and bends over, putting her hands on my bound wrists and bringing her face close to mine. She's got that look, the stern one, and my cooling ardour instantly heats up again. Oh god. When she looks at me this way all I can think is how much I want her to hurt me. And my cock gives a desperate throb.

'A cookery book, bitch-boy, have you got one, or not?'

I'm about to play along, give her a defiant 'no', like a steadfast prisoner under torture, trotting out name, rank and number, when I remember that actually, surprisingly enough, I do have one.

So I say, 'Uh, yes. I do, as a matter of fact. In the bedroom, at the bottom of the wardrobe.'

I'm still utterly clueless, but she leaves me hanging and scampers off happily to get it, returning a few moments later, turning the barely familiar volume over in her hands. Her mouth is already forming a teasing question when I interrupt. 'Larry bought it for me, OK, one Christmas as a sort of joke because I said she was the only brunette I would ever consider doing...' My sentence tails off as brunette Mary smirks and raises her eyebrows at me.

But she brushes off any slight on her hair colour as if it were nothing, meant nothing, and says, 'Well, I guess the joke's on Larry, because I think beautiful brunette Nigella is just the person we need right now.' And she flips to the index.

A few seconds and some considered page flipping later, Mary says, 'It seems some cream might help.'

She turns off the stove, carefully removes the delicious-smelling saucepan, places it gently on one of the unused back burners and turns to speak to me directly. 'So I'm just going to pop out for a moment.'

'What?' I say, my vulnerability quotient suddenly increasing by about one million per cent and becoming so not sexy. She cannot seriously mean she is going to leave the house with me tied to my chair like this.

Unconsciously, I pull a little at the ribbon that holds my left wrist to the armrest and, just as Mary had warned me it would, the wide flat fabric twists into a narrow cord as I put it under strain, changing from a reasonably comfortable restriction into something as vicious as cheesewire. I wince as it digs into my wrist and my breathing gets a little heavier. Mary looks at me and bites her lip. She has a very particular look in her eyes, and I know exactly why. I'm struggling, but I can't get loose. I really can't. Even if I want to. And I do want to. And this confirmation of my utter helplessness is turning her on. It's turning me on. In fact, I seem to be oscillating between being scared and being so aroused I almost levitate out of my chair. I'm confused. Freaked out. Hard as a rock.

I can tell from the way her mouth twitches that she probably wants to kiss me right now. And I want her to kiss me. It's one of the things that does it for us. One of our things. Every time there is a little flash of pain. My pain. There and gone. A slap or a pinch or a nasty unexpected bite. A hiss and a struggle and a groan. We kiss. Kiss it better. Kiss it worse.

But right now Mary doesn't kiss me. She bottles it up and turns away. She has a plan. She's double-checking that the stove is off, that the pan is cooling, that the house isn't going to burn down with me trapped inside.

'I'll be two secs,' she says. She grabs her mobile phone from the counter top and pushes it into my right hand, always super-safety-conscious. 'I'm sure your mum will have some cream.'

I don't even get a chance to ask 'WTF?' before she's gone. I look at the little silver mobile phone in my hand. I pull at the ribbons a bit more, but only succeed in making them even thinner and more uncomfortable. Something my cock is still so hard about.

I look out at the dark garden, trying to make out shapes in the blackness, terrified someone might be there, waiting to pounce. Manipulating the phone with one hand, I keep one finger hovering over the '9' key, just in case.

And then, not quite within the promised 'two secs' window but close enough, Mary's back, holding a small pot.

'I knew your mum would help me out. She's the type who'd have cream in. I told her I was making profiteroles for you. I think she approved. She thinks you're too thin, you know, but, really, what does she know?' (My mum, it has to be said, utterly loves Mary, and will probably love her even more now she is showing her domestic goddess credentials.)

She starts pouring the contents of the pot into her pan. 'Mary . . .?' I want to ask her what she is doing, but realise, less than one word into the query, that I am about to find out.

Mary is smiling at me. She's holding a saucepan full of chocolate and cream, dipping a fingertip in to check it isn't too hot to touch. And then she says, half apologetically, 'It's such a terrible cliché, I know, but somehow, you're so beautiful, you make even the hoariest old clichés all new and shiny.' She sticks her fingers into the warm chocolaty goo, steps forward and, in a sudden urgent movement, smears it from my chin right down my cool, naked chest, smiling a lusty, hazy, heady smile that seems to rush through my body, exactly like the warm chocolate melting all over me.

'I just like the idea of you being, I don't know, dirty, I guess,' she says, shrugging lightly.

We both look at the thick stripe of chocolate that runs down my chest. It's warm and it tickles a bit where it is dripping. I want to touch it, a rebellious part of me is desperate to wipe it away, clean it off. It's so sticky and tickly, but I know I'm helpless. And I know better now than to try and struggle against those cruel ribbons.

Mary bends her head and runs her tongue from my navel, up my stomach and along that neat groove that divides my pecs, licking her way up the chocolate stripe until she's lapping at my jaw line.

'Mmm,' she says, indistinctly, 'tastes nice anyway. Good recipe. Shame you can't have any, but you are always saying you need to watch what you eat.'

And it's true. I am always saying it. Because I do need to be careful. I can't exercise like I used to and weights don't burn fat . . .

But that train of thought is vanishing. I'm quickly becoming more and more incoherent as my cock gets harder and harder, thanks to Mary's continued kittenish tongue flicks across my chest, neck, stomach, chin.

Then she uses her hand to smear the chocolate more, pushing it further into my lap, down and around the waistband of my jeans. Under the denim. My cock strains to meet her hand, desperate for even the slightest graze, but gets nothing.

Next, she wipes a deliberately chocolately hand across my left cheek. My tongue comes out, half on instinct, trying to lick at the dark sweetness covering my face, but I can't reach it. Suddenly I want to taste the chocolate more than anything. I stretch, my tongue straining just like my cock was a moment ago. The chocolate is tantalisingly close, but I can't get at any of it. I moan out loud with the delicious frustration of it all.

Mary leans closer; she has a little chocolate on her lips and tongue. I think she is going to kiss me, but she stops. She stops just a shade more than a tongue's length from my mouth. Out of reach. I'm still aching for chocolate. And aching for her even more. I moan again. I don't have any choice about it. I moan and I writhe. I pull on the ribbons even though I know I shouldn't. My wrists are already covered in stripes of red soreness.

And then Mary reaches out, very suddenly, and twists both my nipples at once, hard. She's done this to me many times before, and every other time she has done it I have cried out as the pain shot through me like a lightning bolt straight to my cock. Hot and jagged and fast and nasty. But this time, in a variation on our usual hurt-comfort games, at the same time as she twists, Mary kisses me, pressing her hot-chocolate lips against mine so that my cry is swallowed up in her mouth and the lightning bolt of pain is twisty and strange, mixed with the pleasure of sweetness and chocolate and desires satisfied. It still reaches my cock, though, which seems to double in size, although that can't be possible.

She pulls out of the kiss and smiles at me. I want her to touch my cock. I wish I could touch it myself.

But I know her so, so well now. I know that's still a long way off. So all I can do is squirm hopelessly, pull at the ribbons that are cutting into my wrists and make a noise of keening, desperate frustration.

Mary dips a finger into her saucepan of smooth glossy chocolate. She leans over me, her hair brushing my shoulders. I can't tell what she's doing. The angles are wrong and I can't quite see. I can feel the warmth again as she smears more chocolate across my chest, grazing my erect nipples, making me twist and squirm.

'I've been thinking about writing on you,' she says, almost to herself as she continues to daub. 'Marking your body. Marking my territory. It seems so hot to do that. I love your body so much. I want to decorate it. It's such a beautiful thing. And I can't quite believe it belongs to me.'

She moves her head a little and then I can see that she has written the word 'slut' right across my chest in chocolate. When I see that I bite my lip with arousal, but I stop twisting. I don't want to spoil her work.

She writes all over me. All over my chest and stomach. She writes 'bitch-boy' and 'whore' and 'filthy' and 'cripple' and all the while I moan for her, trying not to writhe when hot splatters drip from her fingers and land on my stomach.

By the end, when there's no more flesh left for her to adorn, I'm so painfully aroused that I am pleading and begging incoherently. Not asking for her to do any more or any less, just saying, 'yes' and 'no' and 'please' and 'Mary'. Over and over. I so want to come, but there is nothing I can do to relieve my frustration, with my hands tied. I feel even more helpless as she leans forward to play at licking me clean and draws one nipple, hard, into her mouth, nibbling and teasing at my chest, until I'm a frantic squirming mess.

And finally her tongue creeps downwards. She opens up the buttons of my jeans, slowly, one by one. And then, at last, I feel her. Warm and wet and smooth against my poor, swollen cock. When she opens her mouth around it, it's almost too much for a moment, almost too much to bear. I yell and scream and cut my wrists some more on the tight ribbons, as she glides up and down, her throat feeling like hot, damp velvet. And it's not long – less than a minute – before Mary is licking me clean of come as well as chocolate.

And this is pretty standard for Mary and me. I'm a fretting confused, mixed-up boy by day, worrying about every aspect of my relationship, but a panting mess at night, giving it all over to her, leaving all my doubts outside the bedroom, along with my clothes.

As our relationship rolls on well into March, past the six-week mark and beyond, and the weather starts to warm up a little, we still show no signs of cooling down.

When I'm with Mary, wrapped up tight in her little sex cocoon, where only rules of Mary-logic apply, I forget about those dark little clouds that keep on floating into view as I joyously expand my sexual horizons. I just forget.

I forget about Larry and his continued presence on the periphery of my life, reminding me of The Way We Were, and how everything I used to think was so cool, was, in fact, so not. And I forget about Eleanor and her sexy undulating walk and flippy blonde hair and the way that, one strange day, I thought she might be trying to come on to me, though I'm now almost sure she was just teasing me for having an erection from her touching me. I've worked with Eleanor at physio once or twice since that incident and nothing else has happened – although that could be because Mary hasn't repeated her particular brand of evil cock-teasing. Unfortunately.

I forget everything else because Mary seems to know how to switch off my brain as effortlessly as she switches on my cock. She's just unstoppable. It seems like every night she has a new twist on our already twisted relationship. She just keeps on pulling it out of the bag.

She does indeed, as promised on our very first meeting, get on her knees one night and lick my footplate. And it is one of the most erotic things I have ever seen. She moans softly as she runs her tongue along the bright metal, caressing the tread of my tyres with her hands. It feels almost like she's licking and caressing a part of me. And I'm frantic for that mouth to be on my cock, long before she has done all she wants.

Another night, a night of coffees and insomnia and wrongness, she keeps me up into the darkest, tiniest hours of the morning, asking me questions. She asks me about what happened to me, about the accident, about how it felt then, how it feels now. She touches my body and asks where I have sensation and where I don't and where it varies. She makes me describes Being-David-Malkovich over and over until I run out of adjectives, out of words, out of thoughts. I keep going until I feel like she could step inside my body and feel every feeling I do, and nothing would be a surprise. She shows me that my body – my changed, spoiled, abnormal body – is her own personal Song of

Solomon. It's a very weird feeling, and one I'm not sure I'm used to yet.

As the night gets darker so do her questions. She says, 'If you weren't in your chair, how would you move?'

'What do you mean?' I roll over in the bed so I can rub against her, pressing close.

'I mean, well, would you crawl around? What could you do?'

'I couldn't really crawl, like, up on my knees. I could pull myself along though. My arms are pretty strong.' I feel her shiver against me.

She swallows slowly, and then says, 'So, sort of on your belly?'

'Yes, just like that.'

'I'd like to see you doing that.'

'Why?' I say with a teasing smile. Because, of course, I know why.

'I just would. Show me.'

So I do. Suddenly the lights are on and I'm in my chair, heading into the living room where there is most floor space. I let her gently help me on to the carpet and watch me drag myself across the floor on my stomach, the best I can. I'm still naked and I feel utterly vulnerable. My whole world contracts. I suddenly feel this strange wave of sensation, as if I am utterly dependent on Mary right now. And I like it. It's everything I shouldn't like, but I do. I feel like I need this. Like I'm addicted to her. And her bizarre way of thinking.

I'm crawling for her. A weird, fucked-up creature dragging itself across the carpet. And, god, I really shouldn't like this so much. It's every kind of objectification. But sparks of arousal are flying all over my body. I can scarcely tell which parts of me are which. I want to scream at her to take me. Use me. Make me into a mere thing. I want her to stride across the floor to me and fuck me. Force herself inside me. Own me.

But I don't. I don't because even in my own zoned-out state I can tell she's lost in her own rapture. She wouldn't even hear me. 'Tell me why you're doing that,' she says, as she stares at me crawling, squirming on the floor, her voice so ragged it's barely recognisable.

'For you.'

'No, no, tell me why you have to move like that.'

I change my path and start to drag myself towards her, meeting her eyes from way down on the floor. 'Because I can't get up.'

I can tell how much this is turning her on and it arouses me to see her almost frozen to the spot with desire. My cock is so painfully hard now, burning against the carpet as I continue towards her.

She stares at me in silence after that, until I reach her and run a desperate, wanting hand up her bare leg, trying desperately to reach her cunt. As my hand grazes her upper thigh, she takes half a step back-wards, pulling deliciously just my out of reach. And I whimper. Begging. Helpless. Everything she loves.

Then, suddenly, she growls like an animal and flips me over with preternatural strength, and we fuck until I feel sure she's worn away the carpet beneath me.

And after that, while we are still lying there, a sweating mass of heaving chests and smarting carpet burns, that's when I say it. I don't know why.

I say, 'I love you.'

Mary pulls herself up and rolls on to her side to look at me. She's frowning. 'No you don't,' she says, quite curtly. She sounds like she is chastising me – her voice is all who's-a-naughty-boy-then?

'What?' I complain, 'I do.'

'No, you don't, you just like getting a lot of regular sex.'

I'm taken aback by this reaction. I didn't think Mary thought that of me. I'm really not that shallow. Really. I've had lots of sex before and I've never said this to anyone. I wasn't hoping for a matching declaration or anything. But I could have done without a telling off.

'No,' I stammer, not sure what to say next, 'no, well, not that I don't like having lots of sex. But that's not why. It's just I do . . . oh, damnit, don't make me say it twice. I just do, OK.'

'Really?' She smiles, a very slow, very bad, very oh-shit-what-have-I-let-myself-in-for smile. 'Can you prove it?' she says.

I don't know how to answer that. 'Er, no, I don't think so.' I'm floundering.

'Oh, I bet you could. I bet we could find a way.' And I wouldn't have thought it possible, but the expression on Mary's face has become even more chilling and thrilling.

Did I just walk into something? Yeah, yeah, unfortunate turn of phrase.

Mary

In truth, I'm not sure what this relationship is, or how long it will last. I'm not even sure if I haven't made a big mistake in not letting this just be the one-night stand it was probably meant to be. In a lot of ways David brings out the worst in me. He makes me bad. He buys me a ticket to the bad place and saves me a seat on the bus. But, whatever, I'm on board now. I might as well enjoy the ride. And it isn't hard to enjoy it.

I do feel guilty sometimes. I can't help it. I find myself awake in the dark, worrying about whether what I'm doing to David is wrong in some way. Whether he really wants this. Whether he thinks that this is all he can get, so he is going along with whatever depravity I sling his way.

Oh, but, his cock does say different. His cock tells me over and over how much he likes it. (And his mouth does once or twice.)

But as for his declaration of love, I just don't know what to think about that.

So I don't think about it. I don't need to. I get on with other stuff. I work on my dissertation, I have sex with David and I go to work at the restaurant. That's where Thomas comes in. Remember that bus to the bad place? I just got an upgrade.

Oh, Thomas! Because, sorry though I might be to lose his sexy sneer, I'm guiltily thrilled that the previously super aloof Thomas is being friendlier and friendlier to me these last couple of weeks. Suddenly Thomas and I are best mates. A fact I am finding so ridiculously thrilling that it's quite an embarrassment. I have my suspicions as to why Thomas has thawed a little towards me too, and they are very exciting suspicions, very exciting indeed.

A couple of weeks ago, I came in to work after a rather fun time the night before, playing with David and some ribbons and some chocolate sauce. I'd had to improvise the recipe, with some help from The Domestic Goddess, but I was rather proud of it. I had ended up talking to one of the junior chefs about the entire thing. Well, initially we were just sharing chocolate recipes, but somehow I was so high about my own sexual prowess that the conversation eventually took in the S and M aspect too.

I'd never been quite so loose-lipped about my sexual proclivities at work before. I still hadn't talked about the wheelchair fetish thing, of course – I kept a tight lid on that – but I might have gone on and mentioned a few more of my kink-lite escapades with David – the bondage, the nipple clamps, that sort of thing. And I reckon some of that gossip must have reached Thomas's perfectly shaped ears, because suddenly he was my best friend and confidante, desperate to hear more.

And he did.

Thomas started cornering me when I went out for fag breaks. Every time I slipped outside, he'd appear. And I seem to be smoking quite regularly these days, whatever I might be telling myself about only-under-duress.

My increasing nicotine intake might have had something to with the fact that, ever since the day I spilled my sexuality to that chef, I didn't need to be skulking out by the bins for more than a minute before Thomas would join me and start to fish for sexy titbits.

And in the last few weeks, since I started having regular behind-the-bins confessionals with Thomas, he has told me some very interesting things.

The first hint was tiny, but I've spent enough time spotting signs like this in men – signs that they might just enjoy the kinds of things I enjoy – not to miss this one. (Especially when it falls from the mouth of a babe as pretty as this.)

The truth is, there are lots of men who, whether they admit it or not, really get off on being tied up, struck, ordered around, made helpless, all the stuff that gets me hot too – but they do fall into certain categories. And some are easier to spot than others.

Although I can't quite believe I didn't suss Thomas's secret deviant tendencies before. What with all that sullen-faced waiting of tables, taking orders with a moody grimace plastered across his face, he might as well have been carrying a sign saying 'Won't someone, please, give me the sound spanking I deserve?' But that's hindsight for you, I guess.

And it really doesn't matter that I didn't pick up on that, because as soon as Thomas got confirmation of the way I kink he started becoming another kind of bottom-boy altogether. He switched to something a lot more obvious.

(Which, deep down, I am still a little sad about. The old Thomas was more of a David-style secret-repressed-deviant-desires-type boy, which is much more my type. But I can't complain. Because I would never, ever have hatched a plan to seduce old-style Thomas. New-style Thomas, however – too easy.)

The first time it happened was about two weeks ago, the day after I'd had that conversation with the chef. Thomas joined me for a smoke by the bins, twisted the conversation round to sex like a pro, and confessed, between quick nervous drags, that it must be fun ordering David around in bed.

I coughed a bit. I was a bit confused, because this was such early days that I hadn't figured that Thomas even knew I was kinky. In fact, at first I jumped the wrong way and thought he meant that I took the upper hand because David was disabled. So I was about to splutter a correction, when Thomas, as if spotting the ambiguity, quickly added, 'You know, tying him up and stuff.'

'Yeah,' I said, with some relief – and it was at this point that I realised that Thomas had never met David and so almost certainly didn't know he was disabled. I was grateful that my ciggie sucking had held me back from a too hasty chastising. (Although Thomas would probably have enjoyed that.)

'Yeah. All that stuff,' Thomas said, his bravado suddenly seeming to switch into a kind of delicious bashfulness without any warning.

So I took a chance. An easy risk, really. Hardly a risk at all. Or, at least, a very-likely-to-pay-off risk, considering the way Thomas was suddenly acting all deferential and trying as hard as he could to make me talk bondage-sex. 'He likes me being in control,' I said. 'A lot of men like that kind of thing.'

'Mmm,' said Thomas, looking down at the ground. Looking at his shoes and then looking at mine. My current shoes weren't at all fancy. They were the brown clod-hoppers with the big heel that I wear a lot when I want to feel tall without comprising on comfort. (In truth I very rarely feel like compromising on comfort.)

I really liked Thomas looking at my shoes, though. But I didn't say anything.

But right then there was a humungous crash from somewhere in the kitchens and our conversation died suddenly on the dirty concrete, where we crushed our fag butts under our oh-so-fascinating shoes, before rushing inside and into conscientious mop-wielding action.

A few days later – not the next shift we had

together, but the one after that – Thomas found me outside again, and this time he didn't even go through the motions of taking one of my fags, he just said, almost demanded, 'How did you know David would like being tied up?'

'I don't know. I could just tell.'

'Can you always tell?'

'I don't think so. How would I know? I don't think I've ever got it wrong.' (Well, maybe once or twice.)

Thomas went quiet. He bent over in the doorway, pushing his hands deep into his pockets and looking up at me. I remember noticing how dishevelled he was looking. His shirt was half untucked and his hair was even more wild and out of place than usual. He held my gaze for quite a long time, not saying anything, until I gave up waiting and put out my finished fag, before making to push past him back into the kitchens.

But he stopped me, with one hand on my shoulder. 'I've always wanted to try it,' he said fast and nervy, with his face so close to mine I could smell the peppermint and coffee on his breath.

I smiled and pushed him away from me, gentle and firm, as I continued past. But just before I broke physical contact with him, I whispered, 'You really should.'

The next time we were on duty together, things started to get really heated between us, bristly-prickly with sexual tension. He told me, almost out of nowhere, that he'd like to be tied up and spanked. As submissive sexual fantasies go his wasn't the most imaginative one in the world, but Thomas is young and pretty so – much as I hate the kinky clichés – I forgave him his lack of originality.

But afterwards I thought of David. Dear sweet endlessly fuckable David and how unimaginable it was that he should confess to fantasising about something like that.

So, although David will for ever be my over-complicated dreamboy, these little chats with Thomas, well, they got me through the shifts. And they would never have been anything else – I swear, there would have been no evil plan – if it wasn't for what Thomas confessed next. OK, I'm not saying it never crossed my mind. I'm not saying Thomas's confessions didn't make me wish and hope I'd find a way to help him fulfil his twisted dreams, but there was no way I was going to jeopardise what I had with David. No way, until . . .

The next time we were taking a well-earned break, Thomas decided it was time for a little more share and share alike and told me that he thought he was a little bit bisexual – although he'd never tried anything with a bloke.

And the minute he said that, my mind was racing. I couldn't help thinking about how much Thomas looks like David. Thomas is a little younger, a little cockier and, of course, he doesn't have David's excess baggage. But they could almost be brothers. And that made me think very bad thoughts about the two of them.

So I'm weak. But no one alive could resist the prospect of such prettiness squared. And right after that confession came the one from David, that he loved me. And so, when I asked him if he was willing to prove it, I had something specific in mind. And with Thomas apparently wanting to unravel his tangled sexuality, my plan keeps everyone happy. God, I'm practically a fairy godmother here.

* * *

Thomas is working a double section today, because Stacey is off. (Party girl Stacey, in fact, has turned out to be something of a slacker.) Anyway, that means we're full-on for the entire shift, so our little nightly chat doesn't happen until really late. Meaning I have to wait it out before I get to make my very indecent proposal.

Somewhere out in the dark depths of the town a clock is chiming midnight, and so I'm settling down with the other pumpkins, smoking a cigarette out by the dustbins. And, two drags in, Thomas appears holding a glass of water.

He eyes up my fag packet with a greedy glimmer. 'Hey Mary,' he says, 'can I have one of those?'

'Sure,' I say, flipping open the pack and proffering it, although I know he doesn't normally smoke. Then again I don't normally smoke – well, only under duress, and I think this might well count as duress.

I don't do fancy. I end up just going for the most blatant tactic possible and inviting Thomas back to my place as soon as the shift is over. I don't know what he thinks I mean by that. He doesn't ask what David would think, even though it's pretty obvious that I'm offering him sex. So I guess Thomas must have me down as such a stupendous pervert that things like monogamy are meaningless in my depraved little world.

But it doesn't really matter what Thomas thinks of my morality. I have my plan to consider. So when Thomas's death-trap of a car judders to a halt outside my flat, I smile in the dark and say, 'Actually, Thomas, I wonder if you could give me a lift to my boyfriend's place.'

'Your boyfriend? You mean David? Oh, sorry. I

thought you wanted...' His words fade away as he revs the engine, burying his confusion, about to pull away. So far, so good.

We have to stop at traffic lights a few moments later and, with the car stationary, I feel confident I am not going to cause an accident when I say, 'No, Thomas, I think you should take me to my boyfriend's place for exactly what you thought we'd be doing in my place.' I hate that sentence as soon as I've uttered it – the words seem to clump up inelegantly in my mouth. I wish I'd planned what to say better. The lights change just before I finish speaking and Thomas pulls away.

I wait in the dark, listening to the appalling sounds coming from the engine of Thomas's car. Thomas doesn't say anything until he has finished manoeuvring and can afford to give me a questioning glance. 'What?' he says, which is fair enough as my last statement was rather befuddled.

'Well,' I reply, 'you said you were curious about trying something with a guy ...'

I stop.

I start.

'And I thought things might be more fun with the three of us. You and David and I. The more the merrier and all that.' Oh god, there really ought to be some manual of kinky etiquette somewhere that tells you never, ever to use the phrase 'the more the merrier' when proposing group sex. I really need to get a copy of that manual. I'll check Amazon, first chance I get.

But right now I have more pressing worries. I've said what I've said now, so all I can do is hold my breath. This is where it can all go so very wrong.

I squeeze my eyes shut and say a quick prayer to

Morrissey – would Morrissey even approve of what I'm doing? – 'Oh please, please, please let me get what I want.'

'Are you serious?' says Thomas, after a few seconds of forever.

'I am deadly fucking serious,' I say, trying to lighten the tone by making an amusing mock-serious face, which is wasted on Thomas as we're already out on the ring road and he has the roundabouts as well as the world's most fucked gear box to distract him.

'Wow, er, you mean I'm going to meet David and you're going to do all the things you do with David but with both of us?'

'Er, yeah. Maybe. Probably.' I'm being vague. Although I do have a plan; I always have a plan. But right now I'm more concerned with whether I can take Thomas's excited query as a consent.

And I don't know, although Thomas makes it sound so weird and furtive, it really isn't like that at all. Honestly.

I give Thomas a couple of directions, showing him where to pull off the ring road and directing him into the sprawling suburban close where David's bungalow squats in the darkness. Thomas's breathing seems more laboured and deep. I wonder if he's excited, if he has an erection. Would that be dangerous? I've never driven a car or had an erection so I don't know how well (or badly) the two combine. But, what with that on top of everything else, I'm starting to feel quite glad we've arrived in one piece.

Poor Thomas, having all this pervery sprung on him. OK, he knew all along that I was not in the sexual mainstream – that was always kind of the point. But, still, I'd pretty much given him the impression, however obliquely, that I was bringing him back to my place for one-on-one kinky sex, and then, next thing he knows, I'm pitching him into something rather more life-changing. If things go the way I want, memories will be made tonight. Dirty memories. The kind of memories that get dragged out and replayed on cold lonely nights.

I guess maybe a brighter man might have figured out where I was heading a little earlier, put two and two together with the fact that he had given me far too much info on his suspicions about his own fluid sexuality. But not Thomas. So he's still reeling right now. I reach over and give his thigh a little squeeze and then kiss him on the cheek as he creaks the handbrake on.

Then Thomas says, 'Are you sure David is going to be OK with this?'

'Yeah. Um, well, I reckon.' I pause for a moment's consideration. Maybe springing this out of the blue isn't the best of ideas. 'I'd better text him.'

'Text!' Thomas almost jumps out of his seat at this suggestion. 'OK.'

For a couple of awkward minutes we sit in the car listening to the soft melodic beeping noise my keypad makes as I send David a warning text. And when the reply comes – one perfect word that makes me shiver with excitement – I throw open the car door purposefully and head in the direction of my perfect fantasy made real.

It isn't just the sheer stupid excitement of boy on boy that is calling to me. It isn't just the way my boys look like perfect echoes of each other, two beautiful freaks. It isn't just the way they are equal and opposite bad boys, one so ready to spill his deviant desires to me, the other one locked up so tight he can barely even whisper what he wants. And it isn't just the bare mathematics of two heads (giving head) being better than one. It's the really twisted mind-fuck part of it that is doing it for me. Surprise, surprise.

It's the way Thomas is, what, twenty-three, so about a year younger than David before his accident, making Thomas a perfect earthly representation of everything David was. Then. Making Thomas and David perfect – living, breathing – before-and-after pictures of David's horrible cursed life-changing accident. The way I can say to David, look, that's what you were, everything you were from the heart-throb face to the fully functioning legs, and, you know what, David, I like the 'after' version of you so much better.

And it's these thoughts, and the future echoes of the conversation I am going to have with David later, where I explain all this stuff to his wide-eyed, sexsated body, that occupy me as I jump out of the car and head for the house.

I'm 99.9 per cent sure Thomas is going to follow me, but there is a little part of my brain that is wondering if he might just rev the engine and roar off over the horizon – not that his car has the acceleration to roar off anywhere. But I'm not absolutely certain until I hear his door clunk shut and footsteps come up behind me.

He's still following me when I pick my way down David's darkened hall, and when I emerge into the living room.

The text I sent to David from the car had said, in slightly cringeworthy txt-speak, 'U love me? Will u suck cock 4 me?' and his reply was just one word, a shiver-inducing 'Anything.'

I suppose he might not have figured that the cock I had in mind would be attached to Thomas rather than to me. He might well have thought I meant a strap-on or something. I think I have mentioned fucking him with a strap-on on more than one occasion, but I'm not that much of a fan of such things these days. Quite apart from anything else, they remind me far too much of Gavin (or whatever his name actually was). And, well, they're OK, but, for me, plastic or silicone can never compete with warm, pulsing flesh and blood.

But, whatever he expected, David manages to look reasonably placid as I walk in, smiling. He's sitting in his chair watching TV, dressed in his usual uniform of a nice pair of jeans and a white T-shirt, smiling at me, with a can of Coke in his hand.

And then, just when the anticipation inside me starts to peak, just when the tension I have created so artfully, so carefully, starts to feel so thin and taut that I think it might snap – it does. It all falls apart.

It starts with Thomas, who has followed me into the room, suddenly saying, 'Holy crap! What the fuck is this?'

I turn around smiling, loving it, still oblivious. I just think Thomas is playing with me. Teasing. (I'm in total denial.)

'Well, Thomas, as you know, I thought you and David might like to get to know each other,' I purr.

Oh, I so should be hearing alarm bells. Thomas's confused outburst isn't what should be happening. But I'm not quite geared up to save the day right now. I'm getting ahead of myself. I'm already picturing Thomas and David touching each other, their hands gentle on each other's faces – and then hard and twisting in each other's hair, as their mouths clash and crash. Rough. Rougher with each other than I would ever be. Vicious, needy, real.

I have never seen them in the same room before, and it feels like the first time I really notice how similar they look. Take a proper inventory. With their dark, luscious curly hair and messy Hollywood-starlet mouths, they could be brothers. And isn't that wrong? And – wronger still – now I'm picturing them like that, imaginary brothers fooling around together, touching each other. Oh, so very wrong. So very right.

I'm thinking about all of this, but above all else I'm thinking about David's hot, red, red-hot mouth closing around Thomas's sweet soft-skinned cock, and Thomas's head tipping back, as his knees start to buckle and his insides melt. And all these thoughts are making it very hard for me to focus on the part of the room which contains Thomas, and his ever-increasing alarm and surprise, which is where my attention really ought to be.

I finally notice that something might be going on when Thomas says, 'No.'

I look at him, still not quite getting it. Still partly marooned on sex-fantasy island.

Thomas swallows. 'I mean, what? I mean, sorry.' He pauses. He stands and swallows again, harder, and then, 'I don't get it.'

I bite my bottom lip, starting to become aware of a strange dropping sensation in my stomach that isn't excitement. Then I say, my voice edged with panic, 'Don't back out now, Thomas. Relax. It's nothing heavy, darling, not if you don't want it to be. It's just a little bit of fun with both of us.'

'But.' Thomas is pointing at David. 'But why is he

... why is he in that wheelchair? What's that all about? It's all fucked up.'

'What?' says David, sounding confused maybe, or tired, or angry. Oh, god knows what David thinks right now, I haven't even begun to consider. 'What's fucked up?' David goes on, almost shouting. 'Why am I sitting in the chair? So I could get myself this from the kitchen.' He waggles his Coke. 'Or, if you prefer, because otherwise I'd be sitting on the floor. Why do you think I'm in a wheelchair?'

And that's when I finally realise. That's when I know I've lost it. My perfect mood is turned to ashes, blowing away in the wind. Neither of my boys sound remotely like figures from a super-sexy fantasy-made-real, they both sound pissed off and impatient. And oh god, they really don't like each other. At all.

In fact, Thomas is only a breath away from baring his teeth as he looks at David and all but snarls, 'I don't fucking know, mate. If you want to make out you're in a wheelchair then fine, that's your thing, but Jesus...' And he seems to give up with David and turns to me, his face softening a little but his eyes still angry, confused, hurt. 'Look, I'm sorry, Mary, this is too much for me.' And he's starting to disappear from view, backing down the dark hall – literally backing out – until he is just an oblique angle and a nose. Oh shit. Shit, shit, shit.

Naturally, I follow him. And he's about to open the front door when I reach out and put my hand on his upper arm. Oh god, his bicep is so firm and delicious under my fingers. A young man's easy physique – he must be ten years younger than me. Without sanction a greedy section of my mind starts picturing him naked. What a body. He hasn't worked for it – not like

David and his endless (over-compensatory) bench pressing – but it's no less beautiful for that. He turns his elegant face to me, mottled and weird with the jagged streetlight coming in bits and pieces through the textured UPVC in the door.

'What's wrong, Thomas?' I say to his earnest expression.

'What's wrong? God! Do you really need me to . . . I don't know. I knew you were a bit kinky and I liked that about you, but this is too rich for me. I'm sorry. I didn't mean to give you the wrong impression.'

'But, Thomas, I don't get it. I thought you would be into this. I thought you wanted to try it. Explore. David hasn't either, hasn't been with another man, I mean. So I thought it could be good for both of you. It would certainly be good for me.' I give him a sexy smile in the half-light, hoping it's not too presumptuous.

'But.' Thomas turns his head a little more towards me and I can see how confused he looks. 'I just don't get what you're doing. I mean, do you want me to be in a wheelchair too?'

'What? No.' Eh? 'Look, Thomas, do you think . . .?' Then I finally realise what he's trying to say. 'Thomas, David isn't pretending to be disabled. He actually is disabled.'

It's dark in the hall. Shadows are falling across Thomas's face, and it's too dark to see if it changes, but his tone of voice certainly does. He seems to suddenly change the way he feels about the whole situation. 'He is? Really?' Thomas says, his voice soft, concerned, almost pitying. 'Then why does he want to, you know, why does he . . .?' Thomas turns away from the door a little, as if a threat has been removed.

His shoulders sag a little. 'Oh, sorry. I thought it was

meant to be me and him. Is it not that, then? Is it going to be me and you while he watches or something? Is that what you have to do?'

'No, it bloody isn't,' David suddenly shouts from the other end of the hall. He looks almost cinematic, silhouetted in the doorway, and his rage seems to hit us with such force we could both be catapulted through the door and into the street. 'She does not fuck other men while I watch,' he shouts, his voice breaking a little with, what? Hurt? Humiliation? Something else beginning with H? 'God, why are you trying to make this into more of a freakshow than it already is?'

And up until that outburst maybe some unrealistically hopeful part of me was still hanging on to the idea that I might be able to turn this round, but one look at Thomas's under-lit face, and I know that I've blown it so far it's practically in orbit. Fuck. And that's the last time I pray to bleeding Morrissey.

David

There are many words for what Thomas is, but none of them sum him up quite as well as 'wanker'. And wanking is exactly what he's going to spend the rest of his evening doing, now I've banished him from my kingdom without so much as a single kiss from my girlfriend. Stupid git.

And yeah, too right I'm angry. You might expect me to be angry with Mary for pulling that little stunt, making me feel spectacularly inadequate. I mean, bringing another guy back? What was she thinking? That that would make me feel super cool about being a cripple? That I would so love her wanting an able-bodied man as well? That I would feel great about the fact that I couldn't satisfy her on my own? And, of course, put like that, it does look pretty awful. Which it should. But the weird thing is, I kind of get it. I get what Mary was trying to do. She can be a bit selfish when it comes to fulfilling her own perverted desires, it's true. But I'm used to that. I even quite like it.

I have to give her credit for something, because, in a weird way, the events of this evening go to show how far I've come. It's amazing to think I am all open-mouth-shocked about someone not wanting to engage in sexual shenanigans with me because I'm in a wheelchair. Before Mary I had basically retired from sexual life for good. And now I really can't believe this. I can't believe I'm so upset that some dumbass pretty boy has strolled out into the night without letting me suck his cock.

Not that I would want to suck the cock of such a ridiculous prancing prick, obviously, but it would have made Mary smile and, well, making Mary happy is one of my priorities. Or at least it was, before she went and brought that stupid arse into my house for ill-thought-out three-way sex.

I'm fine with the fact that Mary didn't warn me about what was coming. I can even get off on that to a certain extent. But I'm pretty pissed off about the fact that she didn't warn *him*.

I mean, how could she not think to tell him I was in a wheelchair? Did she think he wouldn't notice?

Mary

Fuck!

Fuckity, fuckity, fuck!

But, damnit, I am not letting this evening and all its sexually supercharged moodiness go to waste. It doesn't take long for me to put my disappointment aside and regroup. Time for simple pleasures. Soothing familiarity.

Ergo, I decide to tie David up. And once I realise this is what I want, I want to do it straightaway. I want to rush. I'm greedy to binge on sex. Block out the pain of my humiliating failure with the doping power of endorphins. Because that is the trouble of liking being the one in control, the one on the top: if you make a mistake it can spoil everything.

Luckily David doesn't take much persuading once I tell him my plans. He still looks a little spacey, a little adrenalised from his rage against the Thomas, so maybe he welcomes the chance to give it all up. Or maybe he is as frustrated as I am and eager for the soothingly familiar rituals and the soothingly familiar orgasms.

It almost feels weird to ask him though, to have to ask if it's OK for me to have my wicked way. I don't usually ask these days. A smile and a look is often all it takes. But tonight, because of the circumstances, I find myself explaining, asking, 'Can I tie you up?' and enjoying his blush when he says, 'Sure.'

And then I'm off, rummaging for the nicest sheep-skin-lined wrist cuffs – still seeking the simple comforts – and him on the bed already squirming all over the place, moaning and wanting. Everything else forgotten. Such a desperate little whore. And so, so perfect.

He struggles feebly as I fix his wrists, gazing up at my handiwork.

'Is all that really necessary?' he says, with a laugh somewhere in his voice.

I look at what I'm doing. I'm wrapping extra lengths of chain round his wrists and the bedframe. It looks lovely but, I admit, it might be slight overkill. I shrug and pull it all tighter, forcing both his wrists up higher.

He gasps as his body stretches taut, and struggles some more. 'Well, if you like, but you really don't need to tie me down so much – I'm not going to run away, you know.'

'I know,' I whisper and graze the pad of my thumb down the thin, sensitive skin of his forearm. 'But the less you can move, the more I like it.' I swallow hard, because he looks so amazing like this. His beautiful body tormented and displayed. Delicious. Thomas is disappearing fast from my mind. Thomas is nothing in comparison with this. He's just a ghost of a memory of a dream. It's as if he never happened.

'Would you like it if I couldn't move my arms at all?' David whispers, darkly. 'If they were like my legs?'

'Yes,' I say, my voice dropping too, lower and lower down the scale until it could honestly be described as husky, and I rock my hips against his erection, trying to show him exactly how I feel with a precise bit of friction.

He looks at me, his eyes all sparkly and teasing, aglow with the knowledge of where I keep my magic buttons, and I know, I just know, that he is about to press one of them. Hard.

'What about if I couldn't move any part of my body? I've met a couple of guys at the social club; all they can do is blink. What if I were like that?'

I lean forward and lick his temple. 'If all you could do was blink, I'd blindfold you every night and fuck you so hard you'd have to spend your entire Disability Living Allowance on new mattresses.'

He moans a greedy moan, and I lean over to kiss him messily on the lips. He tastes exquisite, like some obscure kind of dirty, musky honey. 'But I wouldn't be able to feel it,' he mutters into my mouth, as I pull away.

'Well, I'd have to describe it to you, wouldn't I?' I scoot back down his bound body as I speak, dropping kisses on to his alabaster chest between words. 'Blow by blow.' And I let my lips close languorously round his cock. If his mouth tasted delicious, this is sublime; I'm drowning in a great cloud of earthy, animal pheromones, brushing against his quiet, cool legs — so beautiful to me — and right up close to his magma-heated core.

Somewhere deep inside me I know what he's doing. Why he's talking about this subject, which is undeniably hot, but slightly offbeat for him. David doesn't normally talk about his disability when he's in bed — that's my job — and he certainly wouldn't talk about his being more disabled to turn me on. Except when he's just had his position threatened by Thomas-two-legs, of course. And, although I hide it, that place deep inside me knows that bringing Thomas home without doing the proper groundwork first was one of the worst moves I've ever made.

David might have been offering himself up to me, claiming he was willing to do anything. But there were limits. There are always limits. And in my lust-crazed state, I didn't bother to check where the lines were drawn.

David

Mary moves above me. She's tied me tighter than usual. Added a little bit more strain. And although that tiny extra tension was nothing when she first applied it, as time has worn on it has started to burn. What was just a slow warm feeling under my arms is becoming an inferno.

And, god, I like it so much. I need this. I can't imagine life without it. What has she made of me?

It isn't long before I can think of nothing else. My dirty conversation dries in my mouth, Mary climbs on top of me and I barely notice how hot and tight and wet she is inside. I only notice how, as she moves up and down, my underarms burn more and more.

And she knows. I don't know how she knows, but she does. She dips her head and runs her tongue across my armpit. Over and over. It's not a soft and soothing balm, but a nasty, rasping little tongue, right where my body is hurting the most. And I moan, louder and louder, with every stroke.

Then, after an eternity of strict restraints and taut skin and rasping tongue, when I come it's amazing. I jerk on the wrist cuffs and they pull tighter and it makes me come harder and pull even more. Everything escalates, and it's like I'm trapped in a loop of ever-increasing feedback ecstasy.

It's really that good.

But it doesn't take the underlying nasty feelings away. The sex and bliss and ohmigod lies on top, but I know that all the bad stuff is still there, deep down, underneath. That feeling that Mary fucked up. And no matter how hard she makes me come, things are never going to be the same again.

Because it's funny – actually it's ironic – that despite all the weirdness and reservations I have had over the time I've been with Mary, the one thing I always trusted her about was sex. Being with her was the best sex I have ever had. And the most frequent. Even the edgier kinky stuff, which, truth be told, I enjoy a lot more than I let on to her. Maybe she brought out a side of me that I'd rather have kept hidden.

But I can't deny that this sex-wallpaper covers all the many, many cracks in my relationship with Mary. Or, at least, it did.

Because it feels like Mary's let me down by misjudging things with Thomas. And just to underline how much she has lost her usual astute touch tonight, she doesn't even seem to have realised what she's done. So maybe that's why I do the thing I do next.

Or maybe I just want to punish her. Want to make her feel bad right now like I feel bad. Or maybe I don't want to be this Mr Cripple anymore, who might be good enough for a pervert like Mary but certainly isn't good enough for a real person.

Or maybe it's just an accident.

Accidents will happen. Fucking tell me about it.

The 'accidents' happen two days later. I do two really bad things, one after the other. One at physio, one at the social club. I don't know why I do them, or if I even mean to do them. Obviously there must be a connection to the whole Thomas fuck-up, but I don't know if I would have done either of the bad things if it hadn't been for the conversation I had with my Callum, my physiotherapist, right beforehand.

Before I got to physio I might have said I was getting over the whole Thomas thing. Mary and I had just spent the whole weekend in bed, and by the time I've reeled from Friday night's horror to Tuesday's physio I'm on the up.

Except that as soon as I'm rolling through the hospital's doors I feel all weird about it again. And that's not a big surprise. I mean, I might not be a genius when it comes to the workings of the human mind, but I can see why being at physio might remind me of that whole mess – Thomas strolling into my living room and calling me a pervert for being in a wheelchair.

So I'm already antsy when Callum sits down and starts what I can only describe as a woefully mistimed heart-to-heart.

'Look,' he says fixing me with an earnest expression. We're sitting at a white plastic table, the sort you'd find in a suburban garden, in a corner of the big gymnasium. Eleanor is there too, for some reason. I don't know why; she hasn't said anything.

'I've been meaning to have a chat with you for a while,' Callum continues, 'about your progress.'

'What about it?' I say, with a small shrug.

'Well, look, David, there's no easy way to broach this, but ...' And it's then that I notice that Callum seems very uneasy, and start to feel a bit uneasy myself.

'Well, don't look at me for help,' I say, trying to lighten the heavy mood, 'you're the one who gets paid for being here.'

Callum smiles, but his tone doesn't get any brighter. 'OK, David, the fact is, I want to ask you, is walking still your ultimate goal?'

Woah! And just like that urban 4x4 two years ago, I never saw that one coming. I don't know how long it is before I manage an answer, but at last I say, 'I don't know.' And I look down into my can of Coke so I don't have to look at Callum. 'You tell me. You're the doctor.' (Although I know he isn't.)

Callum says, 'Well, I don't know any better than you, David. No one knows. A lot of it is down to what you want.' He fixes me with a placid look.

'Well, if it's that simple,' I say, not sparing the sarcasm, 'if it's just down to what I want, then I'll walk home right now. And I'll have a ten-inch cock that comes fifty-pound notes while I'm at it.' I sigh. 'Don't give me that mind-over-matter shit. Please. Like everyone in a chair is there because they haven't got the willpower not to be. It's so insulting.'

Callum looks hurt, and I'm rather glad. 'Look, David,' he says, his face changing. He's got that look, that here's-the-bad-news look. He swallows. 'That's not really what I meant at all. You know I don't want to patronise you, but at your stage you might want to think about whether walking is the right goal for you or whether learning to live with your disability would make you happier longer term.'

I open and close my mouth. I don't know what to say.

Eleanor, who hasn't spoken once through this whole conversation, puts an encouraging hand on my forearm and says, 'Don't give up, David.'

Callum looks at her, a bit surprised and somewhat pissed off. 'Yes, well,' he says, 'no one is saying anything about giving up. It's just about what's right for you.'

Eleanor gives me another squeeze on the arm as my mouth drops open and my eyes start to prickle ominously.

So I guess it is mainly to impress Eleanor that I fix Callum with what I like to think is a steely gaze and say, passionately, 'Walking is my goal. It has always been my goal and it will stay my goal until I walk out of here.'

After that I probably spend far too much of the rest of the session staring at Eleanor, thinking manly, heroic thoughts, because after the session has finished, while I'm buying another Coke from the machine in the hall, she comes up and stands right behind me. So I guess my staring must have been interpreted as a come-on. Well, in that case it was interpreted right.

It's funny, because I've heard other people – other people in chairs – say that after a while the chair itself starts to feel like a part of their body. That they don't like people touching their chairs without permission. But I always thought that was bollocks. Until now, when Eleanor leans forward a little and her polyester-clad breasts brush against the back of my handles. She might as well be rubbing her tits against my cock, the way it makes me feel. And remember, Eleanor is a trainee physiotherapist – she knows all about the whole chair/part-of-the-body thing. It's a come-on – or maybe a reply to my come-on. And it lasts less than a second.

I grab my Coke and Eleanor leans over me and starts to press the buttons on the front of the machine herself. She buys the same drink as me.

With me parked up in front of her she can't reach the slot at the bottom of the machine to take the Coke when it rattles into the tray, so I grab it for her and hand it over. She lets her fingers trail on mine as she takes the icy can.

Oh shit, she really means this.

Now, Mary might have been the only woman to give me the nod in two years, but once upon a time I knew exactly what to do in this kind of situation. And now I almost wish I didn't. I almost wish I was just some tongue-tied fool in the face of Eleanor and her seductive fingers and breasts. And I can't help myself. I rise to the occasion.

I couldn't escape even if I wanted to, not without running over her toes – but I don't want to. Not at all. She's made her move; she's waiting for me to make the next. And I know exactly what the next move is.

'Hey,' I say, tipping my head back so I'm looking at her and sort of up her nose. She has a pretty nose, but straight up the nostrils is not a good look on anyone. Maybe this viewpoint will help to steel my pathetic, faithless resolve (yeah, right). 'Hey,' I say again, 'you could have shared mine.' And I hold up my can.

Eleanor smiles. 'Really?' she says, managing to end the word with a very slight pout. Unflattering angles aside, this really works for me. Really stokes my already smouldering fire.

And I suppose it's no surprise when Eleanor, spurred on by my dirtiest smile, leans down and kisses me. Her lips are cool; she tastes a little like toothpaste. I feel the zingy tingle from her mouth creep right through my body. Every last inch is refreshed. Clean and minty. It feels like Eleanor, in her baggy white uniform and her practical white shoes, has purged a kind of darkness from me.

When I pull my head away from hers I should feel bad, dirty, a cheater, but I don't, I feel clean and sparkly.

We don't say anything else. It's almost like we said

it all in the kiss. A statement of mutual intent. And, with that statement made, Eleanor takes a step backwards and I do an elegant turn and glide off down the corridor to physio, feeling like some kind of sex god.

Not feeling even the tiniest twinge of remorse, I go over to the social club and hang out there. I get yet another Coke from the machine, though I already feel a bit buzzy and over-caffeinated, and end up talking to Andy, as usual. But I'm still in this strange place, mentally, and I talk to him in a way I probably haven't before.

He starts asking me about sex and Mary and how things are going in the whole erection-getting department. And when I tell him that things are great, Andy starts to sing Mary's praises, going on about how sexy she is and how lucky I am.

That isn't what I want to hear right now. After what just happened with Eleanor the last thing I want to consider is how wonderful Mary is and how lucky I am. So, I don't know, I'm buzzy and pissed off and, well, just in a funny sort of a mood, so I say, 'Yeah, but there's a few things you don't know about Mary.'

Andy smiles. He obviously thinks I am referring to Mary's kinky tastes. And I am.

'You know what she really likes,' I say, my voice full of low-register sexy promise, which makes Andy grin a dirty grin, 'she really likes the fact I can't walk.'

Woah! Andy looks as if he has just had 50,000 volts up the arse. It takes him a while to respond. 'You mean Mary is a devo?'

'I don't know. What's a devo?'

'A devotee. Someone who shags cripples because it turns them on.' Then he pauses and looks a bit vexed.

'It turns on the devos, that is, not the cripples, if you see what I mean.'

'Oh, well, in that case, yes, that about sums her up.'

'Shit.' Andy still looks shocked. He's gone white. 'I thought she was so nice. Just a sweet straightforward girl. Fond of the kinky sex, but ... oh mate,' and he reaches out and puts a hand on my shoulder, 'I'm so sorry.'

Now this is weird. Yeah, I'm pissed off with Mary. And yeah, I just kissed Eleanor. But I'm not ready to consign Mary to the pages of my sexual history. And Andy's readiness to commiserate seems to be making me want to spring to her defence. 'Oh, don't be sorry. I'm having a good time. I mean, there are issues, obviously, but I'm having my brains shagged out – like I said, no problem there.'

Andy looks confused. 'When did you find out?'

'Find out? Well, I've always known, really. I didn't mention it before because Mary doesn't like people knowing. She thinks they might react badly.'

'Look, mate.' Andy's voice has taken an oddly urgent tone, as if he's about to tell me something I ought to have known sooner. 'Devos are not good news. It might seem that way, but a good-looking guy like you ought to be concentrating on finding someone who'll love him for who he really is.'

Mary

David's been a little strange these last few days. I know it's because of Friday and Thomas, but I don't know what to do about it.

He got back from his physiotherapy session today in some kind of weird mood, because instead of coming over to pick me up like we'd arranged, he just sent me a text saying he was too tired.

So I'm trying to turn a negative into a positive by spending the evening working on my dissertation. But I haven't increased my word count by more than about five hundred when I find myself on the phone arranging to meet Mercury for a drink.

Despite my current problems, though, we don't talk about David. I've been with David almost two months and this is the first time I don't want to talk about him, even though there is stuff to discuss. I feel pretty much all Davided out.

Over two of Monroe's finest and most intoxicating pink creamy cocktails, Mercury does his very best to take my mind off my troubles and my sulky, skulky boyfriend.

'Oh, darling,' he says, gushing a bit, as he has a tendency to do when he is trying to cheer me up, 'I did think of you over the weekend. In fact it's such a shame that you are no longer a single girl, because I found the perfect someone for a girl like you, or, should I say, someones.'

While Mercury is making this teasing statement, I am trying to remove the crème-caramel moustache that my cocktail has left on my top lip, first with my tongue and then with my bottom lip and then finally wiping it away with the back of my hand. There are enough moustaches in this place without me adding to the quota. 'Tell me more,' I say coquettishly, once I am satisfied my face is cleanish. 'I might be more or less a smug married these days, but surely I can at least hear about the thrills I'm missing out on.'

Mercury smiles a brief but eager smile; clearly he cannot wait to tell all. 'I was introduced to two English

Lit undergraduates the other day. Second years. Both taking the same course. Twins. Identical twins.'

Mercury pauses here, just long enough for me to hear my blood start to pump harder – all over my body, but especially between my legs. I've been developing a real kink for the idea of brothers. Twins would be even better. Identical twins would leave me in a dead faint on the floor.

Of course, I don't doubt for a minute that Mercury knows all this. Even if I haven't told him directly he has an uncanny knack for reading between the lines when it comes to my ever-evolving kinks.

'Mmm, well,' Mercury continues, 'I do know that for something as exciting as identical twins we might forgive them not quite meeting our usual aesthetic standards, but in this case such allowances don't need to be made because they are both delightful. Each as delightful as the other. Like perfect peas in a perfect pod. And the thing is, although they are both working very hard, somehow I think they need a little extra push. Some extra tuition, I thought. Firm discipline.'

Mercury grins his dirty old man grin. And I'm grateful, he knows just what to spin to take my mind off horror and hurt and heartbreak. 'And you wouldn't be treading on my toes if you decided to take the job on. I'm far too old for this sort of thing anyway. But it would definitely take a creature of your talents to tame them. Kinky as hell, those two. It's so obvious. They're both those terrible gothic types. You know the sort, all studded dog collars and clumsy eye makeup. Almost but not quite enough to disguise how pretty they are. And I know a lot of that sort does it for "fashion",' Mercury says, not making the quote sign with his fingers, but you can hear the quotation marks in the way he says the word, 'or the sheer perverse pleasure of looking as unappealing as possible. But believe me, these two, they like the feeling of a little scrap of leather across their throats. Dirty bitches. It isn't just wishful thinking; I've spent the last thirty years observing these things.'

I smile at Mercury. I've all but drained my glass of its delicious concoction of something very sweet and very creamy and very, very alcoholic. 'Mercury,' I say slowly, 'sweetie, I know you're just being nice, charitable even, but I am with David. Even if he is being a bit of a prissy arsehole at the moment. You know, we're going to get over it. We have to get over it, because, well, he's the one. I'm in love with him.'

I really ought to get around to saying that to David himself sometime.

Much later, at home in bed, I can't help thinking about Mercury's deliciously evil words about those deviant twins. I'm a little drunk, and a little too used to all the sex I can handle, and I find myself pacing the floor. Bored and restless. And extremely sexually frustrated.

I end up on the computer, tracking down the boys Mercury told me about. I know their names and the subjects they are taking so it doesn't take long to find a photograph of each of them on the university's website. And Mercury is right. They are hot. They're not wearing the gothic shit he described; maybe they decided to keep it normal for the university's photo shoot. In fact, they look almost too clean-cut here, with their overly square jaws and short-back-and-sides dark hair.

Nice. Maybe not my type, exactly. A bit square-jawed and big-toothed. But, what with the twin thing and the kink thing, I'd probably make allowances. In a parallel life, of course.

But even later, even darker, even drunker, I'm still thinking about them. About tying one of them down on the bed and ordering his brother to suck his cock. Watching those two perfect reflections become one entity.

Instructing the poor tied-down suckee not to come, while the sucker receives the opposite order – to bring his brother to orgasm as quickly as possible – and then sitting back and watching them battle it out, as one brother sucks and teases with all his might, while the other fights his ropes and his urgent, hopeless need.

I run this fantasy over and over, backwards and forwards, while I trail idle fingers over my cunt, masturbating slowly, deliberately.

But after a while of this, a delicious drawn-out while of fantasising, I find that when I finally come, I'm not thinking about either of the brothers. When I come, I'm thinking about David. Thinking about his hard powerful arms tied down on the bed and his bruised-fruit mouth stuffed with a gag. I'm saying his name and twisting in the sheets. And even as I come, right in the blissful peak of the moment, the fact that David isn't lying beside me makes me feel utterly lonely. Hollow and empty inside.

David

It's been a few days since my crappy-boyfriend double whammy of kissing Eleanor and telling Andy that Mary is a devo. And now Mary wants to meet me after physio, at the social club, which is a tricky one because I know Andy will be there and he so isn't Mary's best friend right now.

But I can't seem to persuade her not to come. She was a bit funny about the fact that I stood her up after Tuesday's session. I guess that's why she wants to meet me this time. Make sure I don't do it again.

That might have been only three days ago, but Mary's been a little odd ever since it happened. She used to act super cool most of the time. She was always the more casual one. The one who made me feel like I was over-keen and over-eager. But now, all of a sudden, the balance of power seems to have flipped. She's been the first one to call or text in the morning for three days in a row. Today she suggested meeting me at the social club. And I always used to be the one chasing around after her.

But later, at my physio session, I forget about Mary. I forget about the fact that I haven't managed to put her off coming to the social club and that Andy is bound to say something to her. And that it won't be pretty. Unlike Eleanor, who looks stunning this morning, which is most of the reason why my looming unpleasantness with Mary and Andy isn't preying on my mind half as much as it should be.

I'm sitting in my chair, thinking, as it happens, about what Callum said to me last time and the whole 'is walking my ultimate goal?' thing, when Eleanor comes over and sits down next to me.

'Hey,' she says quietly, 'you want to go somewhere after? I've got a break owed to me.'

I'd love to. Fuck. I've been thinking about her since

we kissed on Tuesday. But this really isn't a good time. Not with the Big Bang about to detonate. I say, 'No. I promised Andy I'd be at the social club.'

I should have said something else. Done the decent thing. Been good. I should have given her a 'no' that really meant no, a sentence with the words 'my girl-friend' in it. But I don't do that, and I've given her a 'no' that means 'maybe'.

And as Eleanor says, 'Next week then?' I feel awful, and I feel great.

Mary

I have this thing about David's social club. It makes me feel a bit uncomfortable. I think someone there might know. Know my secret. Might know about me and David.

Obviously, I hardly shout the reason I find him so attractive from the rooftops, and most of the time I know that the way I feel is so out-there that no one would even dream it, anyway. Not here though. Here I need to be all the more careful not to let anything slip. Because a look or a turn of phrase that would be ignored anywhere else might set alarm bells ringing here. Paranoid, *moi*?

I mean, I don't know for sure, but I'm pretty certain that going out with gorgeous guys like David because of their disability, rather than some tenuous notion of 'who they really are', is frowned upon here. Well, frowned upon everywhere, actually.

But I decided to come here today, because I've been feeling a bit distant from David these past few days. In fact, for exactly a week. Things have been, well, non-honeymoon-period-y ever since that mistake with

Thomas. It's probably only a blip, though. A little bump in the road. Inevitable, right?

Either way, Operation Be-a-Better-Girlfriend is underway. Hindered by the fact that, for some reason, David didn't seem that keen on me coming here today. But who knows why that would be, what with David being so moody lately.

I arrive at the club before David and feel a bit uncomfortable, hanging around on the periphery. Actually, I feel like an interloper – as if without David's presence I don't have a right to be here.

I talk to a girl I know slightly called Roberta. She's OK, but I only know her because she hangs around a lot with this guy called Andy, who David is really tight with.

Andy doesn't seem to be here either, which is a shame because I really like him. Well, everyone likes Andy. He does likeable extremely well. But I take care not to like him too much, because when we first met David got a bit funny about me being so friendly with him. Actually David was jealous. He was jealous because he thought that I would go off with Andy for some kinky fun – as if I found all blokes in wheelchairs interchangeable. It's not like that. I think I defused the situation by telling David that Andy was too old for me or something, which is kind of true, but not the whole truth. That is probably something much more intangible and slippery. But, short version, all disabled guys are not interchangeable for me and I need a lot more than just the wheelchair.

But, having said that, it's not like I never get any jollies at David's social club – far from it. There was this cute blonde here one time whom I could have followed home like a salivating dog, except that, well, why would I?

Meanwhile, my conversation with Roberta isn't exactly sparkling. She seems to have something on her mind. Possibly Andy. Ever since I've started coming here Roberta has been so blatantly, desperately in love with Andy it's unreal. No one seems to have noticed except me. I did tell David about my suspicions once and he just said he didn't think Andy would be interested. Anyway, whatever the reason for Roberta's slightly away-with-the-fairies demeanour, I'm very grateful when David finally cruises through the doors.

I go over to him and give him a kiss. I want a cup of tea, but he's already got a Coke in his hand, so I wander over to the counter on my own. When I get back with my black-no-sugar, he's talking to Andy, who has appeared from somewhere. They seem to be arguing about something.

A few short steps later and I've overheard enough to realise that they are arguing about me.

'I can't believe you've brought her here,' Andy is hissing, loud enough for it to be clearly audible, and I know right away that I am 'her' – who else could he mean? I hang back a few paces to hear more. Neither of them has noticed me, they are too into each other.

'She wanted to come. She kept on about it,' David replies, and ouch, that hurts.

'But after you found out she was –'

'Don't, Andy, we're OK with it. It's cool.'

And that's about all I can take. As I wade in I notice Roberta is next to Andy giving me super-evils. It feel like the whole room is looking at me, but I force myself to keep my nerve. 'Found out I was what?' I spit, my teeth and nails coming out, my hair bristling. Of course

I know what. I know what this is. This is the thing I was most scared of. This is the place where I always knew it would come out. And somehow, right in the moment, while this is happening, I also realise that I always knew it would be Andy who unmasked me.

And it's Andy who is squaring up to me right now. Even in his wheelchair he's a big guy and an imposing sight with his chest puffed out and his hackles set to stun.

'Found out what you were. What you want him for.'

'Which is what exactly?'

Andy looks at me. His expression changes. He starts off kind of angry, but then, scant seconds later, he just looks sad. 'How could you?' he says, quite calmly. 'He's such a lovely guy. Why can't you just leave him alone?'

I wish I could explain things to Andy. I wish I could make him understand what our relationship is like. In fact, what I truly wish is that this showdown had happened a week ago, when things with David were so blissful and ecstatic, because now things are sliding and I almost feel like Andy's words are a death knell. However, even if that is the case, there is no way I am letting him have the satisfaction of knowing that.

'Well, if that's what you think, why don't you ask him if he wants me to leave him alone? Actually, it's him who won't leave me alone.' I spit out the words, wanting to sound as angry as I feel.

'Yeah, right,' says Roberta, who is folding her arms and looking weirdly at me. She probably thinks I fancy Andy – her Andy – because, obviously, I can't wait to jump any man in a wheelchair. And she can fuck right off if she thinks I'm going to defend myself on that one, because I'm so not explaining that to anyone right now. How can I? I can't even explain it to myself.

But tough as I might be talking, there's a nasty lump forming at the back of my throat. I can feel it getting larger, making it harder and harder to talk, until I realise that if I don't stop having this conversation pretty damn quickly I am going to cry. 'Ask him, then.' I say quickly, as my voice starts to sound a bit weird. 'Ask him if wants me to leave him alone.'

And I know that if David doesn't back me up right now, I am out of here without him. No choice.

'OK,' says Andy. 'David?'

'What?' says David, as if he hasn't been a part of the conversation.

'Do you want her to leave you alone?' says Andy, rolling his eyes as he speaks, clearly as infuriated as I am by David's deliberate dumb insolence.

'Um.' David bites his lip. 'Um, shit, Andy, do we have to do this?'

Andy cocks his head in my direction. 'Her idea.'

'Fuck, David,' I say. Roberta snorts. Which makes me realise: I bet she'd love to. Fuck David, that is. Hell, how come I'm getting all the heat when, if anything, Roberta is the one who's got her tongue hanging out for every guy round here who's in a wheelchair?

'Oh god,' says David, so pissed off I can smell it. 'This is fucking stupid. I love Mary, you dumbass. I. Love. Her. Of course I want to be with her. And she always told me what she likes about me, that I'm in a chair, but I don't care. That isn't all she likes about me. She likes me because I'm hot. And I am. And she showed me that. I love her and I love having sex with her.'

And, oh my god, my heart just soars. I never saw that coming.

I must be super buoyed up by this vote of confidence because then, as David says, 'And I love having sex with her,' I butt in with, 'And I'm going to go out to his car with him right now and have sex with him.' And as I turn to go I take David with me, pushing him in his chair, which feels weird and wrong, because I have never pushed him before when he wasn't tied up, but I'm so fired up I have to do this fast.

When we get outside I don't know whether we are going to have sex in his car. It's not something we've ever done before. I'm not a spontaneous sex person. I've got nothing against it – I'm in favour of most sex – but, personally, my heart belongs to pre-planned, equipment-heavy, fully choreographed stuff. However, this might be an important exception.

Then David the mind-reader says, 'We'd better, you know, they might be watching.'

David

I'm not one for over-analysing things, but I have to say, after one of the weirdest conversations of my life: what the hell was all that about?

I mean, really, what did they expect me to say, Andy, Mary et al.? Of course I don't want Mary to leave me, or to leave me alone. Am I so pathetic that I'd let some perverted woman have sex with me even though I wished she wouldn't? I thought Andy knew me better than that.

God, I wish I'd kept my mouth shut about the whole thing, but at least it looks like I'm going to get some sex, which is always nice.

I get in the back of the car, sliding my way across the seat. I take a guess that Mary's never had sex in a car before – she isn't the rough-and-ready type. Well, here, finally, is a domain where I can take the lead, because I have done this once or twice before, so at least I know which door of the car to open.

Mary catches on quick and dismantles my abandoned chair super fast, like she's on *The Krypton Factor*, before slamming it in the boot. Then she climbs in on top of me. Her weight pins me down on the seat. She's straddling me and I can't move an inch. As she bends her head to press her mouth against mine, I feel hot and dirty. That kiss with Eleanor flashes into my mind. I've been such a bad boy. I need to be treated like a bad boy.

But luckily Mary always treats me like that anyway.

Mary

'Bad boy,' I whisper in David's ear after I've done with kissing him. I can feel him squirming underneath me. For a back-seat-of-the-car quickie this is feeling rather good. I like it. I've got David pretty much trapped beneath me, panting and wanting in a way that makes me burn and catch my breath.

And I find myself heading back from his ear to his mouth, like the hopeless addict I am. He tastes of Coca-Cola, like he often does, fizzy and sour-sweet.

Next, his tongue is in my mouth, soft yet firm. I love his tongue. I know he worries about his cock sometimes and complains it isn't the permanent bar of steel it was before his accident (although I've never known it to be a problem), but he more than makes up for it with his tongue's expertise. And he's making me crave his tongue right now, the way he's swooping and dipping around my mouth.

With some difficulty I stop kissing him and shuffle up his body. As I shift and twist against the car roof, he smirks at me from his sexily supine position across the backseat. I know just how to wipe that smile off his face. I replace it with, well, I replace it with me!

It's a very precarious position I end up in. I have to support myself against the window. I'm so uncomfortable that for a moment I can't believe I am ever going to get off like this. But then I feel his tongue on me, lazy and yet urgent, and I realise that all this contortionism is so worth it. I can feel his breath too, dancing round his tongue, desperate gasps, as I all but smother him.

I squirm, carefully, trying to find positions that make me gasp even more. David hasn't got much manoeuvrability, so it's up to me to provide the movement, sliding over him, using him, using his face, like a sex toy.

Objectifying David like this – it's too good. It doesn't take me long to stop thinking about anything outside the world of the car. And then I can't think about anything except the quickest route to my orgasm.

I can hear David undoing the zip of his fly and then the slightest but most gorgeous tell-tale noises as he starts to play with his cock. I wonder what it is about this that is turning him on so much he has to touch himself. The fact that he can't move, that he can't breathe anything except me, that he is having his face fucked as if he is an inanimate object? With David, it could be any or all of these.

These thoughts are driving me on. Driving me on so fast that I'm pushing myself against David again and again, riding his mouth, slamming into him, drowning him. I can hear his hand start to move faster. The more

I get into it the more he does. Lifting us both up. Him – me – him – me. Pushing us both higher and higher, as each of us gets turned on by the other's obvious arousal. Him by the way I am using him, me by the way he is loving being used.

But when I come – and it isn't long – I feel a tiny sad feeling, just the tip of the edge of a feeling, but definitely there. The feeling of regret that my relationship is dying. And although the sex is still good – still great, even – that's not going to be enough to keep it alive. In fact, the great sex just makes the whole bittersweet thing so much more bitter, so much less sweet, because I am losing something that I am truly going to miss.

I look over towards the hospital. Maybe I am looking to see if any of my detractors from the social club have come out to watch us. There's no one I recognise, but there is someone. A tall blonde woman in a plain white uniform is standing by one of the fire exits. She's quite a long way away, but she's definitely looking at us.

David

I don't know where I am with Mary any more. She seems quieter, almost pissed off, but I don't know why. I guess it must be because she knows it was me who told Andy she was a devo. I haven't admitted it, but she's probably worked it out for herself. Actually, we haven't talked about what happened at the social club. We aren't really talking at all now. We're drifting.

After the showdown at the social club we drift through the next four days or so in a weird sort of stupor. We eat and watch TV and fuck, and we find a million other ways not to talk.

Unsurprisingly, when I next leave for physio, Mary doesn't say anything about coming along to the social club.

Which is no excuse for the next terrible thing I do. I'm not trying to make excuses for anything. But, then again, I'm not saying this is all my fault. This all started when Mary brought Thomas home. Let us not forget who took something that was going great and started meddling.

Let's just say there are – and continue to be – faults on both sides with this whole stupid thing. And by the whole stupid thing I don't just mean the stupid, humiliating mess that ensued when she brought Thomas home, but also the weird coolness that has grown between us ever since (continued great sex notwithstanding) and only been fed even more by all the crap at the social club.

But, regarding this next great blow to our relationship, well, yeah, this one is all my fault.

All I can say is that Mary and I are at our lowest point since we met. And I'm at physio. And Eleanor is there. Which, as I said, is no excuse, but think of this as merely a list of the various events that led up to Eleanor and me having sex in the cavernous disabled toilet just behind the gym at physio.

But it's just, I don't know, I think I just want things to be simpler. Cleaner. And Eleanor is in every way simpler than Mary. What she wants from me is simpler. The reason she wants me is simpler. Let's face it, she's just simpler.

* * * *

One of the things that surprised me, when I first became eligible to use disabled toilets, is how much nicer they are than the regular kind. After twenty-four years of using public toilets that were like, well, like public toilets, disabled toilets came as something of a revelation. Most of them are airy, spacious and sparkling clean, and to top it all some of them even have beds.

Well, maybe they aren't beds exactly, more like low-slung hammocky things, but they're as big as a reasonable single bed. I think they're meant for people with much more serious disabilities than mine. People who have to deal with incontinence and are disabled enough to need assistants to help them while they lie down on the hammocky things. At least, I assume that's what they are for. They can't be intended to make disabled toilets into shag palaces, unless someone other than Mary is really keen to see cripples getting some.

Seriously, once you get your mitts on a RADAR key, you have access to a network of pretty nifty impromptu love dens. I mean, this doesn't exactly make up for all the difficulties and inconvenience caused by, say, not being able to get into a nightclub ever again, but it comes in useful if one is embarking on a new career as a faithless slut, as I appear to be.

I'm lying on the bed-type thing. My jeans are on the floor. I'm sprawled, stretched out in my white T-shirt and white underpants and I feel great. I feel hot. I feel really sexy. I've seen Mary looking down at me when I'm in this position and state of undress, with pure lust lighting her eyes. I know this is a good look.

It does seem a little strange that we have got this

far without Eleanor saying a word about my chair, or the fact that I can't walk. Even though it is, if anything, more relevant to her than it ever could be to Mary, what with her profession and everything. But she hasn't mentioned it. That might be because we haven't said much at all. We've got this far with nothing much more than smouldering glances and some frantic snogging.

But she didn't say a word when I transferred from the chair into this bed. And right now it's almost like I'm not disabled at all. Well, except for the fact that I wouldn't have known about this fantastic location otherwise.

Eleanor is unpopping the poppers of her white uniform, occasionally slipping me a cheeky glance. She's lovely. Being cute. Mary is never cute.

'That must be the least sexy nurse's uniform ever,' I say as she shucks it down her body and steps out of the puddle of polyester.

Eleanor giggles, actually giggles, and says, 'I'm not a nurse.'

'Yeah, I know.'

'And anyway, I have got a real nurse's uniform – well, not a real one but, you know, a dirty one. The sort you wear with white fishnet stockings and white stilettos.'

'Really?' I pull myself up with my arms so I am halfway to sitting, and give her a very interested look. 'Well, you'll have to show me that some time.'

Eleanor just smiles and carries on taking off her white bra and then her matching white knickers. She leaves on her white hold-ups and sensible white clog-type shoes. This looks ridiculously sexy. My cock seems to pulse when I look at her. Eleanor is so white, so pale; she makes me think of marble statues of angels, with her fuzz of the lightest blonde hair and her princess-pale skin.

While she was undressing I was doing likewise, squirming – far less prettily – out of my pants and T-shirt and shoving them on to the floor. I notice that all our clothes, other than my indigo jeans, are white. Weird.

Eleanor walks towards me and stops by the jutting boniness of my left hipbone. She gestures towards my body and says, 'May I?' as if she is about to board the QE2 or something.

'Be my guest.'

Eleanor giggles again – it is slightly less endearing this time – and straddles me slowly. 'I've never been on the top before,' she says. But she doesn't make a bad job of it, sliding herself down over me and wiggling her firm body in a way that creates delicious friction. I'm hard enough that she could take me right away if she wanted. But she leans forward and kisses me for a while first, nuzzling my neck and worrying my ear-lobe.

So far, so textbook sexy, but I'm not going to get away so lightly. That little Jiminy Cricket on my shoulder is starting to chirrup. Pointing out the obvious. That this is so very wrong. And after that I can't stop thinking about how wrong this is. And that makes me think about Mary. About how angry she would be if she found out. It makes me feel so bad at first that I almost tell Eleanor to stop. But then something happens. I stop feeling bad. I start feeling turned on.

As gorgeous Eleanor bounces up and down on my cock, I find myself picturing Mary walking in on us.

With a shout of anger she banishes Eleanor and turns her fury on me, lying there helpless in front of her, naked and hard. She barely speaks to me, her face full of rage. She pulls out a familiar pair of handcuffs and fixes my wrist to the top part of the frame of the bed/ hammock and then takes a step away from me and watches me squirm.

'Oh dear, oh dear,' she mutters, pacing around me as I twist in the handcuffs to keep her in view. 'Bad boy.'

'Sorry –' I begin but she whips in quick and puts a finger to my lips.

'Oh no,' she says, 'it's too late for that now.'

'What are you going to do?' I say, suddenly deliciously scared.

'Well,' Mary says, coming back over to the bed, so close that she's almost looming over me, 'if you really can't keep it in your pants, then I'll have to help you to behave.'

Then she flips me over, something I guess she wouldn't be able to do in real life, even if I weren't cuffed. But this isn't real life and so she does. And I'm suddenly more helpless, as a gag and a blindfold appear out of nowhere and are strapped around my face, but not before I catch a glimpse of Mary's crotch and the enormous phallic object protruding from it.

Then she's on top of me, pressing against my back, hissing in my ear, 'I guess Thomas wasn't up to the job of fucking you, but I am.'

Something hard and smooth nudges against me, opening me up. Fucking me. Too hard. Too fast. Too soon. I scream out because it hurts. It might be a good kind of hurt but I can hardly tell, the sensation is so intense, so big, so overwhelming, so real. But this isn't real. Eleanor is real. Eleanor, up above me, right now.

And it is at this moment that I find myself ragged with desire and tuning back in to Eleanor's bounces and rolls. I find myself coming, hot and confusing, and just wrong. Not just the cheating-on-my-girlfriend wrong of earlier, but a weird, fucked-up kind of wrong. Wrong.

When Eleanor has straightened up and dressed and has helped me back into my chair, she asks me what's up. I don't tell her. She asks me why I'm so quiet. Again, I don't tell her. She probably thinks I'm feeling guilty about cheating on my girlfriend, which obviously I should be. But I'm not. I'm feeling more guilty about the way I just cheated on Eleanor. Thinking of Mary. Thinking of the weirdest kinked-out shit with Mary. While having beautiful, sweet, vanilla sex with a pretty girl like Eleanor.

What's wrong with me? What has Mary done to me?

I should probably get all this worked out before I sleep with Eleanor again. If I even *should* sleep with Eleanor again.

Or anyone for that matter.

After a quick query that establishes Mary isn't coming to the social club, Eleanor asks to come with me herself. I agree, avoiding telling her why Mary isn't coming along today.

The trouble is, I had decided I wasn't going to go along myself. But now Eleanor is coming, I'm committed.

As I roll in, Andy practically collars me with 'So, no Mary?'

'No,' I say, instantly pissed off, 'she didn't really fancy it. Surprise, surprise.'

'Well, good,' says Andy, easily as snarly and snarky as I am, 'because I don't think she's going to be welcome here any more.' And then he looks up and says, 'Hi, Eleanor.' Almost as if he's only just noticed her standing there.

Eleanor furrows her pretty brow. 'Mary?' she says, 'Mary's your girlfriend, right?'

I nod my head, guiltily.

'So why . . .' Eleanor looks from me to Andy and back again, 'why isn't Mary welcome here?'

Andy laughs and it sounds nasty. Bitter. 'Because,' he says, with deliberate slowness, 'she's a devo. She's only into David because he's in a chair.'

Eleanor gasps and says, 'God, David . . .' But then she stops and looks plainly horrified.

'Don't,' I say, but she does anyway.

'God, I mean, don't you mind? She's just into you because of . . .? Oh, god!'

'Er, no,' I mutter, answering a question that I don't think Eleanor actually asked. 'Um, I don't know.'

'God, well, what'll happen when you're walking again then?'

I look from Eleanor to Andy. 'When I . . .'

But the words fail to come, because I feel like my brain has just exploded with things that just never occurred to me before. I really never thought . . .

I swallow. I have to say something. 'It wouldn't make any difference.' I say it so quickly that the words run together, because I know it isn't true. Or at least I think it isn't true.

'Really?' says Andy, 'I wouldn't be so sure, not the way she was talking the other day.'

'Well, it's not like that,' I blurt. 'Yeah, she's into the fact I can't walk, but she's also into me. And if, I mean, when I walk, she'll still want to be with me, because she loves me and I love her. And no one . . .' I'm looking at Andy, talking to Andy, but suddenly I remember that Eleanor is standing beside me.

I look up at her and her mouth is open. She says something quietly. I can't quite hear but it sounds like 'You love her?'

But I never said I didn't.

My brain is scrabbling for something to say to counteract what I've just done, but it's too late and too fucked-up and all I can do is watch as Eleanor shakes her head at me, turns and runs from the room.

'Oops,' say Andy, 'looks like you're fucking up all over the place.'

'Oh, fuck off!' I say to him.

I'm about to leave myself, maybe go home and spend the evening quietly screaming in a darkened room, when Andy says, 'Ask Mary, ask her what she'll do when you can walk again. Just ask her. For me.'

What a wanker!

Mary

Despite everything, despite the fact that I've known for a week or so that my relationship is dying a slow death, I never had any plans for facing up to it. Why should I? Every relationship I've ever been in has just sort of fizzled out – until now.

I arrive at David's that evening, let myself in and head for his bedroom-cum-office. He's at his computer, but he stops typing when I come in and gets right to it, opening the conversation with 'We need to talk.' But I still don't twig that anything in particular is wrong. Or about to go wrong. Spectacularly wrong.

'Sure,' I say, and plonk myself down on the bed and wait for the talk to begin. And then end. So we can move on. To sex.

'OK,' says David, clearly expecting a slightly different reaction. 'Um. Look. There's something I need to tell you. Ask you about. Something that came up at physio today. And, well, I was wondering how you'd feel about it.'

I go cold. Maybe I have a premonition or something. 'What?'

'Why do you think I go to physiotherapy?'

'What?'

'Why do you think –?'

'No, no,' I interrupt him, 'no, I heard you the first time. I just ... What do you mean, why do you go? Gee, I don't know, are there some sexy nurses there?'

David goes rather pale when I say this. He looks annoyed. More annoyed. I could kick myself. This clearly isn't the time for jokes.

'I go because I'm going to walk. I'm going to walk again, Mary. You do realise that, don't you?'

I shake my head. I'm sort of smiling. I don't know why. I shouldn't be. 'No,' I say, very quietly. 'No you aren't. It's been too long, David. Two years. You really aren't.' And when I say that I don't know what I'm saying. I don't know what I'm thinking.

There's a moment's pause. David stares at me, hard, like he's trying to see into my soul or something. And then he says, 'Oh my god. I didn't believe them. But this really is a deal-breaker for you, isn't it?'

Oh. My. God. I get it now. I realise what he's getting at. And my heart sinks. Not this. Not now. 'What? No! No. I mean yes, no, yes. I don't know.' I cover all bases in too-quick succession; it's enough to make Vicky Pollard look decisive. 'I don't know if it's like that. Not exactly . . .' I lose my thread as I listen to myself, wondering if my babble will hold the answer to how I feel.

So this is where this conversation happens. I had been wondering when it would turn up and whether it would mean the end of everything.

I just don't know. After my musings on Thomas I know for sure that I prefer this David – the disabled David of the now, rather than the able David of the past – but as for potential future Davids, I don't know if it's as simple and clear-cut as it might appear. I just don't know if David's disability is the all-important factor. The only important factor. I don't know for sure if it's a deal-breaker or not. All I can say is, 'Get better then, if you are going to, and then I'll have to see.'

Because that's the truth.

He opens and closes his mouth, unable to speak. He is so hurt. When he does finally start to talk he's so quiet. There's hardly any voice there. And he's got it all wrong. 'I knew you liked me being helpless. I knew you liked having power over me. And, yes, I knew you liked the chair. But I don't think I really realised that it was all about the chair. Only about the chair. But it is, isn't it? You have just had a highly fulfilling one-month-long relationship with my wheelchair.'

I don't even want to process that right now. So I find another way to discuss this. 'Did your physio say you were getting better?'

'He said I might. I mean, nothing is guaranteed, but I've been improving. And, actually I've been improving more since . . .'

But he doesn't finish the sentence. Maybe at some other time we could have worked this one through, worked it out, but not now. Our relationship is too damaged to bear this conversation. Too broken.

I stand up, pick up my coat, which I'd dropped on the floor, and start to put it on. 'I'm sorry,' I say, fastening the buttons so fast I fumble over most of them and end up taking twice as long. 'I think I should go.'

'Yes,' he says.

'I'd better go,' I say, again.

'Yes,' he says, 'I think you'd better.'

And I leave.

At home I find Carrie sitting on the sofa watching the first episode of a new reality TV show. It's only just started and there's currently an overexcited woman on screen shouting her way through the introduction of a series of social misfits and the kind of extroverts that I thought existed only in my nightmares. I sit down on the sofa and say nothing. I wait until the first ad break before I burst into stupid, embarrassing tears.

David

I'm pretty sure that the mess that calls itself my relationship with Mary Taylor was an episode in which I was more innocent victim than wrongdoer.

The cold hard fact is, it wasn't me that was kinky for some poor disabled boy, shagged him into confused submission and then walked out when I heard he might regain the use of his legs, was it? I've checked and it definitely wasn't me that did that.

So why am I sitting here, less than a week after the irretrievable breakdown, staring into the yawning abyss of a Sunday and being punished by having to spend the day having lunch with my mum, my odious wide-boy brother and his delightfully annoying girl-friend Trixie?

Incidentally, I'm pretty sure that Trixie isn't Trixie's real name, but she wants to be a pop star so she probably thinks Trixie is a better bet than Sharon or Belinda or whatever her parents decided to call her. Which might make her sound quite interesting, but Trixie is not the type who you hang around with thinking, god, I'll be able to say I knew her before she was famous. Far from it. Trixie's being-a-pop-star cam-paign seems to consist mainly of lounging round liv-ing off Simon's earnings and occasionally auditioning for some frighteningly awful telly talent show. Unfor-tunately for Trixie she never makes the screen as she isn't good enough to get through to the next level, nor is she awful or weird enough to get in on the car-crash-viewing ticket. I would feel a bit sorry for her if she weren't so stupid and loud and annoying.

But the most annoying thing about Trixie, the sca-rily annoying factor, is the there-but-for-the-grace-of-god thing. See, when Simon and Trixie first got together a few years ago, before my accident, I thought that skinny blonde showbizzy Trixie was hot stuff. My type. It gives me shivers now to think about that.

So I'm sitting there, listening to Trixie explaining, at length, how twenty-seven might seem over the hill but really it isn't too late for her to hit the Big Time, just so long as she gets the right song at the right time, and has a killer hook/killer video combination like Kylie's *Can't Get You out of My Head*. Yeah. Right. Trixie has a merely passable singing voice and, whatever she might think, she is too old. I've got more chance of being the next Kylie than she has. It's never going to happen.

While I am busy not listening to her latest the-world-revolves-around-me tale of stardom lost, I keep glancing over at my brother's hair, which is so full of gel it manages to be both slickly wet and dry and crispy. The harsh chemical rasp of the gel is so sharp in the central-heating-cranked-up-to-the-max-even-though-it-is-nearly-fucking-April air that I can practically taste it in the gravy.

God, this is awful! Were my family always so awful? I haven't spent much time with them while I've been with Mary. Were they so unbearable before? I find it hard to remember. I find it hard to remember much about my life before I met Mary.

Just when it feels like I'm in the seventh circle of hell, knocking shoulders with Judas, mum says, 'So how's Mary? You should have brought her along so she could meet Simon and Trixie.'

Imagine my horror as I feel a lump in my throat and my eyes start to prickle, and not because of Simon's over-gelled hair. I'm having to fight not to start sobbing at the table.

Both Simon and Trixie turn to me with full-on expectant what-the-cripple-has-a-girlfriend? beams on their faces. My heart sinks through the soles of my shoes and into the tastelessly patterned carpet.

'Um.'

Oh god. Just do it. Lance the boil. 'Mary and I broke up.'

'Oh, sweetheart!' My mum sounds completely distraught. 'What happened?'

I'd love to tell my mum the truth here. I think the me that I was before I met Mary would have absolutely revelled in destroying my mum's misguided vision of what a perfect woman Mary was. But I've changed. A bit. These days I decide against breaking my mum's heart any more than I have to. What I actually say is, 'Don't know really, just didn't work out.'

'Hey, well, don't worry, little brother. Her loss, eh?' says Simon, probably spouting the same meaningless clichés as he does when he's selling over-priced pads down in London town. Wanker.

Luckily, my sad news gives me an excuse to leave lunch early and skive off back home. OK, I miss out on my mum's pear crumble, but I also miss out the collective sympathies of my mum, a wannabe and a wanker, so fair deals.

I think about calling Eleanor when I get home. But I don't want to have to face the fall-out from the last time I saw her. So I don't. I don't call. Besides, what's the best thing that could happen if I called Eleanor? I could end up having sex with her – and I don't want to have sex with her any more. I'm pretty sure I'd end up thinking about Mary. And I'm trying not to think about Mary, as far as possible.

God, Eleanor! I don't think I could even get it up for her now, even though I have the most fantastic it's-not-you-it's-me excuse, in that I'm a poor disabled boy and since my accident my cock just isn't what it was.

But I don't want to go down that road with Eleanor. She'd probably put me on an intensive exercise and therapy programme for my cock. And I can't help thinking that that wouldn't be as much fun as it might sound to someone like, say, Larry.

Mary

Carrie, all is forgiven. I feel like such a bitch for all the bad things I've ever thought about her in the past, because actually she is really nice. Maybe she is one of those people who come out of themselves in a crisis. And this is a crisis, after all, with the emphasis on 'cry'.

After my blubfest on the sofa on Friday night, she has been nothing short of an angel, an angel bearing comfort food. She's taken care of me for days, while I've sobbed and snotted all over the upholstery, calling in sick to work and existing on nothing but sleep, junk food and that reality show which was on the night I got home, and which Carrie and I are already hopelessly hooked on, only two days in.

And now it's Sunday and, while I'm semi-comatose in front of the *Hollyoaks* omnibus, Carrie's been out and got me tissues and ice cream and huge slabs of Dairy Milk. What's even better is she hasn't probed me for details. Which is a really good thing, as I can't think of a way of telling this story that makes me sound anywhere near reasonable.

But there is one person I can talk to, who, if not exactly understanding, at least can be relied on to know what it means to be the bad guy in a relationship. Mercury is coming over for lunch.

* * *

'So,' I say, taking a steadying glug of the tea St Carrie has made me, and I launching into a prepared poor-me routine. 'Here's what happened, version one, I am *très* kinky for the boys who can't walk. When I found one in the local library I took him home and had my wicked, wicked way. Then, after initially writing him off as a one-night-stand, I decided he was worth some more of my time, so I sought him out and shagged him senseless for a month or so, until I got bored and needed yet more disgusting kink, so I tried to get him to fuck a sort of able-bodied version of himself, but that all went wrong, and then all his disabled pals found out what I was up to, so I practically made him choose between them or me, and he chose me, and then, when I find out that he might regain his ability to walk, I totally freak out, and tell him that if he walks again I won't be attracted to him any more. Not good, huh?'

'Tut tut, indeed,' says Mercury sarcastically, regarding his mug of tea with suspicion.

'Yeah, I know, pretty damning. In my defence, though, I'd like to say that it's not what it looks like. Really. I did do all those things, but, well, it wasn't really like that. And I know it might seem like we finally split because I couldn't handle the fact he might walk again. Which would make that bloody bastard Andy right – that I am evil and just after David for his disability. But the thing is, *he* was only interested in *me* because of his disability. He would never have gone for someone like me. Someone older. Someone without the required long flippy hair and long flippy legs.'

I pause for breath and Mercury takes the chance to

point out that I do, actually, have legs. But I ignore him and plough on with the case for the defence. 'I knew he was settling for me. He's so good-looking, I mean fucking incredible. I've seen a lot of people not notice because they can't see past the chair, but you should see old photos of him before, or how girls react when he's driving or something and they can't tell. Shit. And talking of photos, I've also seen photos of some of the girls he dated before his accident and they all look like bloody supermodels, for god's sake . . .'

I dry up at this point, as Mercury gives me a heavy-browed steady-on look. 'OK, well, glamour models then, maybe not Kates or Naomis, but easily Abis. I know for certain that he wouldn't have bothered with me if it wasn't for the fact that he's currently keeping his self-esteem in an old paper bag. As soon as he's walking again – if that really is what's going to happen – he won't be interested in me, he'll be back being a player. It's not me that wouldn't be interested if he were walking again – it's him!'

Mercury looses the laugh he's been trying to suppress since I said 'Abis'. 'For god's sake, darling,' he splutters, barely intelligibly, 'breathe.'

I take a deep and much-needed breath.

'Look, sweetie,' Mercury continues, once he is satisfied I'm not going to asphyxiate, 'first of all I think you'd be so much better off if you admitted that, despite your eloquent soliloquy on the subject, you *are* pissed off with him because he might walk again. That awkward fact has shattered some of your precious little dreams and ruined some of your smugness about finding your Mr Perfect. And that's not a crime, you know. That's what you like about him – the fact that he can't walk. Besides, would it be better if you were with him but wishing and hoping for a miracle cure that would make him more normal?'

'But his walking or not walking, it's not everything.'

Mercury shrugs. 'No one ever said it was.'

Then, just before Mercury starts giving me an ethically induced migraine, Carrie announces that lunch is ready. I notice that Mercury still hasn't touched his tea and shudder inside at the thought of what he will make of her heavy-on-the-tofu, light-on-the-actually-tasting-of-anything cooking.

David

There's never anything on television on a Sunday night except stupid reality shows. That's my excuse. That's why I'm doing this. That's why I'm sitting in my chair. Naked.

It's almost a kind of revenge, because she would so love to see this.

I'm all ready. Before I stripped off I spent ten minutes or so using the internet the way it was intended. Just me, my mouse and the directory in my bookmarks folder euphemistically marked 'other'.

Right now, probably because I've been looking at porn and thinking about Mary, my cock is burning. It's so hard and tight and aching that it is pressed flat against my belly. Unignorable. Making its presence felt.

I'm too eager to wait. Greedy. I touch it. Reaching down and just grazing the back of my hand along its sensitised length. Slowly. Lightly. And, oh, I want to tease this out. Make it good. Make it as good as she would. I try to control myself the way Mary would control me. Toying with myself like she would.

But I can't.

I can't wait. My hand is gripping my cock. Tight. Tighter. I'm there. Right there. Falling. Losing it.

My tight fist moves faster.

'Mary,' I say out loud. Her face fills my mind. Just her smile is more, a million times more erotic and potent than the finest hardcore that the internet is willing to provide (at least, without a subscription). And she's nodding her head, she's permitting me.

And then I come. Hard and soft and perfect.

Now, just take that sad little scene and replay it about fifty million times and that's my life. That's how I spent the first month after Mary left me.

Part Three: **April**

Mary

I'm lying on my bed watching this reality show that I seem to have become addicted to. It seems to be about which one of a group of talentless weirdos can become the most irrelevant minor celebrity.

Right now they're being herded into a film pre-mière, because these days everyone makes their movie selections based one how many Z-listers are interested in a free ticket.

But don't let that description of the show make you think I'm being scathing about it – I'm just being honest, and I honestly love this show, right now. But I'm not really watching it. I'm just pretending. And I'm pretending because watching trashy TV is rather humiliating for the person who's kneeling naked at the end of my bed. And that humiliation is nice for both of us.

I'm wearing these beautiful new shoes I won on eBay. David introduced me to eBay – I was a late bloomer with all things beginning with 'e' – but now I'm addicted, especially when it comes to finding delicious shoes. These ones are bottle-green with a neat T-bar strap and a big fat heel. Real Alice in Wonderland shoes. They're also slick and shiny patent, and something about patent leather says lickable to me. Which is what Thomas is doing right now, licking my too pretty emerald slippers. It's all too delicious. Almost as delicious as the way I'm nestled in the super-soft bedclothes wearing these perfect shoes and nothing else.

As I watch gorgeous Thomas's gorgeous tongue sliding over the elegant curves of my rounded toes, I do wonder just why this is so sexy. Him licking my shoes. It's so weird, and cliché, and yet also bizarre. But it's wonderful. That tumble of dark, messy curls, that divine sullen mouth, that red tongue and the sparkling dewy-leaf look of the leather . . .

Mmm.

But as his tongue slides over and over, and his closed-eyed expression wavers between ecstasy and something even more zoned-out, I have to tell myself that, as with so many things in my twisted life, I don't have to understand it to love it. And, oh god, do I love it.

My voice sounds so low and husky-dusky when I say, 'Don't forget the soles, baby.'

Thomas was such an easy option for me. It was such a lazy move to replace David with his obvious heir. It took me a shamefully short time to do it too. Less than a week after David and I split.

That Sunday, after I had had lunch with Carrie and Mercury, I managed to stagger into La Lucas and I had Thomas in my bed – well, tied to it – that night. Inevitable, really.

Oh, it's not pretty, and I'm not proud, but the facts were these: David and I had split, Thomas looks a lot like David, Thomas was clearly interested, available, easy and kinky. It was too easy. I am too weak. And this is the result: a rebound so fast my teeth are still rattling. It's just for fun, of course. Thomas. It's just a sex thing. And an I-don't-want-to-be-on-my-own thing. On my own I might do too much thinking and end up realising what I've lost. Can't have that.

Much better this way. Less depressing. More sex.

It took Mercury to point out the other thing. By suddenly climbing into bed with Thomas I might well be trying to show David that a fully-functioning, up-and-walking version of him was just fine by me. Maybe there's something in that. Maybe. Or there would be, if David had any idea I was sleeping with Thomas. If David and I were even talking.

David doesn't return my calls. Or my texts. Or my emails. I haven't tried going to his house. What would be the point? I get the message. Or rather, I get the complete lack of messages.

'You know what I'd like to do now?' Thomas says, when I finally tell him my shoes are clean enough.

'No, I don't, but I'd really like to know.' And I really would too, because over the last few weeks I've discovered that Thomas is full of wonderful surprises.

'Well, you know I told you I thought I might be bisexual, ages ago, outside the restaurant one time.'

'Yeah.' I sit up a little, suddenly even more interested.

'Well, I don't think I am.'

'Oh, Thomas.' I deflate like a balloon. 'I thought you were going to tell me something nice.' I make a comical pout. 'You got me all interested and everything.'

'Sorry.' Thomas dips his head. I don't know if anyone else in the world can manage to do a coy look that lights up the room, other than Thomas. Well, maybe just him and Princess Di.

I'm not really cross with Thomas, I'm mostly feigning. Sure, Thomas's revelation that he isn't bi after all is a little disappointing, but now I don't have a beautiful warped reflection to pair him with, Thomas's tastes in that direction are meaningless.

'Well, actually,' Thomas goes on, still giving me that princessy smoulder, 'I don't think that fact should spoil any of your dirty plans – if you still have them – because I think I might still get off on being told to do it with a guy for you. Um...' He stops talking and squirms a bit against me. Funny boy. He just can't hide a thing. I can't believe I ever thought of him as some kind of unattainable sex god.

'Well, that's good,' I say with a laugh, and then, when Thomas doesn't say anything more, I prompt him. 'I think you were going to tell me what you'd like to do.'

'Oh yes, well, you know what I think it might be? What I want, you know. What made me think I might be bisexual,' he says, still so ridiculously bright and upbeat. I can't help comparing him to David, who would do anything to avoid having to admit liking anything even remotely deviant. Even though David's hidden kinks, I'm willing to bet, would make poor Thomas look like Julie Andrews.

But I shouldn't compare Thomas to David (or to Julie Andrews). And I certainly shouldn't keep thinking about how much Thomas looks like David and how if I half close my eyes . . .

I've done a few things with Thomas that I maybe shouldn't have. I've tied him to a dining chair and taunted him. I've tied his legs together and made him drag himself across the floor, naked. I've climbed on top of him and called him David.

After what happened the night I took him home and he freaked at the sight of David in his chair, I did wonder if this would be OK with him, but I've got away with it so far. I've said before that Thomas isn't the sharpest of knives, so maybe he never made the connection.

But the Thomas freakage-factor is probably why I've decided to draw the line at getting him to sit in an actual wheelchair.

Or maybe the real reason I've done that is just more basic. More obvious. Maybe I couldn't take the sight of Thomas sitting in a wheelchair. After all, the whole point of this diversion with Thomas is that I don't want it to make me think about David. Well, no more than is inevitable. I might have to face the fact that I am going to think about David, at least a little bit, every time I have sex for the rest of my life.

I've moved on now, anyhow. Well, I've realised that there is more to Thomas than using him to fill the David-shaped hole in my life. There's a lot Thomas isn't – like clever – but for now I'm quite happy to waste time concentrating on what Thomas is – like pretty.

Oh, and full of ideas and enthusiasm. 'I think I'd really like to dress up. You know, in clothes. Do you have any clothes?'

I chuckle and the expression on his face tells me he has no idea why I am amused. 'Of course I have clothes. What sort of clothes do you mean?'

Thomas's voice is bright as ever. 'Kind of slutty clothes.'

'Women's clothes?'

'Yeah, slutty women's clothes.'

Weird thing is, I might not be able to help him here. Despite being an active pursuer of the naughty, the kinky and the bad, I don't really wear the uniform. I've never done the leather catsuit thing – it's always seemed a bit, well, a bit trying too hard. And show me head-to-toe PVC on a non-anorexic woman and I'll show you a decent impression of a giant slug propped on its end. I prefer the idiosyncratic and the interesting to the I'm-so-sexy-it's-actually-painful look. I'm not saying I couldn't do that streetwalker look if I wanted to. I just don't want to.

I don't mind looking like a student. Or even like someone who used to work in PR. But I don't want to look like a whore, even in private – especially in private. I like to look quirky. Even behind closed doors. I hate the clichés. A very good example of the slightly off-beat look I like to work is my old faithful – David's fave – my cherry-print dress, or my navy-blue T-shirt with the Strawberry transfer, or indeed my glistening peacock-glacé shoes. I seem to have a pretty good and kinked-out sex life wearing nothing more exotic than my fancy footwear and nothing else.

OK, it could be said that I have a bit of a shoe thing. I do occasionally feel the urge to be something of a bitch goddess, but it's strictly from the ankles down – or, once in a blue moon, the knees down.

So I probably don't have the kink-o-meter-turned-up-to-eleven wardrobe that young Thomas and his fevered imaginings might be hoping for, but I try and make the best of things. Because the truth is that I am a verrry kinky woman who owns five almost identical pairs of double-dyed jeans and not a single black PVC miniskirt. More than one man in my life has been seriously disappointed by that fact before now. I hope Thomas isn't going to add his name to that list.

'I don't know if I exactly have "slutty women's clothes",' I say, 'but I might have something that will make you look suitably nasty. Have a look.' And I point at the large and largely crappy came-with-the-flat wardrobe. Some student places these days are decked out from cellar to loft in brand-new IKEA stuff, but Carrie's place, including the room she sublets to me, is rather more traditional – everything looks like it only made its way here after someone else had thrown it away. Kind of a step down from shabby-chic. Skip-chic, maybe.

But the old wardrobe is pretty vast, which means Thomas (once I have freed him from his handcuffs) all but disappears inside, in his hunt for sartorial treasures.

When he emerges he's done very, very well. His take on cross-dressing is decidedly more preening-peacock than Frank-n-Furter. Male, yet decorated. Pretty, pretty. Pretty boy.

Around his hips he's tied a silky fringed scarf which shimmers with iridescent colours – royal blue, gold, mauve and lots of vivid sea-green. The glossy fabric emphasises his slim hips and neat little bum. He's knotted it very high and tight on one side, so it's like a brutally skimpy miniskirt. It also looks incredible.

He's teamed it with a satin camisole, also bluey-green and trimmed with cream-coloured lace. It's a sweet little thing that I'd almost forgotten I had. (And I never realised it matched that scarf so well.) There's something very thrilling about the way a whisper of his chest hair is protruding over the top of the camisole's neckline. A precious and fucked-up contrast, reminding me exactly what I'm looking at.

And then there are the accessories. He's found my jewellery box and draped himself in more glittering paste and coloured plastic than I ever remember buying, including some Art Deco-ish snap-on diamante earrings, clunky jet beads in strings and strings around his neck, and a funny gold fabric flower clipped into his ever more wild-looking hair.

He stands up straight as he shows himself to me, like a finishing-school student balancing a book on her head, and meets my eye, proud of his concoction. Very proud – I can see his cock jutting, rude and incongruous, from underneath the taut fabric of the scarf. He raises one eyebrow and says, 'Well?'

'One thing you're missing.' I reach down, unbuckle the green shoes and skim them across the room to him. I'm pretty sure they'll fit – I have biggish feet and they're roomy on me.

He looks very pleased as he reaches down and takes them. I stare at him, hardly breathing, as he slips the shoes on and slowly adjusts each ankle strap, his legs dead straight and his bum jutting in a Hollywood-starlet pose. Wow.

When he straightens up he looks at me again, and his posture's changed. The heels of the shoes have made him cock his hips, stick out his bum, pose for me. One stray dark curl is tumbling into his perfectly co-ordinated green eyes. 'So,' he says, slowly, 'how do I look?'

'Inspiring.'

No time at all later, Thomas, still in his finery, is tied down on my bed. He's struggling a little, but I know my restraints well, they give a little, but nowhere near enough for him to get free. But they are safe and secure enough to allow him some wiggle room. And I like it when they wiggle.

He's face-down. Face-up or face-down is always such a hard decision, but I went for face-down, on his stomach. Maybe I did that because I almost always used to choose face-up with David; I could never resist doing nasty things to David's nipples, either with my fingers or my teeth or with tiny metal clamps. It appealed to my sense of utter fucked-up-ness to inflict cruel sensations on one of the few sexual parts of David's body that were unscathed, as sensitive as ever they were. And it appealed to that warped part of my brain even more to watch how he moved his sculpted torso away from the biting silver teeth as I brought them nearer – straining against the restraints imposed on his body by both me and heartless nature, yet so clearly wanting the pain they promised, down to the last strands of his DNA. That was so David. Pretending not to ache for the pain when his whole body was screaming for it, gooseflesh dancing over his inner arms, blood flushing his cheeks, neck, chest, breath so shallow, so needy as he tried to hide his shameful desires in flat, empty, emotionless words like 'no' and 'Mary' and 'please'. Especially 'please'. The 'please, don't' that we both knew was 'please, do', 'please, more', 'please, oh, god, please'.

I've said it before, I'll say it again, Thomas isn't like David. Thomas is greedy and wanton (and currently gift-wrapped). And Thomas is on his front, arched over a couple of pillows, so his luminescent arse is twinkling at me, his glorious summit.

'You've been a very bad boy. A dirty boy,' I say, gentle

and soft as I reach out and run my hand over that single laws-of-mathematics-defying curve.

'Uh, are you going to spank me?' he says, sexily, but also sounding rather pleased about the prospect, which is a bit strange. Very un-David-like. David would rather put his balls in a vice than admit that he might, just slightly, like something as humiliating as being spanked. But that, exactly that, is one of the things that made David so perfect for me.

Not that Thomas won't do. Thomas is far too pretty to be considered a booby prize.

'Do you want me to spank you?'

There is still something sexy about his slutty needing-it shtick sometimes. Like now, when he says, 'Please, spank me. Please. I need you to. I'm such a bad boy. I deserve it.' And then drops his voice to the lowest of the low when he says, 'Hurt me.'

So pretty. I mean, as tired and worn out a cliché as they come, but, yeah, so pretty. I move closer and slip a soft leather blindfold over his eyes. Even prettier now.

And then I give it just a few beats. Just enough for my silence to unnerve him and make him say, 'You are going to spank me, aren't you?'

I press my lips against his ear. 'Yes. I. Am.'

He pulls his breath in. Hard. I let him flutter for a moment and then go on. 'I am going to spank you for dressing up like such a filthy little slut.'

And there's the first stroke. Quick, no build-up, right on his eager, elegant arse. He yelps, as well he might, and that little sound makes my clit turn itself on, just like that. Flick. Like a light switch. Ooh, nice noises. It's going to be far too wonderful if he's going to make those pathetic noises every time.

'I am also going to spank you for getting a hard cock when you are dressed up like a slut.'

I hit him again. A shade harder. He cries out and tugs at the leather straps around his wrists. He tries to turn his head and look at me, but although his head turns just fine, the blindfold stops him seeing what might be coming next. 'Mary?' he says, and just leaves that hanging for a moment. Then, 'Mary? Please.'

I bend down and whisper again. 'That was just a little warm-up. A tester. Now I'm going to give you your proper punishment. Ten, I think. And I want you to be a good boy for me and keep quiet.'

I see every muscle in his arse go tense.

Making him try to keep quiet is using a little bit of perverse psychology on myself. I love the noises he makes, but I will love them even more if he's trying not to make them.

For the first one, the first slap, ringing and hard enough to hurt my hand, he is stoic and silent. And he keeps this up as I spank his quivering, reddening arse three more times.

Then, for the fifth stroke, I hit him a little harder and he can't hold back an 'Ahh!' followed by a 'sorry'. That makes me squirm on the spot because it's so delicious to hear it all released like that. Plus the apology, oh god, the apology is pure sugar-rush icing.

I climb on to the bed and straddle his upper thighs, inching my hands under the artfully draped peacocky fabric.

'Oh dear me, was that sore? Your poor skin does feel a little heated.' And it does. Oh, wow. It's blazing nastily. My palm is feeling the sting too – time for a little change of tack. 'But I'm afraid I did tell you to keep quiet, so I'm going to have to be strict now, which means no more of this little luxury.' I wrench the slippery fabric away from his sore skin, leaving him bare, gasping with excitement/humiliation/trepidation, and drop my head almost instantly to run my tongue along the perfect dark seam of his arse, revealed like a precious reward. Mmm. He tastes like burnt sugar and the bottom of the sea, and the sudden pheromone hit is almost enough to make me come right there.

'And,' I say, as I come up for air to hear him still groaning with pleasure from that one fleeting piece of tongue action, 'I'm afraid your bad-boy behaviour means I won't be using my hand any more either.'

The paddle is ready on the bedside table, because I knew very well I wouldn't be able to do all I wanted with my hand. Not if I didn't want my palm to hurt every bit as much as poor Thomas's arse.

Luckily the paddle I own is perfect for the job in hand (so to speak). It's a nice simple little thing.

Now, I'm no toy fetishist. Even when I was working and had the money I didn't go in for spending heaps of cash on sexy bits and pieces made from rainforest-endangering exotic woods, or various bits of dead animal – listen to me saving the planet, dear old Carrie would be proud.

Anyway, I got this little paddle from a second-hand stall at a monthly kink market in Bristol. It's just made of wood, smoothed by a history of careful wear and decorated with two heart-shaped holes. It's simple and classic and I like the fact that it had a life before me. It has a history I don't even know about. And its secret history is about to get a new chapter.

I reposition myself slightly to give me room to swing my weapon of choice, and then I slap his naked arse with the paddle. He yells, helpless to keep quiet under this new – firmer, harsher – assault, and bucks against the straps. Oh god, such a pretty move, it really is hurting him. I swallow hard, rub my legs together a little, hoping that Thomas remembers a conversation we had a million years ago about safe words, and hit him again.

He yells again on the second stroke. Screams on the third. I am such a hard-edged sadist sometimes – all the time. I bathe in his pain, it's delicious. It makes my clit buck and pulse between my legs. But I do keep control. I am a good little dominatrix and I behave myself. But it's hard. The Wicked Witch of the West in me wants to let rip as his screams get louder, wants to forget about limits and quotas and numbers and safe words, and just see how hard I can hit him, how loud I can make him scream.

But, as I'm in good-girl mode, Thomas's punishment doesn't last long. Well, not as long as I would like, but plenty long enough for a naive little novice like him. It's with a heart full of regret that I deliver the fifth and final stroke with the paddle.

Each blow, with its ringing, smacking sound and answering yelp of helpless pain, has brought me closer and closer to the edge. But I want more. I want something more – something else – before I give myself over to the blinding force of orgasm. I want more of delicious, dirty, needing-it Thomas.

I dip my head and place the tip of my tongue at the very top of the groove that runs down his arse. And then I make a couple of gentle nudges, venturing a little further down each time.

Thomas moans. He lifts his hot, sore arse higher, trying to get my tongue to venture down lower, deeper inside him. That dark pheromoney taste is still there, getting stronger. Sweet and salt.

My heart starts to beat faster. Oh! I love this so much! I love making them scream from both sides. Pleasure and pain.

And the further I push my way inside Thomas the more I think of that first time with David. That time when I did precisely this, not knowing what would happen. Not knowing, even, if he could get hard. And not knowing what I would think if he couldn't. Not knowing if that would turn me on. Just doing it. Still pressing inside him because it felt right, and because I could sense him responding to me like a musical instrument. I could feel him almost becoming a part of me. Like an extension of me. And then reaching around him – just like I'm doing with Thomas right now – and finding him hard and wet and desperate, thrusting against the bedclothes.

Thomas is hard too. It's not quite the same as it was with David. I don't feel the same shattering symbiosis, but it is very, very good.

And then before I know it, sudden and sharp, Thomas is coming, pulling me out of my David-inspired reverie and into the moment. The moment where Thomas is screaming, tied down on the bed and still wearing a blindfold, his arse red and smarting, and then drenched in cascading pleasure. It's a beautiful thing, and I ride the wave with him until he crashes down the other side into a messy, blurry heap of restrained, straining limbs and far, far too much hair.

And all I need now is a perfect orgasm for me, like a full stop, to finish this whole glorious mess off. And I have the perfect thing in mind.

Before Thomas has fully recovered from his own

rembling peak, I untie and undress him. He's still not coherent enough for orders, so to get him where I want him I use the universal language of gestures and brute force, tangling a hand in his big hair and yanking him off the bed on to the floor. I manage to get him into a kneeling position before snapping his wrists back into the cuffs and smiling down at him.

I bend at the waist to give him a slow and reassuring kiss. Then I pull away from him, step back and strap the delicious shiny green shoes back on to my own feet.

I love the way the heels on these shoes make me feel. I stand in front of Thomas, leaning back against the bedroom wall, the dark glossy curls of my pubic hair only centimetres from his face.

Thomas is a bit more with it by now. He looks at me and gives an I-get-it grin and leans forward, reaching for me with his tongue. I love it when they make that mistake.

Before his tongue reaches its destination, I push him away, tangling my hands again in his gloriously messy bird's-nest hair. And I push down. Because some things never get old. I push his head right down as far as I can, until it almost touches the floor, and then I raise my left foot and place it gently between his shoulder blades. Holding him in place, kneeling, prostrate, with my beautiful glistening right shoe just in front of him. And, novice though he might be, he can hardly say he doesn't know what to do.

Thomas reaches out with his tongue again, but this time his destination is my glossy green toe. His tongue shines the leather once again, over and over, until it glistens and sparkles.

When I feel perfectly pretty, I take my left foot off

his back and hook my toe under his chin. I lift hi
head a little and encourage that clever tongue to star
lapping at my right ankle.

He seems to know what I want immediately and h
gets it so right. He makes delicate kittenish flick
around the place on my ankle where the round bon
protrudes and slides frictionlessly across the front o
my shin, ticklish and delicate, half making me want t
pull away and half making me want to scream fo
more.

But I fight both urges down and keep still and quie
until he begins to move onwards, upwards. Up my lef
leg he glides, not quite going straight but snakin
from side to side. I look down at his face as he work
His concentration. His glistening tongue. His lips, pil
lowy and pretty-pink. His eyes are half closed, rever
ent. He's so into it – so into me.

He passes my knee and takes a detour, sliding acros
a little so he's on the inside, skating up my inner thigh
where the skin is thin and delicate. His progres
almost burns.

I'm panting now. Wanting to feel his hot mouth o
my cunt so much. So greedy and eager that it suddenl
overwhelms me, and I interrupt his graceful progres
to grab him by the hair – that hair, so made for thi
kind of cruelty – and force his face hard against me
And then I literally grind myself into him. We're s
close and intimate like this that I can feel everything
– his caught breath, his surprise and confusion, and
his arousal.

Right now, over and above everything else, my clit
is like a sparkling, over-sensitised point of light and
heat. When his tongue grazes it it's too much. I yelp
and manage to say, 'No, lower down. In me.' And

push at his head a little. His tongue responds to my commands and winds its way further down, deeper and down. He finds a new angle and slides just the tip inside.

I cry out. Twisting and desperate because he is so right there. That is it. That. Is. It.

The wall behind me suddenly seems to be very smooth and very cool. My legs feel wobbly, like columns of water, incapable of supporting my weight. My head tilts back. I'm just not in control of my body anymore.

His tongue finds that spot inside me again and just grazes it. I yell and push his head harder between my legs. I buck against him. Riding him. Forcing him deeper, closer, harder. And when I come, I lose it so much that it's only his body pressing against me that keeps me upright.

After that, I finally do let him go. It's the least I can do. I release him from the handcuffs and collapse on the bed, still buzzing, and watch him dress in his street clothes, like a scene from a dream.

He asks to take the scarf and the camisole with him, and I agree, but draw the line at the shoes. He seems happy with the compromise. And then I'm kissing him goodbye and murmuring at him to let himself out. He still smells of sex. I like the fact he isn't the type to rush to the shower, but walks out proudly into the world with the tell-tale scent of me still staining his face and twined into his hair.

And there he goes. Kinky and gorgeous and mysteriously devoted. Practically perfect and, god, I barely dare think it, but ever so slightly boring compared with . . .

David

At least, with Mary out of the way, I might have saved my business from complete bankruptcy. Truth be told, my compensation money has been the only thing keeping my pathetic freelance endeavours solvent for ages. And that money is running out now. But I can't blame the distraction of my relationship with Mary for this financial time bomb, because it dates back to my old hermit-like days before I met her.

But I've pulled my socks up now. Workwise. Which means I'm trying not to notice that it's exactly one month since Mary and I split up, and to concentrate on what I'm meant to be doing today. Namely, rejigging some web content for one of the university sites, a job Larry wangled me as a freelancer. Yep, time to shape up and face up. Because Mary was just a short-lived episode of madness (mostly on her part) and this – work, family, sexual frustration – is my real life.

So here I am, in my bedroom-cum-office, logging on. But before I sink my teeth into that dynamic database that's giving Larry headaches, I decide to quickly launch my Instant Messenger. And guess who's online. A blast from my cybersexual past. Yep. Slutbox04.

And the really awful thing is that I haven't even thought about her for months – for all the time I've been preoccupied with Mary. (Except for one morning when an eye-wateringly large buttplug arrived in the post. Which – thank all the gods – I managed to hide from Mary just in the nick of time.)

Anyway Miss Slutbox04 (or Mr Slutbox04, I haven't yet ruled that out) is sitting right there online. And I'm here, recently jilted, with nothing more stimulating planned than a big pile of boring work. I have to ping her. Won't she be pleased to have me back in her life?

DragonSlayer666: <Hey>

I check my email while I wait for her to ping me back. But by the time I've deleted twenty unsolicited offers of Viagra she still hasn't. I check again in case she is logged on but not at her computer, but her status is active. I try again with something a bit more chatty.

DragonSlayer666: <Hey. How come you're online? Isn't it the middle of the night there?>

Again, nothing.

DragonSlayer666: <I'm sorry. Are you really pissed off with me?>
Slutbox04: <Fuck you>
DragonSlayer666: <I guess you are then>
Slutbox04: <Too right I am. What's with you?>

Oh, shit.

DragonSlayer666: <Look, I know I haven't been around. I'm sorry. Things came up at home>
Slutbox04: <Right. Well I'm sure the things that came up were real important>

Isn't this going well? I really do have the Midas touch these days — if Midas had turned everything he touched to broken-hearted shitty shit, that is.

Mary has made her feelings clear — she only wants

me for my wheels. Physio is awkward, to say the least
now Eleanor justifiably feels used and more or less
refuses to speak to me. And now this joy. Finding I
can't even chat up a female impersonator on the
interweb any more.

DragonSlayer666: <Look, I really am sorry>
Slutbox04: <Do you remember our last conversation? I
    mean do you even remember it? We had a scene
    going. You had told me not to come. Do you
    remember?>

And I wish I could say that I honestly didn't remember
that, at least have that to salve my conscience, but I
do, of course I remember. It was kind of memorable.
But I didn't think she would actually do it. I didn't
think she was serious. I thought we were just messing
about. Just indulging in a bit of sexy talk to get each
other off. I didn't think either of us would be giving it
a second thought away from the computer screen.

DragonSlayer666: <Yes. I do remember>
Slutbox04: <I didn't know whether it was even part of it.
    You know, when you disappeared from the net. But
    then after it had been more than a week I realised
    you were some kind of user. A pathetic Horny Net
    Geek, getting your rocks off pretending to be a master.
    Ordering some girl about and then running away as
    soon as you'd splattered your keyboard>
DragonSlayer666: <Oh come on. You know that isn't
    true. If I were just a Horny Net Geek I wouldn't be
    here now, would I?>
Slutbox04: <So what are you doing here?>

And when she says that, I think maybe she is still interested. I think for a moment that I might be able to win her round, to turn a bit of sexy grrr and have her drooling and panting hard enough to be in danger of shorting out her laptop. But I don't do it. I don't even try.

And I don't try because cyberkicks with nameless, faceless Slutbox04 just don't appeal any more. Five minutes ago I thought this was what I wanted, but now I realise it isn't. So I'm going to tell her the truth. In fact, I'm going to tell her the very thing that made Mary hot for my rollerboy action. And not to get her off. My world view hasn't done so much of a three-sixty that I now think all I need to do is flash my tyre treads at a girl to have her fainting all over me. But maybe I've decided that hiding who I am isn't where I'm at any more.

So here goes.

DragonSlayer666: <Look, I'll tell you the truth, I met someone. Offline. And I know I should have at least pinged you and told you about that instead of leaving you hanging, but this was a kind of intense thing and intense things don't happen to me that often>

Slutbox04: <Really? You surprise me. Because I thought guys who spent all their time on the net surfing for cyber sex chat were the ones who got lucky all the time (<– joke)>

DragonSlayer666: <Yeah, OK, I'll give you that one. But the fact is. Well, you know that photo I emailed you? The one of me on my motorbike?>

Slutbox04: <Oh don't even bother. I know that that isn't really you>

DragonSlayer666: <Well. No. That's where you're wrong, actually. It is me. But it's me before I had the accident>

Slutbox04: <Accident? You had an accident on the bike?>

DragonSlayer666: <Actually no, not on the bike, but still a traffic accident>

Slutbox04: <What kind of accident?>

DragonSlayer666: <A bad one. Just over two years ago. I can't walk now. I'm in a wheelchair. That's why I spend so much time chatting up girls like you online. Or at least, why I used to>

Slutbox04: <Shit. Sorry. I can't believe you never told me>

DragonSlayer666: <Yeah, well. Sorry. But that's why this relationship was kind of special. This girl I met, Mary, she was the first. Well. The first in real life since it happened>

Slutbox04: <I see. God, that is so freaky. I never knew. I mean I assumed you were just normal>

DragonSlayer666: <Right>

I don't bother coming over all PC police with her and telling her that I am 'normal'. Apart from anything else I don't even know if that's true.

Slutbox04: <So where is she now? This hot girl? How come you're online? Shouldn't you be with her?>

Oh. Yeah. Kind of forgot I'd have to explain that bit.

DragonSlayer666: <Well, we kind of split up>

Slutbox04: <I see. Hence you pinging me. You reckoned we could just pick up where we left off?>

DragonSlayer666: <No. Really. I just wanted to say hi>

Slutbox04: <Hi>

DragonSlayer666: <Oh don't be like that. We used to have such good times>

There's a long pause before Slutbox04 replies. But eventually this enormous message pings up, swamping my message window.

Slutbox04: <Okay (1) You're still a fucking bastard and you can just fuck off and die, no matter how unfortunate you might be, but (2) As we did used to have a good time, before I say goodbye forever, I'll tell you this for nothing. That girl you were telling me about, you need to get her back. If she's as good as you reckon. And she really better be good if she was good enough for you to just drop me mid-scene for. You really should go get her. Trust me on that. Now don't ping me again, or I will just block you. Bye bye. Have a nice life. And fuck you>

And before I've even finished reading that, she's gone, offline and out of my life.

And she's so right about me needing to get Mary back. Worryingly perceptive, in fact. So I guess that solves one mystery: Slutbox04 must really be female if she can be that incisive about human nature – just a girl with rather unconventional tastes when it comes to usernames.

Mary

A while later and I'm alone in my room, working a bit, brooding a bit, replaying my scene with Thomas in my head for a little thrill, recasting it with David in the starring role for a far more guilty but far more thrilling thrill. Essentially I'm just wasting time until I need to get to work, when I hear the doorbell ring. Before I move off the bed, I hear the hall window judder and rattle open (we don't have an entryphone, so the window leaning system saves us a lot of unnecessary exercise).

That rattle means someone else has answered the door, which means I don't have to move from my cosy nest of duvet and laptop. But that someone else has to be Carrie, which means Carrie's at home. I wonder how long she's been around. I've hardly been out of my room since Thomas left and I never heard her come in in all that time. I was sure she was out when Thomas showed up, and I assumed we were alone in the flat. Meaning she must have come back while I was distracted. Gulp. Oops. Were we very loud? I try not to think about it.

I can't hear the conversation Carrie's having with the person who rang the doorbell, but it seems to go on for a while. In the end my curiosity overcomes my desire to hide my head under the duvet, so I get up off the bed and peer into the hall.

'Look, she's busy. It's not a good time,' Carrie is yelling, leaning so far out of the window that from my end she is nothing but a generously padded, purple-velvet-upholstered arse.

Something is shouted from the street in reply.

And then Carrie shouts, 'Look, David,' and it's like someone has flicked my instant override switch, because I don't even think, I can't. I push Carrie to one side so I can lean far too far out of the window next to her. And he's right there.

It feels like someone has put my heart into the washing machine.

David is sitting on the pavement under the window. He looks very small and distant in the gathering dark. He looks good. Lean and hard across his shoulders. Better than I remember. His face has a little shadow dusting of stubble. It looks perfect on him in murky streetlight, defining the precise and perfect angles of his face. Oh god, I just fucking want him so fucking much.

As I appear at the window he cries, 'Mary!' with a kind of angry pain in his voice.

'David!' I shout back. It's almost a reflex. I've wanted him to get in touch with me so much. Now he's here I just don't know what to say, or rather what to shout down into the street.

From across the road a very well-dressed middle-aged woman who has been parking her car shouts, 'For god's sake, let him in, it's freezing cold out here.'

David swivels his body in his chair and shouts, 'Fuck off.' The woman looks unbelievably shocked at this swearing, crippled man.

'He can look after himself,' I shout at her, and she scuttles off, clearly appalled.

'Mary, look, can I come in or something. Can we talk?'

'I have to be at work in half an hour,' I say, and realise straightaway how stupid that is.

'Well, phone in sick then.' David smirks a tiny little smirk. Almost missable, especially with him so far away, but I spot it, because I am looking for it, because I'm smirking too. We used to joke about that. David used to hate me going to work. He never seemed to do

any work himself, so he was always trying to persuade
me to 'phone in sick' because, as he would explain, I
really was pretty sick.

But, as I always used to explain, it's a shitty, piece
meal, no-sick-pay sort of a job, and I don't get paid if I
don't go to work. I already missed three shifts at the
beginning of the month while I cried in bed over
David. I just can't afford not to go in tonight. I won't
be able to pay the rent. 'I can't,' I shout, my voice
losing its hard, hurt edge.

'Well, let me give you a lift then.'

'OK.'

Oh, yes! Yes!

I fling myself down the three flights of stairs to
street level and find David is already sitting in the
driving seat of his red Fiesta, twisting round to fold up
his chair. The car is parked right outside, I notice. Right
in front of my house on the double yellows, which I
suppose is a rather silly dividend for having a disabled
boyfriend. (Not that I have a disabled boyfriend at this
moment in time.) And somehow Mercury floats into
my head at that moment, pointing out that, fetish or
no fetish, it would be far, far worse to go out with
someone in a wheelchair just for the parking
privileges.

I grab David's folded chair and shove it in the boot,
then get into the passenger seat. As I heave the door
closed, David says, 'I had to get some stupid bloke to
ring your doorbell for me.'

I know he's trying to tell me what a sacrifice he's
made by coming here. And I show my appreciation by
taking the first turn at apologising.

'I'm sorry,' I say, 'I don't really know what the fuck

happened. Um, I'm really sorry. About the learning-to-walk-again thing. I'm sorry if I didn't react right to that. I never meant to make you think I'd leave you if you walked.'

'Yeah, I know. I think. I'm not even sure if that was the problem,' David says, pulling away from the kerb and pointing his bonnet in the direction of La Lucas. 'I guess the thing is they don't know if I'll walk anyway. But it is, well, it is possible.'

'Yes, of course. I mean they don't know for sure if you're going to get better or not, do they? And even if you do, well, it could be OK.'

David is quiet for a minute, concentrating on a junction. Then, once we are on the straight and narrow again, he says, 'Could it?'

'Yes. Maybe.'

We stop at some lights and he looks over at me. His face is still and expressionless in the dark, but his voice is suddenly so bitter and nasty. I feel like I've walked right into a trap. 'Well, forgive me if I don't see how, because it's not me, is it? Not for you. It's just the chair.' I feel a sudden dread that David hasn't forgiven me at all. Hasn't come close. I think he might even have lured me into his car just to have another go at me.

'No. It's not that simple.' The lights change and we pull off. My lips feel so dry suddenly that they seem to be cracking like thin ice. I run my tongue over them. The chair is part of you. I want every part of you.' And that, I know, is true.

'Yes, especially the parts that don't work.' His voice is so bitter, so sad, that I can't believe now that I ever thought this was going to be some kind of reconciliation. Now I'm sure he just wants to tell me how sick I am, fifty million times over, perhaps with an extended dance mix thrown in. Perhaps he's right. And perhaps I owe him this.

'Admit it,' he goes on, 'that was what attracted you wasn't it? If I could walk you wouldn't be interested.'

'At first, yes. I'm not going to pretend that wasn't the first thing I saw. But it's more than that. You're you. It's not like I could happily swap you for any other disabled guy, but I'm not denying that your disability is one part of who you are and a very attractive part for me. But I mean, really, so what?'

'So what! So what if you're not interested in me for me, just because of some sick fetish.'

'Why is it sick? We have a good time, don't we? I have a fetish for wheelchairs, you're in a wheelchair. What's the problem?'

We're at the restaurant now. David pulls up outside. 'I want you to want me for me. That's the fucking problem.' His face is red now, he's caught somewhere between anger and tears. 'No wheelchairs. No kinky shit at all.' I'd make a guess now that this isn't the conversation he was hoping for either, but Mercury is still too fresh in my mind, petting me for my sins and pointing out that I really didn't do anything wrong except make a poor unfortunate young man very happy and horny.

'I do want you for you,' I say, pulling myself up to my full self-righteousness. 'And that includes all the things about you that make you different from other people, including the fact you can't walk. So can't you want me for all the things that are different about me, including the fact that your not being able to walk turns me on?'

And that argument is my best shot. That is what

I've been wanting to tell him for a month. If that doesn't work, I've got nothing else.

He looks at his lap for a long time. I hold my breath. 'I don't know,' he says quietly. 'Maybe.'

Suddenly something bangs on my window very loudly. I look up and Thomas is there, peering at me earnestly. I wind the window down.

'Are you OK?' he says.

'Yeah, yeah, I'm fine.'

Thomas looks suspiciously at David, then back at me, 'Good, OK, it's just you looked a little bit upset.'

'Um, well, no everything is fine.'

And maybe it is.

Thomas nods at me and turns away, walking back into the restaurant. I don't know what he thinks. I don't care what he thinks. And what he thinks becomes even less relevant to anything when David says, 'I need to tell you something.'

David

I didn't have to tell her. I could have taken it to my grave. Except I couldn't, could I? Not really. I couldn't forgive Mary without giving her the chance to forgive me. I couldn't let her believe that she was the only sick, selfish fucker in our relationship. And now I know for sure that I really have changed.

Anyway, I hope she gets some comfort from that fact, because nothing else about the story of me shagging Eleanor in a public toilet is going to brighten her day.

'Have I ever met her?' Mary says when I finish the stupid sorry story.

'No. And I think it's best if you don't. In fact I could and probably should move my physio sessions. Dammit, I could stop going to physio. It's going bloody nowhere anyway.' I've never even thought that before, let alone said it out loud. I suddenly remember Callum, and the conversation that made me start to question everything. I remember him saying something about learning to live with my disability.

Mary is frowning at me, as well she might. 'I thought you were getting better, close to a cure or whatnot? Didn't we have, like, a huge row and split up over that?'

I shrug. I come close to a bitter laugh. 'Who knows?' I say. 'Apparently it's all up to me.'

There's a pause and then Mary says, 'I don't really know what to say, about Eleanor, that is.'

'Are you angry?'

'Well, yes, obviously, but I think I understand too. God, this is going to sound so lame-arsed. I know I ought to be slapping you round the face, but, god, I don't know. It's just that you used to be so certain no one would ever want you. It didn't matter what I said or did, you were so convinced that I had something wrong with me and no one else would ever . . . So, in a way, I'm glad.'

I swallow, hard. Is this a dream? Is she going to forgive me?

Then her expression changes and she adds, 'And you did think of me, right? While you were with her?'

'Oh god, yeah. I so did think of you. I didn't want to think of you, but I did. I couldn't help it.'

Mary's face comes alive in a way that makes my heart soar and sink at the same time. 'Course,' she says smartly, 'I will have to punish you for it.'

'Course.'

I meet her eyes – with some difficulty – and say, 'How can I make it up to you? Tell me.'

I know she could say that there were (and still are) faults on both sides, that I don't need to do anything. But, oh, I'm so glad she's not that kind of girl.

'You know what I want,' she says, her voice dropping right down to the bad place.

'Oh yeah,' I reply. Oh good. Oh god.

And then she thinks for a moment and says, 'Actually, the price has gone up since then.'

'Oh.'

Mary

One week of madcap planning later, David is tied down on the bed. Face-down. All four limbs stretched out and roped down. And, because I can never resist overdoing it, I've buckled a thin black collar around his neck, which is doing nothing in particular bondage-wise but looks so very pretty.

Just looking at him I'm getting more and more turned on. I feel like I can hear my engine revving higher and higher. The bondage, the body, and the thing that's going to happen next. Oh, god. I slip my hand into my knickers and my fingers seem to dissolve into sheer liquid heat. My clit is so fizzy and on the edge it feels like it's got pins and needles. Buzzing, sparkling, shards of ice. Too close. Got to calm down.

There's a gag lying on the bedside table. Too big and too red – just like the mouth it might be going in. I'm not sure yet if I am going to use it. David and gags – I don't know how that will work. But maybe the threat of a gag will be fun, will get me somewhere interesting.

God, he looks good, fucking great, in fact. A mess of hair and a tiny apricot arse. 'I could come just from looking at you,' I whisper, my voice carrying in the expectant stillness.

David makes a noise. A sort of sexy moan. Luscious and desperate and loaded. He seems like he isn't into talking right now. He's probably psyching himself up for what's coming. And that's a shame, because there are a few things I want him to say to me. Or, maybe, to confess to me. Stoic mood or not, they just can't wait. And those thoughts make me melt again.

Like an addict I trace my finger once or twice over my clit. I'm such a hopeless case. I walk over to the bed and climb on top of David, leaning down so my dressing-gown-clad body is pressing against his naked back and my lips are at his ear.

'David,' I say in a voice that is lower than low, 'David, I want you to tell me how much you like this.'

'Uh,' David says, a kind of aroused defiance.

'You do, though, don't you? So let me explain. Either you can tell me how much you love being treated like this, how much you are wanting it, needing it and loving it, or you can wear this,' and I grab the gag from the beside table, holding it up so he can see.

Moving his head round as much as he can, David looks at the gag, then at me, then back at the gag. And he nods his head.

Bastard! He'd rather take the gag! He'd rather take the gag than talk about it.

Angry, I shove the big red ball hard into his mouth and pull the straps painfully tight.

Then I climb off the bed and leave the room.

I go into the kitchen, where Thomas is sitting at the table drinking a nervous cup of coffee. Looking at him makes me feel better. My anger melts like snow in springtime and I feel gently warm inside. I think I've done it right this time. Instead of springing Thomas straight into some sexual Neverland I took things slow. Well, and we had a history, by this point. Thomas knew me far better. Trusted me, even.

I had to sit him down and explain about David and me, letting him down gently of course, because our recreational sexy fun was going to have to end. But I think he was OK about that. He never took our diversion seriously anyway. Never thought of me as marriage material – well, serious girlfriend material – or anything. I was always far too old and too weird for that.

Which means Thomas is pretty laidback about being thrown aside now David has returned. It's like he always knew it was going to happen sooner or later.

As for this last little favour he's doing me, well, how lucky am I? By rights this shouldn't have worked. There was no reason to assume Thomas wouldn't be freaked out this time, slower pace or not.

He was a little shy at first, then confused and then just a little embarrassed by what had happened before. But it wasn't long before he was looking me dead in the eye and saying, 'Whatever. Whatever you want. If you tell me to do it, I'll do it. That does it for me.' And then he was as flippant and upbeat as ever.

So here we are. David is tied down. Thomas is ready and waiting in the kitchen, drinking coffee, naked. I'm teetering on the brink. Of everything.

'Are you OK?' I say, sounding and feeling gentle, nurturing. I reach out and brush my thumb across Thomas's cheek.

'Fine,' he replies, breathless and deferential. He looks down to the floor, just a fleeting glance, but I clock it and I know he was checking out my shoes. Thomas's shoe thing is getting so obvious. I'm wearing the green ones. Not really for him. Mostly because they feel perfect for this sort of thing. They give me a little height, the right posture. And besides, they match my robe. The dressing gown I'm wearing is also a jewel-bright green, made of a glossy material that seems to say something to me about decadence.

I have a collar for Thomas too. It matches the one David is wearing, naturally. Without speaking, I lean over to Thomas and slide it around his throat, pulling tight but not too tight. I hear his breath catch. Just a tiny gasp and then a precious moment of stillness. Oh, he likes it.

But for Thomas it doesn't stop at the collar. I attach a lead – a similar strip of thin black leather, with a little chain and a snap hook where it connects. It's pretty much the classic set-up, really. Me in heels (albeit clunky, chunky ones) and floaty belted robe, and Thomas naked, collared, led round on a lead. In fact, I'd almost be getting worried that this was too by-the-book, too cliché, if I didn't have David tied down in the next room ready to spin things out into orbit.

I point to the floor and Thomas slides off the chair on to all fours. My heart rushes into my mouth.

Thomas. Pretty young Thomas. On the floor. Naked. On his knees. I know it's bad. I know I shouldn't, with David tied down in the bedroom.

But how can I not? Thomas. As my dog boy. When am I ever going to get another chance?

I tug on Thomas's lead and bring him closer and closer to me, until his face is nuzzling, his mouth and nose nudging into my crotch. I can feel his tongue, big and swollen like his lips. When I pull back the folds of my robe so he can press it against me, it feels as delicious as ever. I'm just too turned on by all of this, by everything, not to do this. It's only a quickie. Just to take the edge off. It won't detract from the main event. In fact, it will even enhance it.

Besides, isn't this supposed to be David's punishment, right? And we all remember what he is getting punished for. Looking at it that way, what I'm about to do is practically compulsory.

Before Thomas's tongue has grazed me three times I'm already coming, my knuckles whitening where I'm steadying myself on the edge of the kitchen table. I don't bother to stifle the sounds I am making – and I'm a screamer – so I know David has heard. After all, he's heard me come so many times, he can't fail to know what I'm up to. The thought of that, of him listening – tied and gagged – and all the frustration and confusion that would cause, makes me really squirm.

As soon as my legs feel sturdy enough, I let them take me into the bedroom, with Thomas crawling after me on the end of his lead.

David lifts his head as soon as we walk in and looks at me with a weird, and weirdly delicious, mixture of arousal and betrayal.

Oh, David, my poor precious boy.

I drop Thomas's lead and go over to him, bending down to whisper in his ear. 'I know you heard me come. But you do know that you are going to make me come a hundred times harder than that little release with what you are about to do for me right now.'

The only sound he makes is a soft, wet, muffled grunt. Which is the perfect reply.

I leave David on the bed and go back to Thomas, who's still crouching on the floor. 'OK, Thomas,' I say, keeping my voice as level as I can. That's all I need to say, because he knows what I want.

Despite the orgasm I had in the kitchen I can feel my excitement level rise immediately. Just a gentle burn at the moment, but creeping up, and I think I've timed it just right.

I settle down in the corner of the room. I brought several fat cushions with me so I could be sure I would be a comfortable spectator. David's flat is oddly functional. The bedroom carpet isn't deep and soft but a hard-wearing, tough weave that doesn't catch his wheels. He doesn't have a squashy armchair in the corner, but why would he? His comfort priorities are slightly different. Hence, my BYO soft cushions.

From my position, reclining on the floor, I can see the bed perfectly. (I checked out all the eyelines in advance.) I can see David, bound face-down, beautifully helpless. And I can see Thomas, standing up, collared and erect (in every sense) and looking at David, spread for him on the bed.

As I watch, Thomas climbs on to the bed and positions himself, kneeling between David's spread legs. Then he reaches out and touches David's arse with his fingertips, gently exploring, almost reverent. And then, contrastingly sudden and sharp, he dips his head and that incredible tongue touches that exceptional arse.

And as Thomas licks David until he's moaning round his gag, I just watch. Much as I love what I am seeing purely for its own sake, I am also having an out-of-body experience, as I put myself in both of their places. I know exactly how it feels to be doing what Thomas is doing right now. I know how delicious and bittersweet David tastes. And I also know what it is like to be on the twisting, keening receiving end of Thomas's tongue.

But, artistic as it may be, I want a lot more from this evening than a bit of pretty rimming. I want the lot. The ultimate. And they know it. They both do.

It's no time at all before David is ready, and by ready I mean he is straining against the chains around his wrists, lifting his upper body and doing anything he can to get more of Thomas's tongue. In short, he is more or less screaming to be fucked, using everything but his mouth. Thomas sits back on his heels and uses his fingers to slide inside.

David pushes back on to Thomas's hand, but he's so ready, so warm and needy and open, that fingers are not enough already, and Thomas quickly moves on. He slips on a condom, lubes up, repositions himself and then, easy as anything, slides inside.

David turns his head so I can see his face, but – maybe it's the gag – his expression is unreadable. He's glassy-eyed and pink-cheeked. The gag is making him drool a little and I can see glistening wetness round his mouth and on his chin. I love that.

Thomas begins to move, thrusting gently at first,

but his movements quickly become faster, firmer, more urgent, as he gets more excited and it becomes clear that David can take it. Hard.

It starts to get brutal then. It's less about a show for me and more about two men getting each other off. Doing whatever it takes to get there. Brutal and nasty. Thomas dips his head and bites the fleshy angles between David's neck and shoulder. David yells and growls through his gag, urging Thomas on with his body as best he can. And Thomas pushes his hand under David's body and grabs David's erection tightly, pumping hard.

Faster and faster. Vicious friction. They are like one creature, thrusting, jerking, fucking. Animals.

And then Thomas is screaming out. And so is David. And so am I.

Perfect timing.

David

Here's the thing. The thing about the Thomas thing. I did do it for Mary. Because I wanted to show her I was truly sorry. About Eleanor. About everything.

But I also wanted to show her. Show her what I find it so hard – so impossible – to tell her. I wanted to show her how much I like all the bad things she likes. Because I do like them. And, really, I might as well get used to that fact. When it comes to all the nasty kinky filth Mary dishes up – I like it. I love it. I want it. I want her to do whatever she needs to do to me. Whatever she wants. I want her to feel like she owns me.

Whether Mary has awakened tastes that were always there – as she likes to claim – or whether something (Mary, the accident) made me like these things, I don't know. All I know is, this is what I am.

So, although part of it was for Mary, it was also because I wanted to have Thomas fuck me, more than anything. It turned me on.

But, that said, this had better be the last we see of Thomas around here. I'm not a fucking pushover. (And, yeah, I did mean to say that.)

Mary

Three days after Thomas fucked David, I still get all unnecessary if I so much as think about it. So I try to only think about it two or three times a day, four maximum. And actually, now I mention it, so not sticking to that rule.

But that doesn't matter, because I'm in the good place. My good place isn't always the same place, but right now it's my flat, in my bedroom, my bed, nestled under David's arm with my head resting on David's firm yet gently yielding bench-pressed pec, and David's chin resting on the top of my head. A little tuft of David's chest hair is tickling my nose. Various parts of my hot naked flesh are entwined in and over and round various parts of his hot naked flesh. This ultra-intense closeness is delicious and special and better than sex.

Finally, I've got David into bed. Into my own bed. In my own house. I didn't even realise how much I wanted this until he said he wanted to see my place and explained, with a shrug, that it was perfectly possible for him to get up my stairs.

He crawled up. Three flights. Yes, there was much biting of lips and digging of nails into palms on my part, as I tried to keep control while he did that. Oh god. There aren't really even words . . . But it was epic. Beautiful. He was a brave prince climbing my tower. A hero.

It was fucking hot.

But I managed to squish my ardour down hard enough that the evening wasn't short-circuited by me jumping him on the first landing.

So now here I am, in bed with my number-one dirty fantasy. And it's probably going to stay a fantasy for while. David's tired. He shouldn't really have done the stairs thing. Well, no, obviously he should have done it; I just shouldn't have expected any more hot action from him after that.

Thing is, just the idea of David is enough to send me into a raving hormonal frenzy, and being with him day in, day out, is like living in a sexed-up wonderland. Like I'm living in a porn movie, or I would be if had it my way. Because, oh! David! Being with David, just looking at David, makes me want it all the time. cannot leave him alone, and David, though a twenty-four-year-old man, can't quite match my ever-ready pace. Sometimes I feel like I'm practically harassing him, I want it so much.

I can't blame him for saying no occasionally. Fact is, David is still recovering from a serious accident. He is in a wheelchair, which means he spends a lot of time sitting down, which, in turn, can lead to various problems. I don't know a great deal about the medical ins and outs. He seems to want to keep me at arm's length from all that. He doesn't want me to go back to his social club, and he's never wanted me to come to his physio sessions (which he's been skiving off from for the last few days, for obvious reasons). In some ways it's sweet that he doesn't tell me too much about all that medical stuff. That he doesn't want to expose me to all that. But he needs to understand that it's not like I'm going to run a mile if I see the dark (and, frankly, unsexy) side to his disability. I can cope. But there's no rush.

So it happens that sometimes I'm half insane in a blaze of horniness and David, well, David really isn't. And then I need to have a way to take care of myself. And take care of myself I do. I am a grown-up liberated woman, after all. Cuddling up to him and thinking bad, bad thoughts about how he climbed those stairs might even be close to perfection. Might easily be enough to get me there. But close to perfection can be improved upon, there's room for a cherry on top of this cake. A smutty cherry, for preference.

'You used to be a pretty bad boy, didn't you?' I say. Fishing. Blatantly. Fishing for dirty talk.

'I don't know what you mean,' David replies, fully awake now and ignoring the bait like the teaser he is.

'Yes you do. You used to be a real bastard. A real love 'em and leave 'em type.'

'What, find 'em, fuck 'em, forget 'em? All that?'

'Yes. That's exactly what I mean.'

'Well, maybe I was like that, a bit. Long time ago.'

'So tell me about that. I should know about that stuff. All that stuff from before.'

'What? Before I was disabled?'

'Yeah, well, no, well, kind of, but I meant more before me.'

'So what do you want to know?'

'I don't know. Something bad. Something I'll like.'

David

Mary is still in a state of hyper-arousal from the stair-climbing show-stopper. She really loved that. Her cheeks and chest are still flushed. Her lips are still red. Her breathing is shallow. I wonder if she will manage to listen to quite a long story. I hope so, because I have the perfect thing.

I wrap my arms tight around her, and find a husky whisper in my voice, which I know will make this story extra shiver-inducing.

'OK, how about this. It was the summer after I finished uni. I was twenty-two or so, and newly single – I'd just finished with this girl I was seeing in Sheffield. It was a mutual thing, the break-up. We'd just graduated and were both starting on the career ladder, and neither of us wanted a partner cramping our style.

'This was before I got the IT job at the uni here. I think it was a week or so before I started. I wasn't working with Larry then. I'd never met him. So this was before I started on that whole ladykiller lifestyle that Larry and I created together. Before David-the-Player was born. But this – this story I'm about to tell you – was, I suppose, where it started. In a way. It's how I realised that I could be like that. The real birth of all that Mr Loverman stuff.

'See, I'd sort of grown into myself at university. What you see before you. Before that, when I'd just finished my A-levels, I was a bit sort of spoddy, a bit lanky, a bit greasy and zitty, but I bulked up and dried out a bit when I got into my twenties. I looked better than I had ever looked. And I was starting to realise it.

'So that day, the day in question, I was at my mum's house. It was a nice sunny morning, or afternoon, probably, by the time I'd surfaced. My mum was off at work. She worked at the university too, actually; in fact that was how I got that job fixing the computers and shit in the first place: she fixed it up for me. So, anyway, she wasn't there and I'd just got up, pottering in the kitchen, tea, cornflakes, all the breakfasty-jazz, and the doorbell rang.'

I take a breath and Mary interrupts. Typical. I don't think she's ever let me talk for that long before without interrupting. 'What are you wearing?'

'What, in the story?'

'Of course in the story, you're not wearing anything right now, are you?'

'No, sure, well, OK, um, I was wearing my underpants, probably. I wouldn't have been wearing anything in bed, but I would have put my pants on when I went into the kitchen. You know, for hygiene.'

There's a pause. A little gap. I'm about to fill it when Mary says, 'This story is weird.' And her voice sounds slightly different, a little stilted. 'It's weird to hear a story where you are ... you know.'

I do know. I know exactly what she means. 'What? Walking around?'

'Yeah.'

'Yeah. I know what you mean. That is a little weird.' And I don't say any more than that. I don't ask her if she would prefer a story where I couldn't walk. If that would turn her on more. If she can only get off on a story about me if I'm helpless. I don't ask her those questions because I don't ask myself those questions. I don't need to know about that kind of stuff any more.

'Mmm, underpants. Very nice,' Mary purrs in my ear, veering back on-topic.

'They probably weren't very nice under –' I attempt, foolishly.

Mary cuts me off. We both know she doesn't want this story spoiled with a description of my unpleasant student underpants in the name of objective reality. 'Just tell it,' she whispers, insistently, a hard hissing demand. She's getting impatient. Good. I like that. I get goose pimples.

'I answered the door and there was this woman standing there. I recognised her, just. She was my mum's friend from her bridge class. She was a nice-looking woman. Old. Older than my mum. But she was smart and petite, with a tightly pressed skirt over a tightly pressed arse. A neat shiny bob. She looked done. Smart. I liked it.'

'She sounds kind of domineering. Bobbed hair is a dead giveaway,' Mary says with a smirk, patting her own sleek do. 'What did she do for a job?'

Now that was something I was hoping Mary wouldn't ask and so I wouldn't have to tell. It's so not relevant, but I so know what she's going to think. I turn my head away, because I can't bear to see the smug look of triumph on her face when I tell her. I can't bear to see her realise that everything she's ever said about me was right. Every suspicion she's ever had. Every inkling about my sexuality. It's all about to be proved correct. Irrefutably. By something that really was nothing to do with what happened. 'She was in the police.'

'A policewoman!'

'Police officer, yes. It's not awfully relevant to the story, no matter what you might think. And I don't know what her rank was or anything, so don't even ask. And no, she wasn't wearing her uniform. I don't think she was one of the uniformed ones.'

'God, it's all nurses and policewomen with you,' Mary says softly. I don't say anything, but she's giggling so I guess that's OK. 'All right,' Mary says after a few moments of stifled mirth, 'I'm saying nothing. Nothing else.'

'Well, I wasn't even going to mention it, because her being a policewoman had absolutely nothing to do with what happened next. I never thought about it. I swear. It didn't, and doesn't, do anything for me.'

She doesn't believe me. And I know that, although she doesn't pursue it this time, it will be stored away in that marvellously depraved brain of hers, just waiting for the right moment. 'OK, OK, maybe that wasn't important. But her age was.'

'I don't see how.'

'Well, you made a big point of telling me she was older, older than your mum. Which means you must think that fact would turn me on, which means it must have turned you on. Oh, admit it. I mean, I know you must have been attracted to her. Obviously you were, otherwise I don't think much of this story. And I reckon you were hot for her because of her older-woman wiggle. All that knowledge, all that power. Did she educate you, when you were nothing but an innocent, if buffed-up, little twenty-two-year-old?' Mary purrs the last sentence, making the word 'educate', in particular, sound exceedingly nasty.

I laugh, and then say, 'Look, can I just tell the story?' I don't leave her any room to answer, but continue. 'So, I opened the door, and I was in just my underpants. This made me kind of vulnerable – which maybe I did find kind of sexy – but I also had some power because, well, look, there is no nice, no modest, way of putting this, I knew I looked fucking incredible. It wasn't even my fault I looked so good, it was just bloody good timing on her part. My hair was at that in-between-cuts stage where it just looked right without me even trying. It had been quite hot so I had a bit of colour. You know I'm not big on the whole bronzed-Adonis look, but I was working on a rather nice delicately-biscuit-coloured-Adonis look. It worked. I was looking good. And I was practically naked in front of Celia on a midweek afternoon.

'So poor old PC Celia didn't stand a damn chance. I mean, I can't even explain it, but the mutual attraction sparks were flying so fast we were already at the stage where we knew what was happening between us but we were both acting as if we didn't know we were going to have sex. We'd seen pornos; we knew this was like something from a porno. And we both knew we were acting like we didn't know.

'I offered her some tea, which neither of us really wanted, and I got as far as putting the kettle on. When I turned my back to her, she reached out and touched my bare shoulder. And then, well, I don't really know how it happened exactly, it felt like she turned me around and kissed me. But that might be my own embroidery. Maybe I turned around myself and kissed her. Anyway, I turned to face her and we started to kiss.

'Her kisses were different from any I'd ever had before. She was more in control. She held my head so tight I couldn't pull away even if I wanted to. She kissed me like she owned me. And she kissed me until she wanted it to stop.'

'And you liked it,' Mary says, squirming against me.

'And I liked it. I really liked it. And she liked it too. She was really into it. She said stuff like "God, you're so beautiful." I remember that distinctly, she purred it while she touched one of my pecs, really gently. Who could blame her for enjoying it? She probably didn't have many opportunities to get off with buffed-up twenty-two-year-olds, even if I do say so myself.

'We went upstairs. Her idea, but I would have suggested it if she hadn't. I took her into my bedroom. You know the room in my mum's house that has her sewing machine in it now? Well, that used to be my bedroom growing up. It only had a single bed, and I guess if I were more ballsy I'd have gone and fucked her on my mum's bed, but, well, I'm not, and I didn't.

'In my bedroom she pushed me down on the bed, climbed on top of me and started kissing me straight-away, pinning me down on the mattress. I was so hard, so quick. In fact, I was scared I was going to come right away. I didn't, but she seemed to have guessed, because she pulled away from my mouth and said, "Maybe you ought to do something to turn me on. I need to go some to catch up with you, baby." Her voice was so dirty, by the way. In fact it was a bit like yours. She made everything sound so rude!

'She made me stand up and lay down on the bed herself, then pulled her skirt up and her knickers down. I almost didn't know where to look. I was almost shy, faced with the pretty curls of her pubic hair and her expectant expression that said it all.

'I am very ashamed to say that at that point in my life I had never given a woman oral sex. Like I said, I wasn't that much of a stud at uni. I just had the one girlfriend and we were kind of conventional, boring even, in our sexual preferences. We'd tried blow jobs and I'd liked them, but my girlfriend just freaked at the idea of me reciprocating. So that was that. I didn't see any reason to press the point.

'But that afternoon with Celia, I learnt a few things. She showed me just where to press my tongue against her. Where to be firmer, where to be softer. How to listen to her breathing and read how far she was from her peak. She spent hours educating me, as you would say. And I don't know how many times she came, but it was definitely more than once. And when I eventually got to fuck her, she came again.

'What Celia taught me that afternoon became the basis of what I did with all the women I pulled at the university when I started working there. It gave me real extra confidence, you know, because I knew I could give them an earth-shattering time in bed. And I did. I might have been all shag-and-run bad boy, but the shag I gave them was always fucking amazing. If they came so hard they started to hyperventilate and cry, that was my benchmark, that was when I'd be satisfied.'

I stop talking and sigh. I wonder what Mary is going to make of what I've just told her. Which ended up being far more revealing about the person I used to be – the one I like to keep hidden from Mary – than I ever intended.

But I don't need to worry. Mary is more than happy. Something that is confirmed when she rolls over on top of me and slides herself on to my cock, which is very ready for her after reliving my glorious hours with Celia.

Mary is so wet. I guess she liked my story. She puts her mouth to my ear. 'This policewoman who made you service her – did she handcuff you while you did it at all?'

'What?' I say, and I'm about to say no, when I realise what the correct (if inaccurate) answer is. I remember what my goal was when this conversation started, and say, 'yes.'

'And then what?'

'Mary, she handcuffed me and made me go down on her for hours. I wanted to stop. I could hardly breathe, but I had no choice. And anyway she told me that if I didn't do what she wanted she'd take me down the station and interrogate me there ...'

That's all it takes. Mary is coming. I'm coming. And deep down, somewhere a little voice is pointing out that Mary seems to be perfectly capable of getting off on a version of me that isn't disabled at all.

Author's Note

David suffered a T11/T12 spinal crush rather than a complete break. The nerves are difficult to read, meaning the possibility of his recovery is always in doubt.

This book would not have been possible without the wonderful assistance of Mik Scarlet and his wife Diane, who let me ask them lots of personal questions about their sex life. Although I should also point out that any errors are of course mine.

I would also like to thank Pluto, Hazel and Seri, who might not even remember but were the first people to tell me that the idea for this book was not completely crazy.

Visit the Black Lace website at
www.blacklace-books.co.uk

LOOK OUT FOR THE ALL-NEW BLACK LACE BOOKS – AVAILABLE NOW!

All books priced £7.99 in the UK. Please note publication dates apply to the UK only. For other territories, please contact your retailer.

DARKER THAN LOVE
Kristina Lloyd
ISBN 0 352 33279 4

It's 1875, and the morals of Queen Victoria mean nothing to London's wayward and debauched elite. Young but naïve Clarissa Longleigh is visiting London for the first time. She is eager to meet Lord Marldon – the man to whom she's been promised – knowing only that he's handsome, dark and sophisticated. In fact he is depraved, louche, and has a taste for sexual excess.

Clarissa has also struck up a friendship with a young Italian artist, Gabriel. When Marldon hears of this he is incensed, and imprisons Clarissa in his opulent London mansion. When Gabriel tries to free her, he too is captured, and the young lovers find themselves at the mercy of the debauched lord.

Coming in November

DARK DESIGNS
Madelynne Ellis
ISBN 0 352 34075 4

Remy Davies is under pressure as the designer for an opulent gothic wedding. There's the over-stressed bride, a trinity of vampire-obsessed bridesmaids, a wayward groom, and then there's the best man . . . Silk looks like he's been drawn by a *manga* artist; beautiful, exotic, and with a predatory sexuality. Remy has to have him, in her bed and between the pages of her new catalogue. Remy is about to launch herself into the alternative fashion world, and Silk is going to sell it for her whether he knows it or not. But Silk is nobody's toy, and for all his androgyny, he's determinedly heterosexual. Pity, since Remy's biggest fantasy is to see him making out with her Japanese biker, sometime boyfriend, Takeshi.

ASKING FOR TROUBLE
Kristina Lloyd
ISBN 0 352 33362 6

When Beth Bradshaw – the manager of a fashionable bar in the seaside town of Brighton – starts flirting with the handsome Ilya, she becomes a player in a game based purely on sexual brinkmanship. The boundaries between fantasy and reality start to blur as their relationship takes on an increasingly reckless element.

When Ilya's murky past catches up with him, he's determined to involve Beth. Unwilling to extricate herself from their addictive games, she finds herself being drawn deeper into the seedy underbelly of Brighton where things, including Ilya, are far more dangerous than she bargained for.

E SOCIETY OF SIN
n Lacey Taylder
N 0 352 34080 0

perhaps, 'Lust and Laura Ashley'. The Society of Sin is an erotic, gothic
iller set in rural Dorset in the late 19th Century, a period when
ucated women were beginning to question their sexuality.

The Society of Sin was conceived on a hot and sticky summer's
ening inside a mansion house on a large country estate when, after an
um-fuelled night of passion, Lady P and her close friend Samantha
verstock succumbed to desires they had both repressed for years.
w, a year later, they have invited a select few to join their exclusive
ociation. But only genuine hedonists need apply; prospective
mbers are interrogated over a sumptuous dinner then given an
signment' which they must fulfil. Failure to do so results in instant
ulsion and the prospect of being 'named and shamed' in the
clusive circles they currently frequent. However, successful completion
the task opens for them a Pandora's box of pain and pleasure:

Summer sees the arrival of Miss Charlotte Crowsettle, who
mediately falls under Lady P's spell.

NTINUUM
rtia Da Costa
N 0 352 33120 8

en Joanna Darrell agrees to take a break from an office job that has
gun to bore her, she takes her first step into a new continuum of
ange experiences. She is introduced to people whose way of life
olves around the giving and receiving of enjoyable punishment, and
e becomes intrigued enough to experiment. Drawn in by a chain of
ncidences, like Alice in a decadent wonderland, she enters a parallel
rld of perversity and unusual pleasure.

Black Lace Booklist

Information is correct at time of printing. To avoid disappointmen
check availability before ordering. Go to www.blacklace-books.co.u
All books are priced £6.99 unless another price is given.

BLACK LACE BOOKS WITH A CONTEMPORARY SETTING

☐ ON THE EDGE Laura Hamilton	ISBN 0 352 33534 3	£5.	
☐ THE TRANSFORMATION Natasha Rostova	ISBN 0 352 33311 1		
☐ SIN.NET Helena Ravenscroft	ISBN 0 352 33598 X		
☐ TWO WEEKS IN TANGIER Annabel Lee	ISBN 0 352 33599 8		
☐ SYMPHONY X Jasmine Stone	ISBN 0 352 33629 3		
☐ A SECRET PLACE Ella Broussard	ISBN 0 352 33307 3		
☐ GOING TOO FAR Laura Hamilton	ISBN 0 352 33657 9		
☐ RELEASE ME Suki Cunningham	ISBN 0 352 33671 4		
☐ SLAVE TO SUCCESS Kimberley Raines	ISBN 0 352 33687 0		
☐ SHADOWPLAY Portia Da Costa	ISBN 0 352 33313 8		
☐ ARIA APPASSIONATA Julie Hastings	ISBN 0 352 33056 2		
☐ A MULTITUDE OF SINS Kit Mason	ISBN 0 352 33737 0		
☐ COMING ROUND THE MOUNTAIN Tabitha Flyte	ISBN 0 352 33873 3		
☐ FEMININE WILES Karina Moore	ISBN 0 352 33235 2		
☐ MIXED SIGNALS Anna Clare	ISBN 0 352 33889 X		
☐ BLACK LIPSTICK KISSES Monica Belle	ISBN 0 352 33885 7		
☐ GOING DEEP Kimberly Dean	ISBN 0 352 33876 8		
☐ PACKING HEAT Karina Moore	ISBN 0 352 33356 1		
☐ MIXED DOUBLES Zoe le Verdier	ISBN 0 352 33312 X		
☐ UP TO NO GOOD Karen S. Smith	ISBN 0 352 33589 0		
☐ CLUB CRÈME Primula Bond	ISBN 0 352 33907 1		
☐ BONDED Fleur Reynolds	ISBN 0 352 33192 5		
☐ SWITCHING HANDS Alaine Hood	ISBN 0 352 33896 2		
☐ EDEN'S FLESH Robyn Russell	ISBN 0 352 33923 3		
☐ PEEP SHOW Mathilde Madden	ISBN 0 352 33924 1	£7.	
☐ RISKY BUSINESS Lisette Allen	ISBN 0 352 33280 8	£7.	
☐ CAMPAIGN HEAT Gabrielle Marcola	ISBN 0 352 33941 1	£7.	
☐ MS BEHAVIOUR Mini Lee	ISBN 0 352 33962 4	£7.	

BLACK LACE BOOKS WITH AN HISTORICAL SETTING

find out the latest information about Black Lace titles, check out the ebsite: www.blacklace-books.co.uk or send for a booklist with mplete synopses by writing to:

Black Lace Booklist, Virgin Books Ltd
Thames Wharf Studios
Rainville Road
London W6 9HA

ease include an SAE of decent size. Please note only British stamps e valid.

ur privacy policy
e will not disclose information you supply us to any other parties.
e will not disclose any information which identifies you personally to
y person without your express consent.

om time to time we may send out information about Black Lace
oks and special offers. Please tick here if you do not wish to
ceive Black Lace information. ❏

Please send me the books I have ticked above.

Name ....

Address ....

....

....

....

Post Code ....

Send to: Virgin Books Cash Sales, Thames Wharf Studios, Rainville Road, London W6 9HA.

US customers: for prices and details of how to order books for delivery by mail, call 888-330-8477.

Please enclose a cheque or postal order, made payable to Virgin Books Ltd, to the value of the books you have ordered plus postage and packing costs as follows:

UK and BFPO – £1.00 for the first book, 50p for each subsequent book.

Overseas (including Republic of Ireland) – £2.00 for the first book, £1.00 for each subsequent book.

If you would prefer to pay by VISA, ACCESS/MASTERCARD, DINERS CLUB, AMEX or SWITCH, please write your card number and expiry date here:

....

Signature ....

Please allow up to 28 days for delivery.